HEREWARD: SONS OF THE WHITE DRAGON

by Marcus Pitcaithly

MMVIII

"Whet the bright steel,
Sons of the White Dragon!
Kindle the torch,
Daughter of Hengist!
The steel glimmers not for the carving of the banquet,
It is hard, broad, and sharply pointed;
The torch goeth not to the bridal chamber,
It steams and glitters blue with sulphur."
~ Sir Walter Scott, "Ulrica's Death-Song"
(from *Ivanhoe*)

To my parents

First published by Marcus Pitcaithly, January 2008
© Marcus Pitcaithly 2008
ISBN: 978-0-9556864-0-5

CONTENTS

1	*The Prodigal Son*	p. 6
2	*Homecoming*	p. 30
3	*The One-Eyed Man*	p. 55
4	*The Heron*	p. 73
5	*The Treasure of St Edmund*	p. 97
6	*Martin Lightfoot*	p. 115
7	*The Wild Huntsman*	p. 136
8	*The Giants of the Fens*	p. 159
9	*Brainbiter*	p. 181
10	*The Miller's Daughter*	p. 205
11	*The Atheling*	p. 228

MAP OF EASTERN ENGLAND

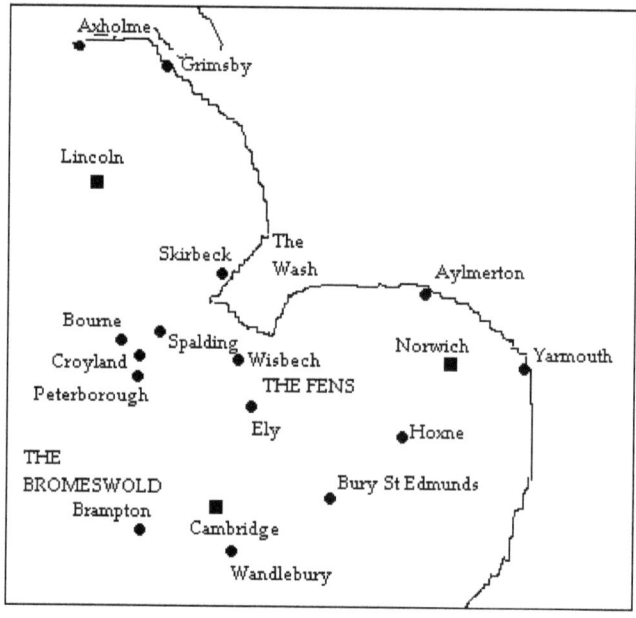

Hereward's part of England is still a wetland area: but in the eleventh century the Fenland was more marsh than dry land. The Isles of Axholme and Ely really were islands, and flat-bottomed boats were most likely the principal means of transport.

England as a whole was also very much a rural environment. The total population was approximately 1.1 million, of whom barely 10% lived in urban surroundings. Towns such as Spalding differed from villages more in amenities than in size; even London housed no more than about 15,000 people, York and Norwich between five and ten thousand, and probably all other cities fewer than five thousand each.

Acknowledgement

In addition to chronicle, legend and my own fantasy, I have drawn on the work of some imaginative writers of the nineteenth and earlier centuries. In particular, it is all but impossible to treat the character of Hereward in fiction without standing on the shoulders of Charles Kingsley and his novel *Hereward the Wake* (1866). I see no reason to be coy about this debt: I would not have approached the subject had I not had much to add, and my Hereward is a very different man from Kingsley's, inhabiting a very different book.

Two characters here depicted – Prior Herluin and Thord Gunnlaugsson – were created by Kingsley, although I have taken both, especially Thord, some distance from their origins. Chapter 10 is inspired by the anonymous play (possibly by Wentworth Smith) *Fair Em, the Miller's Daughter of Manchester* (c. 1590): but, although some of the play's characters and situations are used, the plot is my own.

Hiccafrith, of course, is the old chapbook and fairytale hero Tom Hickathrift, his name rendered into what may be its original form if there is any truth at all in his legend.

Names

I have as a general rule employed the forms of proper names most familiar, or easiest, to modern English speakers (e.g. Edward, not Eadward). I have also tried to minimise duplication: for instance, the second son of Gospatric of Northumbria would have been known to Saxons as Waltheof, but I have called him Waldeve (the Norman form of his name) in order to avoid confusion with Waltheof Siwardsson, who will be a major character in subsequent volumes of Hereward's saga.

Chapter 1: *The Prodigal Son*

Lincoln, 1054.

The Norman monk cleared his throat, squinted at the scroll under the flickering torchlight, and began to read.

"The charges against Hereward son of Askil are as follows. Imprimis, that he and the delinquents he calls his housecarles have burned a farm within the Earldom of Northumbria, and scattered the flocks of that farm, and thereby provoked a counter-raid by the Northumbrians upon the Earldom of Mercia. Item, that he and the said 'housecarles' so-called so called have stolen the plate of his noble father the Lord Askil and the rents of his most noble kinsman the Earl Leofric to pay for ale. Item –" and here he peered severely over the top of the scroll – "that but three days ago he and the said brigands did assault me, Herluin, Prior of Peterborough, with insults and disdainful language and then with violence, and did take from me the money paid in tithe to Holy Mother Church."

The Countess, occupying in her husband's absence the high seat of judgement, shook her head sadly, looking with doleful eyes on the unrepentant youth.

"O Hereward," she murmured, "have you sunk so low as to steal from God and His saints?"

"Lady," replied Hereward, "if this bird of carrion is a saint, I would rather be in Hell than share Heaven with him." His audience were not easy people to shock, but there were gasps at that. The Prior, however, could not suppress a smirk of triumph. It was precisely the response he had hoped his young bugbear would give. Hereward now was damned indeed.

"Do you confess the charges?" interposed the priest who stood by the Countess' side.

Hereward looked him in the eye. He had always had

more respect for Father Wulfwine than for the unctuous prior; and if Wulfwine had beaten him occasionally, he had more often spared him when others would have reached for the tawse; but he knew that his boats were already burned. Besides, however much Herluin had exaggerated, there was enough truth in each charge to make the mud stick – and if he knew the prior, probably a bribed witness ready to swear to every one and more.

"I deny nothing," he replied.

"What am I to do with you?" sighed the Countess. "Your parents are in despair. They say you cannot be ruled."

"These charges lie outside his father's authority in any case," Wulfwine pointed out. "There is no choice now but to inform the Earl Leofric."

"And Leofric will go to the King, and the King will pass sentence of outlawry." The Countess Godiva was fond of Hereward. He was not only her kinsman but her godson, a bond she took very seriously. And, rebellious and irreligious though he had grown in recent years, she was sure he was reclaimable.

"It is no more than the brute deserves," sniffed the Prior.

"He will be in fine company," remarked Wulfwine, with a half-smile to Hereward. "There is scarcely a nobleman at court these days who has not been a forest-wight in his time."

Hereward shrugged his shoulders.

"If you're going to banish me," he said, "get it over with. I've quite a mind to see the world." Godiva shuddered.

"Enough," she said. "Hereward, I love you: but I must love conscience more. I shall write to Earl Leofric and tell him the charges that Prior Herluin has laid, and that you have made no denial. It is almost certain that the King will proclaim you an outlaw, and you will be banished from the realm of England."

Hereward said nothing, but inclined his head, then

turned on his heel and walked out. His godmother let out a sob; Father Wulfwine placed a comforting hand on her shoulder.

"His parents will understand," he said. "It was the only way."

Berkhamsted, December, 1066.

The red-haired horseman cocked his head back, looking up at the gates of Berkhamsted. They were not impressive: low, with worn planking and crumbling edges, feeble beside the gates of great cities he had broken down in the past. But they were still closed.

"They're taking their time," he remarked. "Maybe they do mean to hold out this time."

"Impossible, my lord," replied the man on his right. "This town will crumple like every other."

"There's only one King in England now," chimed in another. But the red-haired man shook his head.

"I am not crowned yet," he said.

For this was William the Norman. Six weeks after his victory at Hastings, he was almost master of England: almost, but not quite. There were pockets of resistance here and there – but here in Berkhamsted was the focus of the English cause. Here was the prince, Edgar, great-nephew of King Edward the Confessor: the man who, if these barbarous English had understood the laws of primogeniture, should have been King in Harold Godwinsson's place – and who had been proclaimed King indeed when Harold fell. While Edgar was at large William could never sit easy on the throne: and he had deferred his coronation until after the prince's submission should be received, so that all England should see they had indeed one King and one alone.

There was a creaking of unoiled hinges, and the gates began to inch open. The Normans fingered their sword-hilts;

it seemed an age before the noise stopped, and out of Berkhamsted there came, on foot, three figures. They were young, and fair-haired; the elder two wore thin moustaches. Though they wore armour they were not dressed for battle: their hauberks were shining and clearly new; their woollen cloaks were clasped with brooches of gold in the shape of horses; they wore no shields, and each carried his highly polished helmet under his right arm, and his scabbarded sword hilt foremost in his left hand. Halting before William, they dropped as one man to their knees.

"My lord of Normandy –" began the youngest.

"Of *England*, boy!" barked one of William's knights. The Duke held up his hand.

"Peace," he said. "Of what you will today; of England soon enough."

"I – I am Edgar, called the Atheling," quavered the youth. William stared. His rival was a child, and not, to the Norman's harsh eyes, a promising one, however handsome. Edgar gulped, and continued, more confidently. "I here surrender my sword, and with it my claim to the throne of England. I acknowledge your lordship, and beg leave to depart the kingdom."

"Denied," said William brusquely. "Who are these burrs who drag at your tail?"

"Th-the Earl Edwin of M-Mercia, and the Earl M-Morcar of Northumbria," stammered the Atheling.

"Who both likewise pledge our fealty to Your Grace," added Edwin eagerly.

"Leofric's brood, eh?" said the Duke. He had heard much of the House of Mercia, but he guessed the blood of their famous grandfather ran very thin in these two. "Ivo – their swords." The knight addressed – the same who had snapped at Edgar – dismounted, and took the three proffered blades. "Your lands and chattels are now mine to dispose of; I will find two more trusty earls – or three, or four. The earldoms were growing over mighty, as my predecessors found to their cost." Edwin and Morcar squirmed. "You can have your pick of their manors, Ivo. I recommend Bourne; they say there's good pig farming round there. Secure Prince Edgar and take him back to camp; these two... gentlemen are free to go. I think I will inspect my newly loyal town of Berkhamsted."

Bruges, three weeks later.

Clang.

Hereward's sword struck sparks off the floor.

His opponent lunged furiously at him, but he neatly sidestepped, swinging his blade upwards, and struck down again, cutting a deep gash in the other swordsman's shield.

Lord Baldwin stirred. This was not what he had expected.

"Have you tried the Breton mead, my lady?" he asked his guest, just a touch too casually. She shook her head.

"I thank your lordship, I prefer wine." Baldwin motioned a servant forward and a cup of wine was provided.

"Your champion seems to be flagging," he remarked.

"He is the Count's champion too," the lady pointed out. "And he has never yet been beaten." The slightly built, saturnine squire lounging against the wall muttered something inaudible.

"What did you say?" asked Baldwin sharply.

"I said, neither has my lord Hereward," replied the squire. He spoke perfect Flemish with only the barest trace of an Irish accent. Baldwin shifted in his seat again.

"There is a first time for everything," he said.

Clang.

The champion arced his blade up and down at Hereward's head, and missed completely, stumbling forward as the Englishman sidestepped once again. Before he could regain his footing, Hereward had kicked his sword out of his hand, and he had fallen headlong.

"Do you yield?" asked Hereward calmly. He was not even out of breath.

"I yield," the champion whispered.

Baldwin burst into applause, joined immediately by the ever sycophantic courtiers and soldiers around him.

"Well done, Englishman! Well done!" he exclaimed. "I have never seen Sir Ascelin discomfited before. He must be getting old!" Ascelin scowled. He was four years younger than Hereward. "You must look to your laurels, Ascelin," Baldwin teased. "Else my father and Lady Torfrida may both look for new champions."

"Sir Ascelin may retain my favour... for the moment," said the lady, her eyes on Hereward.

"You are charitable," said Baldwin. "Lord Hereward – I understand you have not yet been knighted?"

"Nor will I, my lord," replied Hereward. Baldwin's smile vanished.

"Your pardon, Lord Hereward, I'm not sure I understood you."

"It is not the English fashion for one knight to dub another," said Hereward. "If I take my knighthood at a warrior's hands it will be from one who has first beaten me in fair fight." He gave a crooked grin. "Of course, if your lordship would care to take Sir Ascelin's place..?" If a gnat had sneezed in the silence that followed, it would have echoed round the chamber. At last, Baldwin gave a hearty guffaw, and the court a collective sigh of relief.

"Ha! This is an impudent Englishman, is it not?"

"Insolent, my lord," said Torfrida. Again she fixed her eyes on the Englishman's, and spoke deliberately: "Exiled whelp of a conquered race, he thinks himself a hero after one lucky fall." Hereward bristled, but said nothing.

"That wasn't luck," said Baldwin mildly. "Well, gentlemen, shake hands. We are friends here, and this is a time of friendship. When the season is over, we shall discuss the border troubles. The Countess of Guines may not know the meaning of goodwill, but she won't move while the snow lasts."

The two mercenaries faced each other, bowed stiffly, and, with little appearance of affection, extended their hands. They made a curious contrast physically: Hereward shortish, broad, rough-hewn of face, his wild ash-blond hair much longer than was the Flemish fashion – and his remarkable eyes, one blue and one grey; the Norman taller, slenderer, with almost delicate good looks beneath an auburn crop. It was Ascelin who was the ladies' darling; but the lady he had chosen to dedicate his service to was watching Hereward with intent interest. Ascelin did not like what he saw. The Lady Torfrida was a great beauty and a not inconsiderable heiress. Not only that, but the mere fact that she was still unmarried at the age of twenty-two piqued the interest of the knights of the Low Countries: clearly, they said, the man she was waiting for would have to meet a very exacting standard. Half Flanders and most of Artois had been gossiping since she had permitted Ascelin to wear her favour, and he himself had assumed that it was only a matter of time until he left being her servant and became her lord.

"And when Christmas is done and the ice is melted," Baldwin went on, "if the Countess' heart is not melted too, we shall ride against her, we three together in the van – if Sir Ascelin can sit in his saddle after today's whipping!"

Ascelin grimaced. "My lord."

"But for now, we feast. You were lucky to be banished, Lord Hereward: you'll eat better with us than the noblest of your countrymen does this night!"

"I saw you speaking with the courier," Hereward said to his squire as soon as he could break free from the overbearing Baldwin. "What is the word from England?" Martin shuffled his feet. "Tell me the worst."

"It is all over," said Martin. "It was true – Prince

Edgar has renounced the throne. He repeated it publicly, and the Witan accepted his resignation and confirmed William as King. Eldred of York crowned him on Christmas Day in the Abbey, and all the earls did homage."

"Then there is no longer England," said Hereward heavily. "Was there no word of my family?"

"Your father's manors are divided among three of the Norman's followers: Gilbert of Ghent, Ogier fitz Ungomar and Ivo Taillebois. They say your brother Toli remains at Bourne on Ivo's sufferance, with your mother and one maid, and the torches are not lit at night."

"An outlaw has neither country nor kin," said Hereward, half to himself. "Remember the saying: 'My sword is my father, my shield is my mother, my ship is my sister, my horse is my brother.'" Martin could not suppress a smile.

"Your lordship's horse is a mare," he pointed out. Hereward ignored him.

"It was always going to be the way," he said. "Seven thousand warriors would not cross the seas for no reward. William's hawks fly to his lure, and English bones must now be picked clean to keep them fed. But what is that to a landless man?" This time Martin's reply was serious.

"I have known many men who were alone, my lord," he said. "Landless, friendless, kinless. I have been one myself. I don't believe you could ever be so. You will see your mother and your motherland again before you die." Hereward shrugged.

"My wyrd is set fast," he replied. Martin did not agree, but he knew better than to argue. Hereward, like all the Fen people, was as much Danish as Saxon: and the faith of the northern nations in Wyrd, the Mother of Fate, was completely undimmed by their conversion to Christianity, and would not brook question.

In Bourne Hall, as Martin had said, a poor Christmas was kept. Even on Twelfth Night the hearth lay cold, no minstrels sang, no mead was poured, and two guttering candles served for light instead of torches. Toli, Steward of Bourne at the age of fifteen, sat with his mother Edith, hacking at the cheap lump of gristly mutton their maid Rowena had managed to buy for a few pennies in the village; Rowena ate with them, rank forgotten in distress. Edith, wrapped in blankets and worn-out furs, stared blankly at the meat, and shivered.

"You should eat more, Mother," Toli urged. "You need your strength."

"For what?" she asked. It was unanswerable.

"It's this place, sir," said Rowena. "It's wrong to see it like this. It would destroy anybody's spirit who remembered the happier times."

"Rowena's right, Mother," said Toli. "You should go to Aunt Godiva and the holy sisters at Croyland."

Edith turned her head curiously.

"And will you come with me?" she said.

"No," said Toli. "The Earl Morcar entrusted Bourne Hall to Father and Father's responsibilities are now mine. I may have lost my own inheritance but I won't give up Bourne unless it's to the Earl."

"Then I will stay with you," said Edith simply. "I have only one son left. I will not let us be parted." She threw back her head, and began to chant:

"Where is the horse now? Where the rider?
Where the giver of heirlooms?
Where are the seats at the table?
Where are the songs in the hall?
Alas for the bright wine-cup!
Alas for the man in mail!
Alas for the prince's glory!
How is that time gone hence,
Under the cover of darkness,
As if it had never been!"

When the snows had melted and the campaigning season come again, Hereward went to the chamber of the Lady Torfrida. He was admitted by her nurse, a wizened old Lapp woman festooned with charms and amulets. Her mistress was standing in the centre of the room, apparently waiting for him.

"You have something to say to me, Lord Hereward?" she asked coolly.

"Yes."

"Then say it." There was a pause. Hereward was struck once again by the brightness of Torfrida's blue-violet eyes.

"My lady," he said, speaking with some difficulty, "I came... I came to say... goodbye."

"That is an ill omened word, my lord."

"I am going to the frontier," he explained. "There will be a battle. It may not please God that I should return."

"And is the mighty Hereward afraid?" Hereward looked up hotly, ready to deny it, but saw that Torfrida was smiling gently, not mockingly.

"I... I would not go without... without..."

"Whatever it is," she said, "you must go without it if you cannot ask for it. But I can give you something, at least. Kolfrosta!"

"Lady?" said the Lapp.

"The chest." Kolfrosta shot a warning look at her mistress, but nevertheless scuttled over to the oaken chest that stood beneath the window, drew a key from somewhere inside her shapeless gown, and opened it, propping the lid back against the wall.

"I trust what you find in there is to your liking, Lord Hereward," said Torfrida. Hereward peered into the chest, and gasped. Gingerly, he reached into it, and, holding it as if it were as delicate as a flower, lifted out a coat of the finest mesh chainmail. It was no heavier than his winter tunic and looked scarcely less flexible, and it gleamed as if it were made of silver rather than steel; he had never seen workmanship to match it.

"Lady," he breathed, "this is surely the work of the sons of Dvalin!"

"Not quite, my lord," smiled Torfrida.

"Of some enchanter, then?"

"Of Saracens," she replied. "Three hundred years ago, when the infidel had advanced into France itself and only the army of Charles Martel stood in their way, my ancestor, the first Count of St Omer, fought beside him. The Saracens had occupied the Roman theatre of Arles, but Charles burnt it over their heads, and those who escaped fled down the valley. But at Montmajeur they were rallied by a brave African emir whose name is forgotten. He raised the cry of vengeance and the Prophet, and charged into the Christian host: and, light as air though his armour was, they say every lance that struck him broke in shivers, every sword slid off him, every arrow glanced aside, while every blow he struck sheared off a Christian head. At length he rode against Charles himself, and raised his scimitar high; and the general must have been slain, but for the Count of St Omer. For my ancestor flung aside his sword, and hurled himself bodily upon the emir, carrying him from his horse; and on the ground he strangled the man whom no weapon could pierce, and took from his corpse the enchanted armour. No blade has ever pierced it. I want you to have it." Hereward's brow furrowed.

"But what of your champion, Sir Ascelin?" he asked. Torfrida shrugged.

"He will find another lady," she said. "I am not cruel: I will let him wear my favour at least until he returns from this campaign. I am giving you the coat now to preserve your life – that is more important than Ascelin's pride."

Hereward slipped the mailshirt easily over his head, and found it a perfect fit; and he clasped Torfrida to his chest in a sudden embrace. She buried her face in his mailed shoulder; neither of them noticed Kolfrosta rocking back and forth on the balls of her feet, crooning to herself:

"Soon won, soon lost. Soon won, soon lost. Soon won, soon lost."

The Countess Susanne de Guines, armoured *cap-à-pied*, faced Lord Baldwin. It had been expected that when her elderly husband Count Manasses finally gave up the ghost his claims in Flanders would die with him; but the widow had proved determined, and was now ready to bring those claims to battle.

"My lord," she said. "Are you empowered by your father to grant the terms of the County of Guines?"

"I bear full authority," replied Baldwin. "But the borders will not move, nor the tribute drop, unless you can show that the people of Guines cannot afford it."

"Or unless God so wills it."

"Of course." Baldwin dipped his head in acknowledgement of the pious qualification.

"Then shall we let God decide? My army is ready."

"Is this worth the lives of so many men?" demanded Baldwin angrily.

"The men of Guines would rather die than pay for the privilege of letting Flanders tell them who their friends and foes shall be," Susanne retorted. "But there is another way."

"Not if it means Flanders must surrender her rights," insisted Baldwin.

"I refer to an ordeal by combat. Your champion against mine." Ascelin pricked up his ears. This would be a chance to make good his humiliation at the hands of the Englishman.

"Lord Hereward, what do you think of the Countess' suggestion?" asked Baldwin.

"I am ready to fight any man she can produce, sire," Hereward assured him. Ascelin gasped. The Countess looked

Hereward up and down; she remembered the Englishman. He had been brought before Manasses after a shipwreck case a couple of years earlier, and had served him before joining the Count of Flanders: which meant that he knew who Guines' champion would be. That he was prepared to fight him spoke highly of his courage, but she would have thought him more intelligent.

"You have your answer, lady," said Baldwin. "Where is your champion?"

"Holbert!" bawled the Countess. Out of the ranks of Guines lumbered a figure more like a bear than a man, huge, shambling, his heavy armour cobbled together from suits made for smaller men, his very boots sheathed in iron, and in his hand a mace like a tree. Baldwin's jaw dropped. "Well, my lord?" pressed Susanne tauntingly. "Is your champion having second thoughts?"

"Has yours ever had a first?" rejoined Martin. Holbert grunted.

"When I've finished your master, little man," he growled, "I'll use you to pick my teeth." Martin leant down from the saddle so that his face was level with Holbert's. The champion's breath stank.

"All you'll ever eat again in this life are your words," he said.

Hereward vaulted down from his horse and unsheathed Brainbiter.

"If your ladyship will give the signal?" he said. Susanne drew her own sword and raised it skywards; and the champions rushed at one another, shaking the ground like charging bulls.

Hereward landed the first blow; but Brainbiter rebounded off Holbert's armour, jarring his wrists and not even leaving a dent. Holbert's mace fell past his head and thudded into the ground, then again; then the giant struck sideways, knocking the Englishman off his feet. But by the time Holbert could aim what should have been a death-blow,

Hereward was up again, slicing at him from left and then right in quick succession. Still he made no impression on the armour. Holbert, however, was beginning to breathe heavily; he was not used to facing so quick-footed an opponent. A few minutes later, he was leaning on his mace, gasping for air, and Hereward was still untired. He raised Brainbiter for the kill – then stepped back as a blinding light assailed his eyes. While he blinked and steadied himself, and puzzled what it could have been, a heavy blow to his chest sent him once more sprawling. His helmet fell from his head and rolled away; Holbert hefted his mace into the air to crush his unprotected skull.

The blow never fell. The motion had exposed the gap between helmet and lorica; and as Holbert stepped forward, Hereward, ignoring the pain in his chest, drove Brainbiter upwards and through his enemy's throat. The blood gushed forth as Holbert crashed headlong to the ground, and a groan went up from the men of Guines; Baldwin gave Susanne a satisfied smile. But Ascelin was not smiling; and nor, as he watched the former champion of Flanders, was Martin.

Ascelin scowled still more blackly throughout the victory feast.

"Well," remarked Hereward to Martin, "if he shows the world he hates me, I'm safe enough from him. If he were plotting against me he'd try to appear my friend." And Martin could not argue with that; but still he did not trust the ex-champion.

The day after the feast, Ascelin called on Torfrida in her chamber.

"I saw you smile at the wolfshead," he said accusingly.

"May I not smile where I please?" said Torfrida.

"He is an outlander!" exclaimed Ascelin. "A criminal! I am still your champion!" He dropped to his knees.

"I thought a champion was supposed to serve his

lady, not the other way around," said Torfrida sharply. "That's the difference between a champion and a husband. That's why you're on your knees – which doesn't suit you at all, by the way. Get up."

Ascelin did not move.

"I heard that you entertained him here in your chamber," he said sullenly. "You should have a better care of your reputation."

"I have many visitors," said Torfrida. "Kolfrosta is always here." The old Lapp looked up from her embroidery and mouthed something uncomplimentary in her own language.

"That old witch!" scoffed Ascelin.

"I think it is time you left, and past," said Torfrida quietly. Ascelin got awkwardly to his feet and headed for the door; there, he stopped, and turned.

"You're making a mistake, Torfrida," he said.

"Haven't you forgotten something?" Ascelin frowned uncomprehendingly. "My favour."

"Lady, I beg you –"

"You've done enough begging," said Torfrida coldly. Ascelin's face purpled; but he handed over the silk sleeve, then stalked out, muttering furiously.

In Spalding Keep, Ivo Taillebois was entertaining his neighbour, and fellow sharer in the lands of Askil, Gilbert of Ghent. Taillebois looked not unlike his King: the same reddish hair in severe Norman cut, the same broad frame, prominent jaw and high-coloured face. Both were also men of low background: William the Bastard a tanner's grandson, Ivo a woodcutter's, whence his surname, and whence, perhaps, his constant insistence on his baronial status. Gilbert was older, plumper, more placid, and more plainly dressed, his drab olive-green woollen tunic contrasting with Ivo's in expensive azure linen. He showed, in Ivo's eyes, little sign of how he had acquired a reputation as the wisest and most cunning of King William's knights.

Ivo's jongleur, Loquifer, was plucking at a lyre and chanting a passage from the Song of Roland; the assembled company listened politely, but most wished he would return to jests and juggling. Loquifer's high, nasal voice was unmusical in the extreme.

> "When the Emperor his justice hath achieved,
> His mighty wrath's abated from its heat,
> And Bramimunde has christening received;
> Passes the day, the darkness is grown deep,
> And now that King in 's vaulted chamber sleeps.
> St Gabriel is come from God, and speaks:
> 'Summon the hosts, Charles, of thine Empire,
> Go thou by force into the land of Bire,
> King Vivian thou'lt succour there, at Imphe,
> In the city which pagans have besieged.
> The Christians there implore thee and beseech.'
> Right loth to go, that Emperor was he:
> 'God!' said the King: 'My life is hard indeed!'
> Tears filled his eyes, he tore his snowy beard."

Ivo and his guests dutifully applauded, relieved that it was over.

"Give us a riddle," suggested the host. Loquifer thought for a moment.

"I saw the dead bring forth the living," he said, "and the breath of the living consume the dead; and when the dead was consumed, the living died."

"Something that eats the dead," guessed Ivo. "A wolf, or a crow."

"But the dead don't bring forth wolves and crows," pointed out the prostitute perched on the baron's knee.

"Shut up," said Ivo. "A maggot, then. Born of putrefaction, and when they've eaten all they die."

"No, no, no," Gilbert broke in. "The *breath* of the

living, he said the breath. It can't literally mean eating." Ivo's steward Rollo looked up from the chicken he had been gnawing on.

"A, a wasting disease," he suggested.

"Perhaps it's you, Rollo," sneered Ivo. "You eat enough."

"I have it!" exclaimed Gilbert, snapping his fingers. "Fire. We rub dead sticks together for a spark; the breath of fire is smoke, which marks the consumption of the wood; and when the wood is gone the fire dies."

"Sir Gilbert is wise," said Loquifer.

"You're not paid to flatter him, fool," grunted Ivo.

"I think Loquifer flatters himself," answered Gilbert. "If I penetrate his riddle it is because I think as he does. Now, some would say this makes me a fool; but, if I am wise, it follows that the fool himself is wise because *he* thinks as *I* do."

"You missed your calling, Sir Gilbert," said Loquifer with frank admiration. "You chop logic so well, you should have been a fool."

"Well," said Gilbert, "I am a courtier, which is much the same thing – only without the licence to tell truth."

Ivo yawned. The conversation was getting above his level; he did not care to be reminded that his fool was his intellectual superior.

"Tell us about the English," he ordered. Loquifer grinned.

"The English, my lord?" he said. "Their language makes the grunting of pigs sound more musical than my lute; they wash in the stagnant fens to improve their smell, and it works; the crows that ate English corpses at Hastings vomited for a week afterwards." Ivo and Rollo guffawed. This was more to their taste.

"You wouldn't say so in front of some I've met," said Gilbert.

"No indeed," agreed Loquifer. "It would be over their heads. If I wanted to make an Englishman laugh I should fart.

But that's probably still too sophisticated."

"And my hall at Bourne is still rotting in the unwashed hands of these savages," mused Ivo. "We must do something about that." There was a pause, and he yawned again. Loquifer bit his lip; his employer seemed less engaged than usual.

"Shall I juggle, master?" he inquired. Ivo nodded absently, and lobbed a dried apple at the jester; Loquifer caught it in his right hand as his left produced from behind Gilbert's ear three leather balls; and the juggling began.

As the season drew to a close, the Lord Baldwin proclaimed a boar hunt. Hereward and Torfrida were to ride beside Baldwin and his lady, Richildis; and Martin fussed around his master, tying his cross-garters just so and brushing down his cloak.

"If I were you, my lord," he ventured, "I should wear a coat of mail under my shirt today."

"Hmm?" said Hereward. "I'm sorry, my mind was on the Lady Torfrida. Did I tell you she has asked me to be her champion?"

"Yes, my lord."

"Me – a forest-wight, a wolfshead, an Esau on the face of the earth. A robber of priests, with the law's blessing on every hand that is turned against me."

"My lord – you should wear your hauberk today."

"Oh, no. I'm grateful for your concern, Martin, but Swallow's never thrown me yet. I'll not be coming within reach of the beast's tusks. And my ribs have set well enough since the fight."

"The boar is not the only animal that can bite."

"What?" Martin had his attention now.

"The spear that can penetrate a boar's hide will have little trouble with a man's."

"Who should harm me?" laughed Hereward.

"Sir Ascelin de St Valéry, or any one of a dozen

others," replied the squire. "All are envious that a foreign outlaw too proud to take knighthood from the Count's son should have been the one to slay Holbert of Guines, let alone become the Lady Torfrida's new champion. I've heard enough mutterings of late to know you're not safe today. And then there's what I saw at the fight."

"What was that?"

"The light in your eyes was no accident, master. Ascelin turned his shield in the sun of a purpose." Hereward shook his head.

"Martin, Martin, you've a nasty suspicious mind," he said. "But it will do me no harm to wear the mail, if it'll stop you clucking like a mother hen. Lay it out."

"The boar! The boar!" exclaimed Torfrida. The hunters spurred excitedly forward, as their quarry ducked into the undergrowth with baying hounds close behind it. Hereward, swivelling his spear in his hand, crashed through the bushes after it, the speedy bay mare Swallow carrying him far ahead of the others; until suddenly he found himself alone in an open clearing, with no living creature in sight. Not in sight – but in hearing. Something was breathing which was not himself or Swallow. Hereward flung himself down on Swallow's neck, just as a boar-spear whistled through the space where his head had been; losing his balance, he toppled from the saddle, falling sideways and jarring his shoulder on the ground. As he struggled to get to his feet, he heard the scrape of a sword being drawn; and an armoured figure on horseback trotted into the clearing. The man's face was obscured by his heavy helmet, but Hereward recognised the horse, a tall and heavy Franconian stallion: it belonged to Sir Ascelin de St Valéry.

As Ascelin rode down on him, swinging at his head, Hereward drew his knife and parried the blow. A jolt of pain ran up his arm: the knife was not made to ward off swords, and he had already been injured in the fall. Ascelin circled and trotted back towards him; Hereward, rubbing his arm, could only duck, and fell backwards. But as Ascelin made to raise his sword again, it fell from his fingers and he uttered a howl of pain. An arrow had sprouted from his shoulder; clutching wildly at it, he spurred his horse out of the glade, now eager only to escape whoever had come to Hereward's rescue before the next shaft should find his heart.

Standing between the trees, bow in hand, was Martin Lightfoot.

"You are supposed to be in Bruges," his lord told him. Martin shrugged.

"I don't like leaving things to chance," he said.

"You were right," admitted Hereward ruefully.

"There are three men no man should trust: the knight he has outfought, the merchant he has outbargained and the minstrel he has outsung," said the Irishman.

"Not bad rules," said Hereward. "Have you more?"

"There are three great follies: to show gold in front of a monk, to offer hospitality to a king, and to take a woman at her word."

"You're a cynical dog, Martin."

"But an experienced one." And Martin helped Hereward back into the saddle.

The summer of 1067 was all but done before Sir Ivo Taillebois decided to lay claim to Bourne Hall; and the leaves were turning gold as Rollo and Loquifer, with twelve footsoldiers tramping behind them, wended their way through the woods towards the stewartry of Toli son of Askil. Under the trees, silently watching them, stood a tall man with a patch over his right eye.

"Give us a riddle, fool," commanded Rollo importantly. The jongleur obliged.

"I am dumb but I speak, have no mind but much wisdom; my heart grew on the farm and my skin in the forest; both were killed and tanned, then scarred with spear-points, and from that wounding I came to life again and gave life to the dead."

"Holy St Denis!" exclaimed the steward. "That sounds heathenish to me. One of the old gods? Odin or Baldur?"

"You're a steward, Master Rollo," said the clown. "It's something you should know better than you do."

"Is it, by God?"

"It is, by God and His Mother both. It is a book."

"A book?" Rollo frowned uncomprehendingly. "I see the first part – dumb but it speaks, wisdom without a mind – but what does the rest mean?

"The heart is pages of calfskin, the skin a wooden cover, and the spear-points are steel nibs whose writing preserves the words of the dead," explained Loquifer, not entirely patiently.

"Ah, of course," said Rollo. "Plain as the nose on your face when you put it like that."

"I happen to think the nose on my face is remarkably handsome."

"Ha!" barked the steward, reaching into his saddlebag for a lump of cheese. "You're wasted on the baron. He has no humour; his only wit is to make sport of my belly, as if a healthy appetite were a sin." He took a huge bite of the cheese, and Loquifer muttered something about divine forgiveness; when, on the path ahead, they sighted a bowman with a dead hare at his belt. Rollo spluttered, spraying cheese crumbs. "By God! A poacher! Bring the Saxon ruffian down!" Two soldiers darted forward. The poacher made off as fast as he could, but they soon caught him, and dragged him in front of the steward. "Take his hand," Rollo commanded.

"No, my lord, please," gasped the poacher. He was a youngish man, dark-haired, thin, and his accent was not local or even English; and there was terror in his eyes. "I beg you – "

"You have robbed Sir Ivo Taillebois," said Rollo coldly. "I am his steward. Do you think he would thank me for letting you escape the law?" He turned to one of the soldiers pinioning the captive. "Take his hand." The soldier drew his sword and lopped off the poacher's right hand; the young man dropped to his knees, screaming, and began to burble what sounded like a prayer in a language the Normans did not recognise.

"I didn't like to interrupt, Master Rollo," said Loquifer quietly, "but this isn't actually Sir Ivo's land. It belongs to Ogier the Breton."

"Then we've saved him the trouble," said Rollo. "I just hope he's grateful. Nail up that hand, and let's get on."

"I wish I had been here, at the end," said Baldwin softly. He and Hereward were standing in Bruges Cathedral in the silence of the night, over the coffin of Count Baldwin V of Flanders.

"It could have been any time, my lord," Hereward told him. "The responsibilities of his office lay on you."

"Responsibilities?" echoed Baldwin bitterly. "I was dancing."

"The prince who never revels with his subjects loses their hearts. If luck had decreed he should die while you were hearing a plea or examining the tax records, would that have made a difference?"

"Luck; aye, it was ill luck. And an ill sign for the future. Will this be the sort of luck that marks my reign?"

"Never think it," urged Hereward. "The reign of Baldwin VI will be as long and as glorious as that of Baldwin V, God rest his noble soul."

"Well," said Baldwin, smiling, "at least I have inherited a fine champion." Hereward shuffled his feet.

"My oath was to your father, my lord," he said carefully.

"But you will renew it?" Baldwin looked at him expectantly. "Won't you?"

"I don't know. I would be honoured to serve you,

but... I feel I must return to England. Landless and kinless I may be in law, but in my heart I still have a family and a country. Both writhe under oppression and I miss them both sorely. I shall come back, of course," he added. "I'm still an outlaw there. But I must go." Baldwin laid his hand on Hereward's shoulder.

"Then go, with my blessing," he said. "Will you need a ship?"

"No," said Hereward. "Brunman of Skirbeck is at Antwerp; I'll pay my passage with him." Baldwin frowned.

"Brunman of Skirbeck?" he said. "Isn't he a pirate?"

"Exactly," said Hereward. "He keeps the fastest and best armed ship in the North Sea. Where should I be safer? But there is one favour I must ask your lordship before I leave."

"Name it." Hereward coughed, and looked down; then he met Baldwin's eye.

"Your blessing on my marriage to the Lady Torfrida de St Omer, if she will have me."

"With all my heart."

That was a balmy night in Flanders, but in Lincolnshire the rain was pouring down as Rollo and his train arrived at Bourne Hall. Dismounting, the steward strode up to the main door and knocked sharply.

"This place stinks of Saxons," muttered Loquifer, shivering in the wet. "It will take weeks to scrub the stench out."

The door edged open and a blonde girl peered out, a candle in her hand. Rollo shoved his foot in the door.

"Who's there?" she asked quaveringly.

"Your master's steward, pretty one," he leered.

"Who is it, Rowena?" came a voice from within.

"Normans," said the girl. An instant later, the door was thrown wide open, and out strode Toli. Young the boy might be, but he wore a sword, the Normans noticed, and carried himself with the pride of a king.

"What do you want here?" he demanded.

"I am Rollo," answered the steward haughtily, "steward to Sir Ivo Taillebois, Baron of Spalding and Bourne. I have come to claim Bourne Hall in the name of my master."

"And I am Toli Askilsson," riposted the youth, "cousin and steward to Morcar Alfgarsson, Earl of Northumbria, the only true lord of Bourne, in whose name I command you to depart." Rollo, red with indignation, slapped the presumptuous Englishman's face; in answer, Toli punched the fat Norman, splitting his lip and knocking him sprawling in the mud.

"Oho, you'll regret that, my lad," crowed Loquifer.

"Does anybody else want to press Sir Ivo's claims?" shouted Toli, drawing his sword.

Twelve Norman blades came out of their sheaths as one.

Chapter 2: *Homecoming*

September, 1067.

"This is the Manor of Bourne," declared Toli defiantly, "the inheritance of the House of Mercia, handed down by Earl Leofric to Earl Alfgar and so to Morcar of Northumbria. My father was Askil Tokason, Lord of Ware, Earl Morcar's steward, and he charged me to hold Bourne until the Earl should claim it: and hold it I will, against you and the King and his army if they should come." Twelve Norman swordsmen took a step forward; but only one. They looked uncertainly at Rollo the Steward, still lying full length in the mud where the boy had knocked him.

The fat man propped himself up painfully, wiped the dribble of blood from his mouth, and spat out the command: "Kill him."

The Normans charged. Toli stood his ground: but it was a matter of seconds before the weight of numbers bore him down.

The next day, the *Gannet* arrived on the Lincolnshire coast in fine weather. Brunman's ship was of newfangled style, a hybrid that mingled the designs of lean Viking longship and swag-bellied merchantman to create a beast both fast and capacious, ideally suited to his piratical activities; and in this he had brought Hereward the Outlaw and Martin Lightfoot across the sea from Flanders.

"England," declared the laconic pirate, as Hereward bounded through the surf. The exile fell on the sand and kissed it, as Martin followed unhurriedly.

"After all these years," murmured Hereward. "Thank you, Brunman! I wish you calm seas and much plunder!"

"Thank *you*, my lord," said Brunman, patting his purse. "And good luck. I will deliver Swallow to you in

Skirbeck." The boat had been too small to carry Hereward's horse, who would have to wait to disembark until the *Gannet* could pull up to a quay and lower a gangplank. Hereward disliked parting from her, but trusted Brunman: the pirate knew better than to make an enemy of him.

As the captain rowed back to the ship, Hereward threw back his head and roared:

"I'm home! Home! God's teeth, it's good! Smell the air, Martin."

"It smells of salt, my lord," replied his esquire, "much like the sea air in Flanders or anywhere else."

"By the bones of St Cuthbert," exclaimed Hereward, "you're a cold one. Doesn't it feel glorious to be back in England?" Martin could not remember his master this joyous, even on his wedding day.

"Your lordship forgets", he said, "that I am not English. And nor is England, now. This is an occupied country; and it is best to be careful."

"You're right, of course," said Hereward with a frown. "But my brother still holds Bourne Hall. We'll dine with him there tonight. He was barely walking when I left, you know. Thirteen years..." Misty-eyed reminiscence was as unlike Hereward as crowing jubilation. Martin hoped that his master was in command of all his senses: if they ran into the occupiers, he would need them.

In her chamber in Bruges, the Lady Torfrida was embroidering the image of a white bear, her new lord's chosen symbol. When the door opened, she looked up sharply: she did not care for people who did not knock. But the newcomer had the right to wander where she pleased in what was now the household of Count Baldwin VI, and to ignore courtesies as she saw fit: it was Baldwin's stately wife, the Countess Richildis.

The Countess moved across the room, seeming, in her long duck-egg kirtle, to glide rather than walk, and sat herself neatly down beside Torfrida.

"My lady of Ware," she said. Torfrida bit her tongue, unsure whether this was meant as a compliment or an insult. Her husband had no title: and, had he escaped outlawry and stayed in England to be Lord of Ware and the dozen other properties of Askil, he would never have met Torfrida.

"My lady," she replied guardedly.

"Do you love your new husband?" asked the Countess. Startled by her directness, Torfrida looked up. Richildis' sharp blue eyes pierced into hers.

"Yes, my lady," she said simply.

"That is good," said Richildis. "Do you love him enough to follow him to England?"

"What does your ladyship mean?" asked Torfrida, worried. "He has gone only to visit his family. He can't stay there; he's an outlaw. A wolfshead, as the English say. And he has promised me he'll return."

Richildis shrugged dismissively.

"Return to collect you, perhaps," she said. "If he doesn't send his servant to do that."

"I do not understand," said Torfrida.

"I think you do," said Richildis. "You know the Lord Hereward better than I do; you saw the look in his eyes. He may tell us he means to return to Flanders, he may even believe it himself, but he won't. When he sets foot on Lincolnshire ground again it will be as if he never left, and if he has to fight every Norman in England to stay there he will. You know that in your heart. So I ask you again: are you willing to follow him there?"

Torfrida took a deep breath.

"If he asks it of me, lady," she said, "I will follow him to the ends of the earth."

"Then he is very lucky," said Richildis softly; "and so are you." There was a pause, and Torfrida wondered what the Countess' purpose could be. "Have you heard recently from Sir Ascelin de St Valéry?"

"No, lady," said Torfrida. "Why should I care about him?"

"I understand you did once," said the Countess mildly. "He is in Normandy – he has joined Duke William's army, King William, I should say now, and is fighting against the Count of Maine. But now that he is William's man it is very likely that he will return to England with the King. Perhaps your husband has not seen the last of him."

And, with that, she rose and shimmered out of the room.

"We'll give you a fine dinner at Bourne, Martin," Hereward promised. "Roast pork and fenland ale: proper English fare. I've missed it." He sighed. "I've missed everything."

"That's well enough for tonight, my lord," said Martin, "but are we to survive till then on empty stomachs?"

"You're the bowman," retorted Hereward. "The wood is full of food. Shoot us something."

"And end up like that?" said Martin, pointing. Hereward looked up, and caught his breath. Nailed to a tree by the roadside was a severed human hand. It was not old: the blood was sticky and the skin still pink: but flies were humming round it.

"God in Heaven," breathed Hereward.

"Norman justice," said the squire. "No doubt the man who lost that thought to bag himself a dinner here."

"Swine," muttered Hereward. "Bring it down; if we can't return it to its owner we can take it to the Abbey and get it a Christian burial."

"I'm not carrying that," said Martin.

"Then we'll bury it here," Hereward insisted. "I'll dig while you hunt." The Irishman unslung his bow and moved stealthily forward towards the trees, while Hereward began to scrape at the mossy earth by the roadside with his knife. When he had made a decent-sized hole, he shooed the flies away from the hand and levered it off the tree with the flat of his blade, before dropping it into the hole. "*Requiescat in pace*," he muttered as he patted the earth back into place. Just as he was finishing, a shadow fell across him.

Rising, Hereward found himself face to face – or nearly so, for the stranger was somewhat taller than he – with a grey-bearded man of indeterminate age, wearing a broad-brimmed hat, a long, much repaired cloak, and a patch over his right eye. The patch, like the rest of his clothes, was the greyish blue of an autumn sea: so too was his visible eye, which twinkled like a smiling star, but had, Hereward thought, a hardness to it. In his right hand he held a staff of elm six feet long.

"Do not be afraid," said the one-eyed man. His voice was very deep, but gentle.

"Afraid?" grunted Hereward. "Who says I'm afraid?"

"I am a friend."

"Yes?" said Hereward suspiciously. "Whose? Do you know who I am?"

"You are Hereward, son of Askil, son of Toki of Lincoln, who was banished from these lands thirteen years ago." And Hereward felt that, if the stranger had said "You are King William", or, for that matter, "You are Queen Mathilde", he would in that moment have believed it.

"And you are?"

"I have many names," said the stranger. "You may call me Lysir."

"Well, Lysir," said Hereward, "what do you want with me?" The one-eyed man did not answer, instead asking:

"Why have you come back?"

"To see my family and my home again," said Hereward.

"And is that all?" pressed Lysir.

"What more should there be?"

"Hereward", said Lysir, "is spoken of as a fighting man."

"I fight where I'm paid," said Hereward.

"Did the Lady Gwendolen pay you before you fought Ironhook?"

Hereward shivered. Of course, his past career was famous enough, but it still felt uncanny that Lysir should know such things.

"Tell me what you want, old man," he said.

"First answer me," insisted Lysir.

"I was rewarded afterwards," said Hereward.

"And that is why you fought?" Lysir raised an amused eyebrow. "You faced Ironhook because you saw injustice about to be done. You took up the sword because the law had failed to defend what was right. That is how you earned Brainbiter, and why you are still its master." He gestured at Hereward's sword, whose hilt the outlaw had begun to finger.

"What if I am?" said Hereward.

"Do you not see injustice now?" Lysir pointed to the disturbed earth where the poacher's hand lay buried.

"I didn't come back to be the champion of Saxon England," said Hereward. "That's the business of kings and earls. Edgar Atheling has submitted to William, and all the nobility with him. If he changes his mind I'll be ready to do my bit, so long as I can have my father's lands back and a pardon for my outlawry. But until they cross me, the Normans aren't my concern."

"Then I bid you farewell," said Lysir heavily. "You may not find everything as you expect at Bourne." He strode up to the edge of the trees, then turned back. "Remember the old verse," he said. "Wyrd goes ever as she will." And with that, he was gone.

Hereward was never afterwards sure whether it was the instant Lysir left or some minutes later – not too long, he knew, or he would have noticed the shadows shifting – that Martin came back into his view. Two woodpigeons swung from his belt.

"Did you see which way the one-eyed man went?" asked Hereward.

"What man, my lord?" said Martin curiously. "I've seen nobody but us since we entered the woods."

Bourne Hall.

Rollo turned to a new page of accounts, and munched on an apple. The jester Loquifer was squatting in a corner tuning his lute, while the tearful, terrified English maid hurried about with a tray full of beer mugs, serving the thirsty soldiers. Two of them, badly wounded in the fight with Toli, lay propped up on pallets against the wall; but, even though the holes in their guts were oozing beer, they too were drinking heavily. From time to time the soldiers would exchange leering comments in French, and laugh: Rowena did not know whether to be worried or relieved that she could not understand them.

The steward's mug was empty.

"Girl!" he snapped, waving at the maid. Unlike his companions, the steward spoke English, though his accent was appalling. "Beer. Hurry up, hurry up. And stop snivelling," he added, as she failed to suppress a sob. She hastily replenished his tankard. "This won't do," he declared, jabbing at the page before him, "won't do at all. The Manor of Bourne doesn't seem to have collected its rents in months. No wonder it's such a hovel."

"There was a terrible confusion after the Conquest, sir," said Rowena, as bravely as she could. "And then what with the changes, and the bad harvest, the people hardly had anything, and Lord Toli – that is, we, we hadn't the men to collect it if they had…"

"Be quiet," said the steward. "We will collect every penny of back rent due to the Manor of Bourne. To do otherwise would be to rob the good Lord Ivo. And we'll put these books in proper order – this is shocking. Shocking."

"But sir," protested Rowena, "the tenants can't afford –"

"I told you to be quiet!" roared the steward, leaping to his feet and hurling his beer in her face, scattering documents across the floor. Loquifer, in his corner, sniggered; the soldiers joined in, and soon the whole hall was ringing with laughter, while Rowena stood, dripping, humiliated. Rollo scowled. "Get me another beer," he ordered.

It was dark by the time Hereward and Martin arrived on the outskirts of Bourne. The village was not walled: it was too scattered to be worth the effort: instead the larger farm houses were each defensible, and lesser properties had to be abandoned when freebooters came. In the old days that had meant the Danes; there had never been a chance to defend Bourne against the Normans.

"We're nearly at the Hall now," whispered Hereward. There was no one in sight, but darkness encourages secrecy, especially when one knows one might not be altogether welcome.

"Are you sure it's wise to go straight there, my lord?" asked Martin anxiously. "As sure as night's dark there'll be Norman soldiers there."

"You're right," said Hereward. "My father's retainer Osred has a farm on this side of the village. We'll go there first; he can tell us the lie of the land."

To win past Osred's outer fence was not difficult: it was unmanned, and both men were skilled in siegecraft: but the house itself was a daunting sight. As high as Bourne Hall, although the Hall accommodated only one storey while Osredstun had two, it loomed blackly above them.

"Are you sure this is a farmhouse?" said Martin. "It looks more like a fortress."

"Good men have reason enough to fortify their houses these days," replied Hereward. He leant down to pick up a stone; but before he could throw it the upstairs shutters were thrown back and a torch thrust out of the window.

"Whoever's out there can go to Hell," declared the torch's invisible bearer; "for I'll go there myself before I open the door by night."

"Winter?" said Hereward. "Little Winter, is that you?"

"If you call me little again, stranger," promised the man with the torch, "I'll cut you down to my height and we can talk face to face."

"That's my Winter! That's my brother in arms! Don't you remember your leader? Raiding the barns and orchards when you were even smaller than now?"

"Hereward?" wondered Winter, leaning out to peer into the darkness.

"The same. Hereward the forest-wight, Hereward the exile: I have returned."

"Hereward!" repeated Winter. "Bless me, I took you for a damned Norman! Gwynnog! Father! Up and open the doors – Lord Hereward's back!"

At Bourne Hall, the hide-whole soldiers were by now scarcely in better state than their wounded comrades; Rowena, her dress and her dignity still stained with Rollo's beer, was still serving them, while Loquifer tootled on a recorder. Eventually, however, the steward grew tired of the fool's idea of music.

"Loquifer!" he commanded. "Ask us a riddle."

"I went hunting for a quarry that first preyed on me," said the jester, "and the only beasts I carried home were the ones I didn't catch."

"Too easy," scoffed Rollo, scratching himself. "Fleas. This place is crawling with the bastards."

"You're getting better, Master Rollo," grinned the jester.

"Or you're getting worse," growled the steward. "Give us a harder one."

"I curl at the root," said Loquifer, baring his yellow teeth, "I stand in a bed, I make maids' eyes water, and broad is my head." He repeated the riddle in English for the benefit of the maid; his attempt at the language was still more atrocious than the steward's, but she understood him well enough.

Rollo guffawed; Rowena blushed, then turned away in disgust when she saw the jester eyeing her in evident satisfaction at the effect of his scurrility.

"I give up," said the steward. "It can't be what it sounds like."

"An onion," announced Loquifer triumphantly. There was a pause while the meaning of the riddle sank in; then Rollo gave a great racking sound that might as well have been a cough as a laugh, but was probably both.

"Ha!" he exclaimed at length. "Good. Good. A song. A song, now! Let's have the Hastings Song, to celebrate our famous victory over the Saxon scum."

Loquifer began to strum on his lute.

"When dawn rosy-fingered

Rose over the land," he warbled. The soldiers began to join in.

"And the beams of the sun
Were cast over the world,
The Duke of the Normans
Did give his command..."

"It does an old man's heart good to see you again, my lord Hereward," declared Osred. Hereward had never thought of Osred as old before, but the farmer had indeed aged sorely; his face was deeply lined and his hair snow-white. He could not be much above fifty and looked every day of seventy. His son Winter was little changed: the same sprightly, elfin Winter Hereward remembered: as for Gwynnog, their Welsh servant who had been more like a brother, he had gained a few inches' height and a beard – but he had lost far more. For it was Gwynnog's hand that Hereward had buried in the woods.

Hereward took a swig of ale.

"It makes me feel young to be back among my housecarles," he said. "But your hand – oh, Taillebois' steward will pay for that. I will take his and make him carry it back to his master in his mouth. But how are things at Bourne? How are Mother and Toli bearing up under the yoke?" There was an uncomfortable silence. "Well?" prompted Hereward. "Speak."

"You are too late, my lord," said Gwynnog.

"Too late? What do you mean?"

"It was to Bourne Hall the Norman's steward was riding when he took my hand," the Welshman explained. "He came there last night and marched in at the gate with a dozen men at arms."

"Ivo is the new owner of Bourne Hall," added Osred. "The tanner's grandson has parted your lands three ways."

"Aye, I know," said Hereward. "Between Taillebois, Ogier the Breton and Gilbert of Ghent."

"A Norman, a Breton and a Fleming," remarked Osred. "One from each of the buzzard nations that follow at the destroyer's tail. Do you know them, my lord?"

"Gilbert I knew in Flanders," said Hereward, "and before that in Scotland. He's a rogue, but I believe he has a good heart. These other two I don't know."

"Ivo is a villain," spat Winter. "There have been men here from Spalding who say he laughs at hangings; kills any man that angers him and takes any woman that pleases him. And now he is master of Bourne Hall."

"And you didn't stop this?" Martin demanded.

"What could we do?" retorted Winter. "If we fought, even if we slew these dozen men, the three barons could have another hundred here tomorrow."

"Then", said Hereward, "I would find a way to send two hundred down on them."

"What of my lord's family?" Martin asked.

"They have not been seen since the Normans came," said Gwynnog. "A closed carriage left this morning by the Croyland road; most likely they were in it."

"Is Toli turned such a coward that he wouldn't defend his charge?" wondered Hereward incredulously.

"It would have been madness to fight, my lord," insisted Winter. "With all respect, you've been away most of your brother's life; I know him better than you. He's no coward."

"Well, madness it may be," said Hereward grimly; "but I mean to take back the Hall. "Winter, Gwynnog, you were both ready enough to follow me as children: will you follow Hereward now, as men?"

"If you call on me," declared Gwynnog, "I will stand by you."

"And I," said Winter.

"And I, my lord," added Osred.

Hereward rose, pushing out the bench he had been sitting on.

"I may send for you before morning," he said.

"You will not attempt the Hall tonight?" said Osred. "Not alone?"

"Of course not." Hereward smiled reassuringly. "I'm only going to spy out the land. But I think I will take Brainbiter nonetheless: it is always better to have a sword than not."

The gate of Bourne Hall stood ajar and unguarded; Hereward slipped easily into the yard. There was light in the windows, and raucous voices could be heard on the air.

"By the Duke's command, Harold," they sang,
"You lie here, a king,
That you still may be watcher
O'er the shore and the sea."

But the dead watcher over Bourne Hall was not King Harold. Nailed by a spear-head to the wall above the door was the ghastly, gaping head of a young boy. Hereward did not recognise him by sight: it had been too long, and in any case the vile thing could hardly be said to look human: but he knew with sick shock that it could only be his brother.

"God damn them," he said quietly. "God damn them to the lowest depths of Hell." He raised his foot and kicked the door in.

It was unbarred, and swung open easily. Startled by the noise and draught, Rollo tried to get to his feet, but fell back into his chair, too drunk to rise.

"Who – who are you?" he wheezed.

"My name is Naemansson," said Hereward smoothly. "I am a Dane formerly in the service of the Lord Alfgar; I knew the Lord Askil Tokason, and as I was passing through Bourne I came to pay my respects to his son."

"Well," said the steward, "you've already dipped your head to him." The soldiers tittered; Rowena, unable to bear any more, burst out:

"If Lord Hereward were here you'd sing a different tune!"

"Hereward?" sneered Rollo. "The prodigal son? We needn't fear him; I heard he ran away to Italy with the pay-chest of Count Baldwin's army." He turned to the jester. "Loquifer, dance!" he barked. "Show us how an Englishman dances."

Loquifer began to shuffle and stagger about, like a blind man in drink on the sea; the Normans chuckled appreciatively. Rollo eyed the newcomer's stony face.

"You're not laughing, stranger," he observed.

"I didn't find it amusing," said Hereward.

"Well, I did," declared Rollo. "You shall be rewarded, Loquifer. No stingy Saxon sits in the seat of Bourne now; I am Rollo the Steward, and my hand is open. Name your prize."

"Then I would see the Countess Godiva ride through Lincoln as naked as she rode through Coventry thirty years ago," leered the jester. They were the last words he ever spoke. Before the laughter had died the clown's head was bouncing along the floor, trailing blood and gore; it had rolled several yards before his body fell. Hereward wiped Brainbiter clean.

"Now that's funny," he said.

Rollo got stumblingly to his feet, only to be slashed across the chest and almost cut in half; the soldiers, fumbling drunkenly for their weapons, made to attack the maniacally laughing Englishman, but in their befuddled state they were easily cut down. Not even the wounded were spared. When all fourteen lay dead, Hereward howled to the rafters:

"Behold the Lord of Bourne! I am Hereward! Hereward the outlaw, the champion, the berserker and the viking! I am the fattener of ravens, the darling of wolves and the curse of the widow! I am the land-thief and the sea-thief, slayer of bears and giants, ravager of the world!"

When dawn rose over Bourne Hall the next day, there were fourteen heads above the door.

Croyland Abbey.

The funeral of Toli was well attended, considering the short notice. The Abbot of Croyland conducted the ceremony; Father Wulfwine was there, and the former Countess Godiva, now a nun; also the boy's uncles from the Abbey of Peterborough, Abbot Brand and young Brother Godric, as well as all the leading folk of Bourne. It was a warm autumn day, and birds were singing as the coffin slid into the ground.

"*Requiem aeternam dona ei, Domine,*" Abbot Ulfkytel intoned, "*et lux perpetua luceat ei. Requiescat in pace.*"

"Amen."

Hereward stepped forward, and began to declaim

over his brother's grave as the earth was shovelled in.

> "Wyrd is set fast:
> So quoth the wanderer,
> Mindful of hardship,
> Of wrathful slaughters
> And the fall of his kin.
> All is turbulence
> In this earthly realm;
> Wyrd winds on and changes
> The world under Heaven.
> Here gold is fleeting;
> Here friend is fleeting;
> Here man is fleeting;
> Here clan is fleeting.
> All this earth's props
> Waste into idleness.
> Well bides it with him who seeks mercy,
> Balm from the Father in Heaven:
> There, for us, stands the only fastness."

"There, for us, stands the only fastness," chorused the congregation.

The silence was broken by the fearful clamour of a duck fleeing the talons of a falcon. The Lady Edith broke down, with a long wail.

"Death, death, death!" she cried. "War among men and beasts, war among birds of the air, war in the water beneath and war in Heaven above! Will it never be over? Will it never be over?"

Her sister Godiva gathered her into her arms.

"Not in this world, I fear, lady," said Ulfkytel. There was an uncomfortable pause.

"Forgive me, my lord abbot," said Hereward quietly after a minute, "but we should be on our way. It is not safe for us to stay."

"I stay," declared Edith, steadier now. "I shall never leave Croyland now. Here are buried all my hopes but one; and here I shall rest myself soon enough."

"Mother –"

"It is my last request of you," she said firmly. "My last save this: do not give your heart wholly to vengeance. That is the way to Hell."

"Mother." Hereward bowed his head to receive her blessing, and was granted it. And when the guests departed Croyland, Sister Godiva helped Sister Edith up to the little house where the cells of the few nuns were, and there she stayed.

The others left on the flat-bottomed boats favoured by the marsh folk; Hereward travelled with Wulfwine, Brand and Godric, Martin poling the boat.

"Uncle Brand," said Hereward, almost diffidently, "there is a favour I would ask for myself and my companions now that my brother is laid to rest."

"Ask what you will," said the Abbot.

"It is that we should be made knights."

"Knights, lad?" said Brand. "I thought you had been a belted knight these dozen years."

"After the Norman fashion, dubbed by another fighting man?" said Hereward. "I could have been; but I was too proud. I wanted to show that an English squire could lead any French or Flemish knight, and best them too; I wanted to be able to go to the greatest champion of Europe and say 'You alone are worthy to dub me'. I thought as the Normans do, that it was unmanly to be knighted by a priest. But the truth is, I was not worthy of knighthood."

"Not worthy?"

"I was an enemy to my own kin," Hereward explained. "Banished by Uncle Leofric's request, with my parents supporting him. But I have my mother's blessing on my head now: and I would have an English knighthood, at the hands of a priest." Seeing Brand hesitate, he continued hastily, stripping a gold chain from his neck: "I know I robbed St Peter of his tithes, and I offer this in payment – even with thirteen years' interest, it should more than cover my debt."

"Bless you, lad," said Brand, "bless you, it shall be done. At Peterborough, tomorrow at dawn. Wulfwine, will you dub this renegade a knight? You owe him no less after lending your voice to his banishment."

"I said it would do him good, Father Abbot, and I was right," answered Wulfwine. "He left England a scoundrel and returned a hero. You have the soul of a knight, Lord Hereward, there's no doubting that; and I will give you the accolade."

Hereward was adamant that all five should be knighted: Osred and Winter, Martin and Gwynnog, with him. Knighthood was a new thing in England, introduced in King Edward's reign by his Norman bodyguards: but the pious Confessor had entrusted it to the clergy instead of warriors to bestow the accolade. This caused some uncertainty over whether the low-born could receive it. Gwynnog, whose parents had been slaves in the Marcher country before Osred had bought them from their old master and set them free, objected that he was too humble for such an honour, but Hereward insisted:

"If a priest gives the accolade, then it is an eighth sacrament, and may be given to any man not excommunicate." The Welshman thus quelled his doubts, and knelt beside Hereward and Winter at the altar rail. Martin and Osred, however, would not be persuaded. The old man declared himself unworthy, while Martin said:

"I am a knave, master, born and bred, and you know I will die a knave. I fight with peasant weapons and I don't believe in chivalry; I'm a thief and a cheat and I'd be a mockery of knighthood." He would not be budged.

A few hours after the three childhood friends at Peterborough, another knighthood was bestowed at Spalding: on a black pawn that had advanced across the board despite all Ivo Taillebois could do to stop it.

"And that, I think, is checkmate," said Gilbert of Ghent.

"Damn it," said Ivo, frowning. "Why do you always win?"

"If I told you that you might beat me."

"I think you're cheating," said Ivo.

"It's not possible to cheat at chess," said Gilbert carelessly. Ivo squinted at the pieces, trying to work out what devilry Gilbert had worked on him; whereupon his chaplain entered, a neat, punctilious priest who bowed low to his master.

"What is it, Hugo?" demanded Ivo irritably.

"The Prior of Peterborough is here, my lord," said the priest smoothly. "He says he has urgent news regarding the Manor of Bourne."

"Bring him in," ordered the baron grudgingly.

"I'll get out of your way," offered Gilbert, getting up as Father Hugo slid out of the room.

"Nonsense," said Ivo. "You were given a share in Bourne; this concerns you too."

Hugo ushered in the flushing Prior, and shut the door.

"Prior Herluin," said Ivo. "To what do we owe this pleasure?"

"No pleasure, my lord," said Herluin, wagging his head. "It is my sad duty to inform you that Bourne Hall has been surprised and all your men savagely slaughtered."

"What?" roared Ivo, leaping to his feet.

"The wolfshead Hereward returned unexpectedly from Flanders and conspired with friends and relatives in the village. He is in control of Bourne now."

"All dead, you say?" Ivo repeated.

"Every one."

"Fourteen men! How many English did they take with them?"

"Only the outlaw's brother Toli. They were taken by surprise."

"What is this Hereward?" said Ivo. "A demon? How can fourteen men defending a hall be overwhelmed and kill only one?"

"I know Hereward," Gilbert put in. "In Scotland he killed a bear single-handed. He's a formidable man."

"Well, he shall learn that I am formidable too," declared Ivo.

"There is worse, my lords," said Herluin. Gilbert looked at the Prior curiously: he suspected that a part of him was enjoying delivering this bad news.

"Worse?" snapped Ivo. "How can it be worse?"

"The Abbot of Croyland, and, I grieve to say it, my own abbot, Brand Tokason of Peterborough, are co-conspirators with this Hereward," said Herluin. "Abbot Ulfkytel has given a grave to his brother and shelter to his mother, and with my own eyes I have seen Abbot Brand entertain the wolfshead and his accomplices in Peterborough. Hereward is his nephew. Wulfwine of Ely bestowed knighthood on three of the brigands in the abbey church. It is only at risk of my own life that I have been able to come and warn your lordship."

"I'll burn their abbeys about their ears!" swore the Norman furiously.

"Patience, Ivo," counselled the older knight, laying a hand on his arm. "We don't yet know how widespread the conspiracy is. Maybe the common people don't support this rebellion – but they will if we start attacking monasteries."

"Sir Gilbert is right, my lord," said Hugo.

"Yes; yes," agreed Ivo, somewhat more calmly. "Well, Croyland and Peterborough can rest undisturbed, for the moment. But Bourne! Bourne I will take back, or all my tenants will laugh at me behind their hands. I thank you,

Prior Herluin, for your loyalty."

"No more than my duty, my lord," said Herluin, bowing.

You had best return to Peterborough before you are missed," said Ivo. "I'll ready my men for revenge. Are you with me, Gilbert?"

"I haven't many men in Spalding," said the Fleming, "but if we wait a few days I could gather more. And Sir Ogier could help us too."

"By then half of Lincolnshire might be in flames," said Ivo impatiently. "No, we march now. We'll come on them by night as they came on poor Rollo. I'll wipe this outlaw scourge out of Bourne."

So it came about that, as the sun began to sink late the next afternoon, the two knights were riding at the head of a troop of soldiers, a mounted captain by their side, by the same woodland road where Gwynnog had lost his hand and Hereward had met the one-eyed man.

"It will be dark before we are out of these woods," Gilbert warned.

"So?" said Ivo. "What do you fear – ghosts? Fairies? Our enemies are in Bourne."

"Remember," said the older man, "I know Hereward. He will be expecting a counter-attack."

"But not nearly so soon," Ivo pointed out. "He doesn't know we know he's there, so how can he know we're coming? He'll still be celebrating his victory; we'll probably find him drunk on the floor. And if not – we have enough men. He'll be trapped there; just as poor Rollo was trapped. Rather neat, isn't it?"

"At the very least we should put out scouts and flank guards," insisted Gilbert. "Hereward or no Hereward, this is hostile country."

"You overestimate these English," Ivo told him. "The ones with the brains to fight back haven't the guts to try. Five marks says we won't see a man till we reach the village."

"In that case," said Gilbert, "you owe me five marks." He pointed forward. Standing in their path, in full armour and with Brainbiter held squared before him, was Hereward Askilsson.

"Gilbert of Ghent," he said. "I am sorry to see you among these buzzards."

"You should know me better than that by now, Hereward," said Gilbert. "I take profit where I find it. It's been a long time."

"Not long enough, if this is the company you keep nowadays," said Hereward. "Sir Ivo Taillebois, I order you by God and St Edmund, and in the name of Edgar Atheling the lawful King of England, to turn and ride back to Spalding. Do that and you and your men will be spared. Ride on and you will die, like those you sent before you."

"Murderer!" Ivo shouted.

"No," said Hereward softly; "I am an executioner. Your servants butchered my brother and set his head above the door of his own house: there are fourteen Norman heads there now. Fourteen against one and I slew them all, with this sword." He raised Brainbiter above his head. The orange light of the evening sun, reflected on the blade, made it glow as if it were forged of flame rather than steel. "Do you want to feel it?"

"You're a liar," said Ivo, though there was no certainty in his voice. "And this time it's one against fifty."

"Your soldiers are waiting for you in Hell, Sir Ivo," said Hereward.

"You'll be with them first, Saxon!" swore Ivo, drawing his own sword. But even as he spurred forward, his horse was shot from under him. Out of the woods on both sides of the path came a sudden hail of stones, throwing-axes, even a horse-shoe that clanged off one soldier's helmet; and after them came the English, villagers and cottars armed with hatchets and knives, Winter and Gwynnog directing them while Martin, standing behind Hereward, strung and loosed arrow after arrow.

Staggering to his feet, Ivo again lunged at Hereward, who sidestepped, kicked his feet from under him, and raised Brainbiter for the death-blow; and Ivo Taillebois' life would have ended there had not the captain cantered forward, swinging his axe for Hereward's head. As the Englishman parried the blow, Ivo crawled away, calling pitifully for help.

Gilbert had hung back from the fight, but he did not abandon Ivo. While the captain circled to ride at Hereward again, Gilbert rode swiftly forward, and hauled the Norman up onto his horse. A well-aimed stone from Winter caught the captain between the eyes, and Hereward turned back to Ivo: but Gilbert, who could see the way the battle was going, was already riding as swift as his horse could carry two back to Spalding.

"Beaten," Ivo groaned as they left the wood. "And by those stinking peasants! Oh, I'll make Hereward pay for this."

"At least the King won't hear of your humiliation in Normandy," Gilbert pointed out.

"No," agreed Ivo glumly. "But God alone knows what the Queen will say."

London.

"To William, by the Grace of God King of the English. My lord, the distrust and dissension between your regents is such that the governance of the realm has all but ground to a halt. All of your subjects most devoutly wish for your return –" Queen Mathilde paused in her dictation as the Baron de Warenne entered the chamber. "What's the matter?" she asked irritably. The clerk blotted the letter and silently cursed.

"There is word of rebellion in Lincolnshire, Your Grace," said the baron. "Bourne Hall has been attacked and fourteen men slain."

"Bourne?" echoed the Queen. "Bourne... Who is lord there?"

"Sir Ivo Taillebois, Your Grace."

"That toad," said the Queen, pleased. "Was he among the dead?"

"No, ma'am," said de Warenne regretfully. "His steward, his fool, and twelve soldiers. Sir Ivo has set out to punish the attack, but there is no word yet of his success... or otherwise."

"And who did it?"

"They say it was the mercenary who slew Holbert of Guines."

"Hereward?" mused Mathilde. "So he is in England."

"Your Grace knows him?"

"By reputation only," said the Queen. "He served my father in Flanders; my brothers always spoke well of him. But that was after I had left the Flemish court. I understand he's already outlawed in England; that saves us proclaiming it again, at any rate."

"He has a bloody name," said de Warenne. "Does Your Grace think the King should be informed? Or perhaps one of the Regents?"

"The King has worries enough in Normandy," said Mathilde. "And I am the true Regent, as you know well enough, or you would not have brought this to me." King William, when he departed, had formally left joint rulers of England behind him: his counsellor Ralph Guader, and his brother, Bishop Odo of Bayeux. In fact, so rarely could they agree that, unless the Queen took the decisions, they were not likely to be taken at all. She wondered if, perhaps, this was what William had intended. If England was ungovernable without him, his regents would never grow over mighty, and the rest of his nobles would pray daily for his return. It irked their lordships mightily to be ruled by a woman, and it did not help that Mathilde was barely four feet tall: one baron had been heard to remark that he felt as if he was taking orders from a doll: but they had to concede that things did get done. And, of course, their prayers for the safe homecoming of King William became all the more fervent. "One incident does not make a revolution. This Bourne – it was Hereward's house once, was it not?"

"The Earl Morcar's, Your Grace," said de Warenne. "It was kept for him by his cousin Toli – Hereward's brother."

"And what became of this Toli?"

"I understand Sir Ivo's men killed him."

"Idiots," sighed Mathilde. "Well, they got no more than they deserved." A thought occurred to her. "Wasn't the Manor of Bourne divided?"

"Yes, Your Grace."

"Who else shared in the spoils?"

"Sir Ogier fitz Ungomar, principally. Also Sir Gilbert of Ghent."

The Queen reached her decision.

"Send to Sir Ivo," she told her clerk, "and tell him that he has until Midwinter's Day to bring this Hereward to justice. If he fails, then in the name of the King I shall confiscate his share in the manor of Bourne and transfer it to Sir Ogier – for an appropriate fee."

"My lady," said the clerk, nodding and scribbling. The Queen smiled at the Baron de Warenne.

"That should be the last we'll hear of this rebellion," she said.

Hereward stood alone on the edge of the woods, and chanted softly.

"Wayland himself
By fireworms was wracked,
The brave earl
Hardships endured:
That was overcome;
So may this be."

Lysir stepped from the shadows into a ring of moonlight on the forest floor.

"Welcome, Hereward, son of Askil," he said. "Welcome to your heritage."

Chapter 3: *The One-Eyed Man*

The Wash, 865.

"There it is, boys – England!" exclaimed Prince Ivar. "That's the home of the bastards who threw your king into the snake-pit! The gods have blessed us! I have promised a temple to Frey on the spot where we first make land."

The scullers pulled harder, till their shoulders were fit to crack. At last the longship nudged up onto the sand, and the Danes leapt down into the surf. Prince Ivar remained in his chair: he was not made for leaping. The condition of his bones enforced a sedentary life, though at this moment he was clad in hauberk, helm and shield, to leave no doubt of his intentions towards his father's enemies.

"Here," he said. "Here where the green earth rises above the sand, Frey will have his temple."

While a creel was rigged up to carry the Prince down from the ship, his men bounded up the beach, eager to scout out the land and learn why so rich and green a plain was so empty. They soon found out.

"It's a bog," one man exclaimed. "All bog beyond that first dip. We're on an island."

"Back to ship, then," said the captain; but the Prince held up his hand.

"We must mark this place first," he said. "It is the site of Frey's temple."

"But if it's an island, sire –"

"I made an oath, captain. The gods do not deal kindly with men who go back on their words. Here I decreed the temple and here it will stand."

"If Wyrd lets it stand," muttered the captain. "It's an ill omen, this."

"Well then," said Ivar, with a toothy grin, "we had better ensure that the foundations are fast bound. We must arrange a... special sacrifice."

Bourne, December, 1067.

Bourne Hall had seen a sorry Christmas in 1066. On the feast day itself, when William the Norman was receiving the Crown of England, the Askilssons had huddled round a damp, smoky fire, with one stringy capon to eat between three. Hereward could not work miracles, and his return did not restore the prosperity of the village overnight: and, for all that this could hardly fail to be a happier feast than the last, it would still be a lean one: but of one thing he was determined. The tenants of the Manor would dine with him in Bourne as they had on Yuletides past; and he would give them a boar.

"We need to keep our guard," Martin reminded him. "If Ivo Taillebois knows we are drinking and feasting, he will be minded to come join the revel."

"Ivo will be drinking his own health in Spalding," said Hereward. "If he were going to attack us this winter, he'd have come before the snow. And besides, we have our friends to protect us." Since Hereward's return every thief and outlaw in the area had flocked to Bourne. He had made it clear to them that the price of his protection was that they spare the locals and restrict themselves to robbing the Norman invaders. Most had accepted this; some had not. They had not lived long. "Saddle Swallow."

"Are you going alone?" said Martin.

"Yes. There is nothing I fear in the forest."

Martin sighed, but he knew Hereward well enough to know that he would not be dissuaded. So he saddled the bay mare, and Hereward rode out from Bourne with his spear in hand, to nods and smiles from the villagers, to chase the boar.

Without hounds to scent the quarry, hunting was no easy matter: but the dusting of snow on the ground preserved the tracks of every beast that had passed, and Hereward avoided the paths of men so that those of his prey should not be obscured. It did not take him long to find the distinctive marks of the long cloven hoof, with its two outward-turned vestigial toes, leading down towards the mere. Hereward turned Swallow thither, and she picked her way down the slippery track; rounding a bush, he saw the boar ahead, drinking from a small stream that had not yet frozen. He hefted his spear, and urged Swallow into a trot.

The pig lifted its massive head and looked round, with little concern. By God, he was a fine one. Well over six feet from snout to tail, a great grizzled crest of hair along his back, huge yellowing tusks, and he must have weighed more than four hundred pounds. When Swallow reached a canter, he began to trot away; only as Hereward actually took aim with the spear did the boar pick up speed.

The huge pig squealed as Hereward struck; but he missed the heart. The spear lodged in the monster's shoulder but did not stop him in his flight; instead, he wriggled furiously as he ran, trying to shake the spear free. Hereward, clinging tight to the haft, was wrenched from his saddle and hurtled into the mere; Swallow skidded to a halt while the boar, slowing at last as he began to feel the pain of his injury, limped on, still with the spear sticking in his back.

Hereward floundered to his feet, cursing. Stumbling through the reeds, he tripped, and fell again, smashing more of the thin ice that had formed on the surface of the mire. He came up gasping for breath; he could not remember when he had ever been so cold. But when he tried to stand again, he found he could not. Something heavier than his wet clothes was weighing him down. The water could not be deep – when he had stood an instant ago it had barely reached his knees – but he found that he could not touch the bottom, or at least could not feel it. His legs were already beginning to go numb.

Frightened – a state he was unused to – Hereward scrabbled to remove his waterlogged cloak. He managed to unclasp it, and it sank, but he still could not stand. His breath was getting shorter as the cold bit at his lungs. The solid ground was only a few feet away but when he tried to swim he did not move.

He was on the verge of losing consciousness when a strong hand grasped his. A grey-bearded face swam in and out of view: a face whose left eye smiled kindly and whose right was covered with a patch. Lysir.

Hereward could not tell if the one-eyed man was wading in the mere or walking on the ice, although it should not be strong enough to hold his weight; but he felt himself drawn up from the water as if he were as light as a rag doll, and dragged onto the shore, where he lay, coughing and wheezing.

When he was himself again, Lysir had gone.

"Who is he?" he demanded of the world in general, for the sixth time that afternoon. "Who?"

"Hush," said Martin, adding another jug of hot water to his lord's foot-bath. He was not at all sure that he believed in the one-eyed man. He had never seen him; nor, it seemed, had anyone except Hereward. But Hereward was not given to dreams and visions. And certainly he had been in the mere, and had got out of it, cloakless and spearless but alive.

"I need to know who Lysir really is," insisted Hereward, "and what he wants with me. This is the third time he has appeared."

Rowena refilled Hereward's cup of spiced ale, took the poker from the fire and plunged it into the cup, releasing a hiss of sweet-smelling steam.

"A packman from Lincoln told me", she said, "that folk there said King Harold was alive."

"Men always say that when their leader is slain," said Martin. "If they loved him hope keeps him alive, if they hated him, fear does the same thing. They tell themselves that if Harold returns it'll be as if the Normans had never come, and then they make that *when* Harold returns, so they can live on hope instead of doing anything to free themselves."

"I don't know about that," said Rowena defensively, "but wasn't King Harold shot in the eye?"

"So were many others that day," said Martin dismissively; but Hereward looked thoughtful.

"Harold would be how old now, forty-five, fifty?" he mused. "Lysir could be the right age. He's tall and strong, as they say Harold was; and wherever he lives it's in hiding, as Harold would have to be. And Harold's mother is Danish, which would explain the name."

"Humph," said the sceptical Martin. "Of course, he could just as easily be Woden."

"What?" said Hereward. Rowena crossed herself.

"The heathen god Woden. He had one eye, they say, and a grey beard, and he was tall and strong, and walked the earth among mortals as one of them. He fits as well as Harold." Hereward frowned.

"But Woden was always accompanied by his ravens, was he not?"

"Not when he sent them abroad to bring him news from the corners of the world." Hereward chewed his lip thoughtfully. Martin, who had been joking, wished he had stayed silent: his master appeared to be taking his suggestion seriously. Rowena, who had been piously brought up, shuddered at all this talk of the old gods.

"Woden…" murmured Hereward. "Do you remember the names he used among men?"

"No," said Martin curtly.

"I think Lysir was one of them."

Spalding Keep.

Sir Ivo Taillebois hurled his cup against the wall; it smashed, leaving a dark and ominous wine stain.

"Seven days!" he shouted. "In seven days it will be Midwinter, and if I have not ousted this English pig from Bourne Ogier fitz Ungomar will get the manor."

"It will be little use to him," observed his chaplain.

"It's been nothing but cost to me so far, and a bloody cost at that, but it will all be profit when Hereward is gone," said the knight grimly, "and I mean that profit to be mine."

"The rebels may know by now about the Queen's decree," said the priest. "If they do they will be on their guard – and after the last attack..."

"That will not happen again," snapped Ivo. "How could they know, anyway?"

"News leaks out," said the priest.

"Damn all tattling slaves!" exclaimed the knight. "Listen, Hugo: if they know I have until Midwinter, they'll expect me to come before Midwinter's Eve, won't they? So if I wait until then I won't be expected. And they'll be celebrating too."

"A night attack?" said Father Hugo doubtfully. "At this time of year?"

Ivo waved a dismissive hand.

"The snow's less than two inches deep. Besides, the country round these parts is flat as paper. If it weren't for the damned trees we could see Bourne from here. It'll be a stroll. I'll set out at sunset, and by dawn we'll be masters of Bourne."

"Yes, I remember the tales," said Osred doubtfully. "My granny was Danish – a Denmark Dane, not one of those as had settled in England in King Alfred's time – and when she was young her folk over there still believed in the old gods. But why do you ask?"

"I want to know the name Woden went by when he appeared as a prophet," said Hereward.

"Let me see... Yggur, that was it."

"You are sure?" said Hereward, disappointed.

"Yes. Yggur the prophet, Waer the lover, Hropt the physician, Bruni the charioteer, and Lysir the rover of the seas."

"Lysir?" echoed Hereward, sitting up excitedly.

"Yes," said the old man. "At least…"

"Yes?" Hereward prompted.

"King Hadding prayed to Woden for an ally, and he was sent a one-eyed freebooter called Lysir. He suspected the pirate and the god were the same, but he never knew. And Woden still appeared to Hadding in his own form while he was roving with Lysir. At least, I think that's how it went; it's been a long time."

"Thank you, Osred," said Hereward, grasping the old man's hand, "thank you."

The door swung open, admitting a gust of icy air.

"We found the boar!" announced Winter.

He and Martin were lugging behind them a sledge, with Gwynnog behind steering it, on which lay the massive corpse of the boar Hereward had struck. The point of his spear was still buried in its shoulder, although the shaft had broken off. Even in death the creature was magnificent.

"That'll feed all Bourne from Midwinter to Twelfth Night," declared Osred.

"Maybe not that long," said Hereward with a smile. "But we will begin it on Midwinter's Eve." Increasingly, the Church was of the opinion that feasting should not begin until Christmas Day; but for Hereward, Lent was bad enough, without living on fish through Advent as well. His ancestors had always cooked the Yule Boar on Midwinter's Eve, and he was not about to break the custom. "Martin, get him to the kitchen and help Rowena to prepare him. Osred, Winter, Gwynnog, you may treat my house as yours; but I have business in the woods."

Hereward rode towards the Bromeswold; he did not know where to find Lysir, but the one-eyed man seemed to have the knack of finding him. Not, however, today. He was heading back to Bourne in disappointment, cold and tired, when a thought struck him: and he turned Swallow and headed for the spot beside the mere where Lysir had saved his life.

Lysir was standing by the water's edge, waiting.

"So you have come," he said.

"Who are you?" demanded Hereward.

"I have told you as much as it is given to you to know."

"As much as you choose to give me, you mean."

"Does it matter whose the choice is?" said Lysir. "It has been made and you will not alter it."

"Are you King Harold?"

"I believe there was a man once who said: 'My kingdom is not of this world'."

"If you have nothing to tell me," said Hereward, "then why have you let me find you?"

"Because I have a question for you," said Lysir.

"What is it?" asked Hereward, surprised.

"I have heard that your dearest wish is to be remembered. What I would ask you is: how?"

"What do you mean?"

"It is simple enough," said Lysir. "When men speak of you in after generations, as you hope they will, would you have them speak of Hereward the Strong? Hereward the Crafty? Hereward the Wise?"

"I have tried to be all those things," said Hereward defensively. "But I hope they will say that I was a man of honour."

"Hereward the Honourable..." said Lysir, tasting the name. "Perhaps; perhaps. Is that what they call you now?"

"I don't know," admitted Hereward, wondering why he was discussing this: but he had noticed that Lysir had a way of making him talk about whatever he chose. "I think I am known more for being watchful than for anything more creditable. When I was fighting in Flanders people used to joke that I never slept; they called me Hereward the Wake."

"Hereward the Wake," repeated Lysir. "It is a worthy name. And it is not a name that others have. That is very good."

"That's as may be," said Hereward. "But the name stayed in Flanders. Nobody calls me that in England."

"Then the name must be earned anew in England," said Lysir.

"That will depend on my enemies," said Hereward.

"It need not. You know the Temple of Frey?"

"That place," said Hereward, instinctively crossing himself. He noticed that the gesture did not seem to trouble Lysir: whatever the one-eyed man was, he was apparently not a devil. But devils aplenty were supposed to haunt the old heathen temple out in the Fens.

Hereward had been told the story as a child.

"Ivar had to keep his promise," his old nurse had said. "So a Saxon maiden was buried alive on the island to bind the foundations of the temple.

"Of course, out there on the sea-edge of the Fens, it was easier to avoid than to reach in any case, and even on the high feast days of the old gods it was never full; and the very priests grew to hate the drear and lonely place. And then, when Alfred of Wessex defeated the Danes and made Christians of them, the old gods were cast down. The other temples were mostly made into churches, but that one was abandoned and left to rot. All shun it: even the birds will not fly overhead: and the fishermen pray for the day when it falls back into the sea and the evil is forgotten."

"I see you do know it," said Lysir. "Now, a man who could spend the longest night of the year in the Temple of Frey and come out with his life and reason might well be said to have earned the name of Wake."

"That's insane," said Hereward. "I'd have earned the name of fool and nothing else. Besides, I've promised to entertain my tenants at Bourne on Midwinter's Eve." He added, as an afterthought, "You're welcome to join us, of course."

"I am not a sociable man," said Lysir. "But consider what I have said. It would make a worthy addition to the legend of Hereward." He turned and walked away; the mist enveloped him, and after ten or twenty yards he was invisible. Hereward shook his head and stared: he was sure there had been no mist when he had ridden out of the trees.

"My friends," said Hereward, "I am afraid I will not be able to be with you on Midwinter's Eve."

"Why not, my lord?" asked Osred.

"I intend to spend the night in the Temple of Frey."

The others all exclaimed at once; but Martin was the loudest.

"I have never heard a stupider idea, *my lord*," he declared angrily. "Abandon your guests so you can freeze out in that Godforsaken place, and make yourself look like an enemy of the Church at the same time? In God's name, why?"

"I go there to defy the Devil, not to worship him," said Hereward. "I will be wearing a cross, and let the man who calls me pagan beware."

"That doesn't make it any the wiser."

"Martin is right, my lord," said Rowena. "That is an evil place."

"I'm not talking about the curse," said Martin. "I don't believe in that – there can hardly be any plot of land in the world where there hasn't been a murder done at some time – there's just no *reason* to it. Why do it?"

"For my reputation," said Hereward.

"You want a reputation as a lunatic?"

"Martin," said Hereward, gritting his teeth, "I think you are beginning to forget yourself."

"No, my lord," said Martin, only a little less hotly, "you forget yourself." He turned to Osred and Winter. "What will this do to my lord Hereward's reputation in the village? Speak truly."

"Well..." said Osred unhappily.

"What will it do afterwards?" put in Hereward. "If I come through it alive and sane and show that the curse can be defied?"

"That would be seen as a miracle," said Winter. "Because it *would* be so. I beg you, my lord, not to undertake this dangerous task."

"A miracle?" said Hereward. Winter and Osred nodded; Rowena found herself obliged to agree. Gwynnog did not respond; but he could have made no difference now. Martin saw, if the others did not, that Hereward's mind was made up. "Martin, will you take my place as host?"

"Not I," said Martin, folding his arms.

"Winter, then."

"If that is your wish, my lord," said Winter.

"You do understand?" pressed Hereward. Winter looked at the floor.

"I do, my lord," said Gwynnog. "I do."

As dusk fell on Midwinter's Eve, Ivo Taillebois and his men marched out of Spalding. The last time he had set out against Bourne, he had been ambushed by more rebels than he would have thought the wood could hide: but this time he had scouts ahead and guards on either flank. He would not be taken by surprise again. Besides, the snow would reveal any untoward tracks; and the moon was bright.

Even as the Normans entered the woods, Hereward stepped off his punt onto the tiny dot of land that was Frey's Isle. The temple loomed grimly before him, a wooden prism, its steep roof sagging and broken in places where the ancient timbers had rotted or worn through after centuries of neglect. He could not fathom how it came to be still standing, founded in the unstable sand: perhaps the awful sacrifice truly had bound it with something more than human power.

He strode up to the door, and paused only momentarily before pushing it open. It gave with little resistance, though the hinges grated painfully: and, torch in hand, he stepped inside.

In the centre of the temple was a round hearth. Somebody had piled it with driftwood; there was no telling if it had been done that day or a hundred years before. However long it had been there, Hereward was grateful. He hurried up to the hearth and thrust his torch into the pile of wood; being bone dry, it went up almost immediately, and he was able to examine his surroundings.

They were far from homely. Above, the stars showed through the hole that served as a crude chimney, which was, Hereward noted, far too small to let all the smoke out – no doubt to avoid letting the rain in, but it would make for a stuffy night. The rest of the temple was a cavernous empty space, except at the far end, where there stood a stone altar stained purple-brown with the blood of sacrifices. Above it still stood Frey's totem, the boar Gullinbursti, on whose back the god rode into battle; below it, brought down either by Christian iconoclasts or by the hand of time, lay the great oaken statue of Frey himself, his nose chipped, his neck cracked, one arm and the enormous phallus that was this god's signifier broken off and lying in the dust. His sightless eyes glared sternly upwards; Hereward turned his back on the statue and sat warming himself by the fire. He had not realised how cold he was; as the blood returned to his hands and legs, he decided that this would not be so difficult a night. Outside, the snow began to fall.

"This snow will get worse, my lord," Ivo's steward told him. "Are you sure we are on the right road for Bourne?"

"There is only one road, idiot," growled Ivo. He was beginning to regret bringing the whining Hubert with him: it was at times like this that he missed his old steward, fat Rollo who had fallen beneath Hereward's sword. But Hubert was a handy fighting man.

"But if much more snow falls, we'll hardly be able to tell where the road is," said Hubert.

"The road", replied Ivo through gritted teeth, "is where the trees aren't. Shut up and walk faster, it'll keep you warm."

In Bourne Hall, the revellers had begun to carve slices off the massive boar which was still turning on the spit, dripping sizzling fat into the fire; the spiced ale went round, and raucous carols were sung. Winter and Rowena were both kept too busy to miss Hereward; but Martin sat jabbing with a stick at the cinders which fell from the fire, wondering how his master was faring.

Hereward sat up with a start; he had almost fallen asleep. He was not sure how much time had passed, but was aware of a draught – the door, so stiff before, had blown open – and of a burning thirst. He should not have sat so close to the fire. The flask of beer he had brought would not satisfy this: he would have to fetch water. He got to his feet, stumbling slightly, and headed for the door. Amid the shadows to his right, a deeper blackness than the surroundings caught his eye momentarily, and he turned: but when he looked straight at it there was nothing there. Or had it moved beyond his vision? As he turned back, something hit him hard on the back of the head.

He fell, but was not knocked out; he rolled aside, drawing Brainbiter and driving it wildly upwards, thanking God that he had thought to bring the sword. The still shapeless shadow seemed to be above him now, but the blade connected with nothing, slicing through empty air. Hereward jumped to his feet, cursing the stabbing pain in his head, and slashed wildly about him: but there was nothing. Then all of a sudden he realised that there was: a shadow, as if some tall figure were standing between him and the fire – but with nothing to cast it. Even as he noticed this, Hereward felt fingers fasten around his throat.

The icy grip tightened, claw-like nails digging into his skin, but he could see nothing. Clutching desperately with his left hand at the spot where his enemy's wrist should be, he grasped only the air; he was ready to faint when he chanced to slash through the same space with Brainbiter.

He was never sure afterwards if he imagined the squeal, for all the world the same sound the wounded boar had made: but, whatever had happened, the grip relaxed, and Hereward slumped to the ground, gasping for breath. When he looked up, the shadow had gone. He rubbed his head, and wondered if it had ever been there, or if thirst and drowsiness were playing tricks on his mind. He had had nightmares every bit as real before.

Hurrying out, he gathered up handfuls of snow and pushed them into his mouth, numbing it; as the snow melted he gulped it down. He took a long swig of his beer, melting the snow that remained in his mouth and easing the numbness, and crammed more snow into the flask. The pain in his throat had begun to ease, although that in his head remained, drumming insistently away with every heartbeat.

"Of Matilda's moans
We have heard they were countless,
The lady of Gauti,
So that sorrowful love
Robbed her of all sleep," he chanted.
"That was overcome,
So may this be."

He lifted the little crucifix he wore, and kissed it: and he went back into the temple.

"We're lost," said Hubert, stopping dead.
"We aren't lost," insisted Ivo, "we should have kept straight on at the elder bush."

"You said there was only one road."

"There is. This is just a clearing. It's this damned snow, the whole ground looks the same."

"It's beginning to drift," said Hubert, frowning.

"I don't care," said Ivo. "We'll go back to the elder bush and then on. And don't speak without calling me lord!" The soldiers grinned at each other behind their master's back; but they were also shivering. It was growing very cold.

"Hereward..."

Hereward looked up.

"I'm dreaming," he said loudly.

"No, Hereward. I'm here."

"But you're in Flanders..." Torfrida stood up, and stepped into the firelight, pushing back her kerchief so that her hair was exposed, shining black; the cloth fluttered to the ground.

"Shh..." she said, slinking towards him. He watched, mesmerised, as she drew a little knife from her sleeve, and cut in one move across the top of her gown, so that it fell to the ground, leaving her naked. Hereward gulped. It had been three months and more since he had seen his wife, and she was more beautiful than ever. But she was *not here*.

"Huldra!" he shouted. Torfrida hissed like a cat. Hereward jumped to his feet and grasped her by the shoulders; all the fury he had glimpsed in that instant seemed to leave her, as she raised her dark liquid eyes to look into his. But Hereward, who knew that the Huldra cannot bear to be viewed from behind, spun her roughly round, and found himself holding a rotten log, which crumbled in his hands. He blinked, and looked down: there was no sign of the rotted wood. The smoke from the fire stung his eyes, and he realised that he was having difficulty breathing.

"There's no such thing as the Huldra," he told himself. He was not sure if he believed it, but certainly he knew they had never been seen in England. But then, perhaps that glaring devil Frey had the power to bring them here. *"Vade retro, Satanas,"* he muttered, fingering his crucifix. Whatever the reality of the horrors of the Temple, there would be more to assail his mind ere morning.

> "Fire is blazing," he recited softly,
> "Barrows are opened,
> Burn field and fen.
> Hell's gate gapes,
> Graves open,
> And all is fire
> On the island's edge:
> But no flames flaring
> Will put fear in me:
> My mind shakes not,
> Though yonder the dead
> In the doorway I see."

He looked up, almost expecting to see a revenant standing at the door indeed. There was nothing there; the door was closed, though creaking beneath the battering of the wind. Hereward frowned: the air outside had been almost still not long ago.

Suddenly, a gust caught the door and blew it open once again. The blast hit Hereward with the same force of sheer cold that he remembered feeling when he had fallen into the mere: and the fire, which had died down from its earlier brightness but was still glowing warmly enough, was scattered across the floor, a thousand tiny embers winking out one by one as the cold took them. Hereward's torch had gone out long ago: and, as the embers vanished, the temple turned black.

He felt rather than heard the whoosh of the blade. Ducking just as it whistled over his head, he drew Brainbiter and struck out, meeting something with an unmistakeable clang. He had struck metal, he had not dreamed that: but was it the sword of an adversary, or one of the rusted lamps hanging from the lofty roof?

"*Vade retro!*" shouted Hereward. "God, demon or body from the grave, get you gone! Have here your due – Brainbiter's edge! If you are a living thing, your death will be wretched, and far your spirit will wander, into enemies' power! That I promise!"

He heard something then – a death-cry, or rather the echo of one, as if it were uttered far away: and then, nothing. And he knew he was alone. He shivered, but it was only the cold. There were still a few fragments of scattered driftwood smouldering; he scraped them together, and coaxed the fire back into life.

As the sun rose, and the snow began to fall again, the Normans had still not come out of the woods. They had been reduced to digging, with their swords and axes and their mail-clad hands, to get through the drifts, which were breast-high in places.

"Midwinter's Day," said Hubert. "My lord."

Ivo gave a low, angry growl.

"We turn for home," he said. "I wish Ogier good luck of that accursed manor."

In Bourne, all were asleep; even Martin had nodded off by the fire eventually, troubled by dreams of what Hereward might be facing. Gwynnog stirred, and sat up. He had drunk but sparingly, and his head was clear. He got up, and, holding a plate in the crook of his right arm while he wielded the knife with his remaining hand, carved seven slices off the boar. He was not hungry: but Hereward would need his breakfast.

"None of it was real, was it?" said Hereward. "It was smoke, cold and thirst working on my brain. And hunger. I haven't eaten all night. There is no evil here but what men bring in their minds."

"Whether your enemies were sent by Frey or came from within you, you defeated them," replied Lysir. "That is what matters. Now go home, eat, and sleep."

"Sleep," said Hereward. "Yes, by God, they were wrong about that: I do need sleep." Lysir shook his head.

"They were not wrong," he said. "You have earned your name – Hereward the Wake."

Chapter 4: *The Heron*

Spalding, February 1068.

"Anything good?" whispered Gils excitedly.

"Only the grain," Witta hissed back. "But it's all here! Everything they took last harvest."

"Hand us some down, then."

Witta hefted two sacks of wheat up, resting one on his shoulder while he leant precariously, wobbling on the ladder, to hand the other down to his accomplice. Gils caught it, and Witta was just swinging the second down when the door of the barn was kicked open.

Six Norman soldiers stood outside, and at their head, sword in hand, was Hubert Gervase, steward to Sir Ivo Taillebois, a triumphant sneer on his lips.

"Welcome to Spalding Keep, gentlemen," he said. "I fear your stay will be a short one, but I promise when we send you on it will be to a better place."

Two days later – for Ivo Taillebois did not believe in wasting time – Gils and Witta were marched out into the market square, chained together with two men, Finn and Modi, who had tried to rob the tax chest. A scaffold had been built with a gallows big enough to take four. The populace, who normally enjoyed a good hanging, were subdued, and mostly stayed at home: this could have been any of them, and they knew it. Besides, the weather was looking ominous.

On the scaffold beside the hangman stood Hubert, in whose charge the whole affair was placed, and Ivo's chaplain, Father Hugo Ylard. Father Hugo was not happy: he had frequently urged Ivo to remit the heavy charges on the hungry townsfolk, and, besides, he disliked hangings: but he knew his duty.

"You stand convicted, varyingly," declared Hubert to

the four frightened men, "of attempting to deprive our lord William, by God's Grace King of the English, of his due moneys; and of forcing an entry to the barns of Sir Ivo Taillebois, with intent to commit robbery. The sentence is that you be hanged by the neck until you are dead." In the sparse crowd, Witta's wife began to sob. "Father Hugo, you attest that these four men have been offered the chance to make confession?"

The priest inclined his head.

"They have all availed themselves of it, and received absolution," he said.

"Then let the sentence be executed."

The four men were stood on stools, and the nooses placed around their necks: Gils, Witta, Modi, Finn. The hangman kicked the stool from under Finn, and, as he hung in the air kicking, spasming, clawing at the cord, stepped towards Modi. He never reached him.

A dagger, flung from the crowd, struck the executioner through the heart. Before he had even fallen, a man had rushed the scaffold and cut Finn down. He sliced through the cords that bound the thief's hands, kicked the soldier who had tried to mount the scaffold down into the mud, and set about freeing the others.

If anybody recognised the newcomer, they showed no sign of it. He was a tall, spindly-limbed man, in a very ordinary brown woollen tunic and cloak, his face covered with a crude leather mask. He had cut free Modi and Witta before Ivo reacted.

"Kill him!" roared the knight. Hubert, startled at last into action, drew his sword: the masked man engaged him almost casually, disarming him with a quick twist, then turned back to free Gils. Hubert bent to recover his sword, and Modi clubbed him over the head. He slumped to the ground.

"Stop that man!" screamed Ivo; but by this time two more soldiers had already headed up the scaffold steps – only for the masked man to parry both their thrusts with a lightning-fast back-and-forth motion, then, before they could riposte, slash sideways across both their faces. Streaming blood, they fell back. The four condemned men jumped down from the scaffold.

All of a sudden, the crowd was far thicker than it had been. The square was packed: and into this throng the four men melted, quickly disappearing. The masked man, meanwhile, showing little concern with escape, turned back to face Ivo.

"Who are you?" barked the Norman. "Where does a great gangling heron learn to fight like that? I could use you in my guard; surrender and I'll maybe not hang you."

"A heron is what I am," retorted the masked man. "The river is strong and swift and the heron small and thin, but the heron stands in the flood and snatches fish from the river's very heart. You are the river, Lord Ivo: and I have taken your fish." And with that, he leapt off the scaffold, turning a somersault over the heads of the awestruck soldiers in sheer exuberance, hit the ground feet first and sprinted through a gap that somehow opened up in the crowd and out of the gates of Spalding town.

"I should like to meet this Heron," mused Hereward. "We could do with a swordsman like him."

"No doubt he'll come here soon enough," said Winter. "This is the only refuge in miles for Ivo's enemies, unless he goes to the robber bands in the Fens – and they're worse than the Normans."

"I wonder who he is?" said Hereward. "He must have been a soldier, and probably no common one, to have a skill like that. Only the sons of the nobility are trained so well in the sword."

As he spoke, there was a commotion outside. One of the locals Hereward had recruited to stand sentry over the Hall poked his head round the door.

"Beg pardon, my lord, but there's a rider here says he has a message for you."

"Where has he come from?" asked Hereward.

"Yarmouth, he says."

"Says? Don't you believe him?" The sentry frowned.

"He don't sound like it, my lord. He sounds foreign."

"Norman?" said Hereward sharply.

"No, my lord, not Norman."

"Bring him in."

The messenger was rudely hustled in, the sentry gripping his elbow. He shook himself free with a disgusted "Tchah!", and made an ostentatious show of wiping his heavily embroidered sleeve clean. Hereward recognised him at once, though not by name: he was a page of the Flemish court, who had served Hereward's rival Sir Ascelin de St Valéry until the latter's ignominious flight from Flanders.

"Do you come from the Lady Torfrida?" asked Hereward anxiously. "Is she well?"

"She is well enough," replied the page. "She is in Yarmouth."

"Yarmouth!" Hereward thumped the table. "What on earth is she doing there?" The page shrugged.

"Since your lordship has not returned to Flanders, she has come to be with your lordship in England."

Hereward sank back into his chair, stroking his chin. It was true: he had been away from Flanders for five months, and he missed Torfrida sorely. But he had never found a safe moment to leave Bourne. With Ivo, and his other enemy Ogier the Breton, sitting so close by, the Hall would be attacked the moment he was out of England.

"I must go to her," he said.

"Across half of Norfolk?" said Martin. "The country will be crawling with Normans."

"None of them looking for Hereward Askilsson, who they think is in Lincolnshire," Hereward pointed out. "But I'll go by sea; it'll be less obtrusive, and probably quicker."

"In whose ship?" demanded Martin.

"A ship will not be necessary. I will take a fishing smack." The page wrinkled his lip, but nobody said anything. It *was* a good plan: one more fisherman skirting the coast to Yarmouth would hardly be noticed. As for Torfrida, it might temporarily injure her dignity to be brought back to Bourne in a smack, but she was not a fool and would understand the necessity of it. "I had better leave at once."

"Who can this Heron be?" demanded Ivo yet again. Hubert shrugged helplessly. The conversation had been going round in circles for hours; they had got no further than concluding, as Hereward had, that the masked man was an ex-soldier and probably noble. Hereward's own name had been suggested, but those who had seen him closer than Ivo had quickly informed the knight that he was at least a hand shorter than the Heron and much burlier.

Hubert shrugged helplessly.

"Whoever he is," he said, "we'll catch him soon enough." Ivo grunted. "Would you like to hear Wulfric play, my lord?" Hubert asked ingratiatingly.

Wulfric was Ivo's new jester and tumbler; his predecessor, like Hubert's, had met an end at Hereward's hands. Ivo had to admit that the Englishman was a better singer and a lither tumbler than Loquifer had been, but Wulfric's French was limited, forcing them to converse in English or a mixture of the two – an effort with which Ivo could seldom be bothered.

"Let him juggle," he said. "That doesn't need language."

Wulfric shambled forward. The awkwardness of his normal movements belied the physical agility he displayed in his performances. He scooped up from the table a handful of knives, and began to juggle them with amazing dexterity, now flicking one up behind his own back and catching it as it descended towards his head, now pausing to pull a coin from behind his ear and add it to the cascade; then he snatched up from the table a dried apple and a skewer. Keeping the knives circling, he threw the apple up so that for a few moments it hung spinning above them, then caught it on the point of the skewer as it came down, balancing the skewer on one finger while he juggled the knives with the other hand; then he flicked one knife with a *thunk* into the apple – then a second, then the third, and deftly caught the coin as it descended. The whole hall applauded; Wulfric bowed, and caught the gold piece that Ivo flicked to him.

"Thank you, my lord," he said, bowing again.

"If my soldiers could move like you," said Ivo, "the Heron might never have escaped." Hubert looked at Wulfric curiously: Ivo's words had brought an idea into his head: but he put it from him. The tumbler was a peasant who had never handled a weapon bigger than the knives he juggled with. He was of roughly the right build, but that might be said of a dozen of Ivo's retainers, including the steward himself. It was impossible that he should be the Heron. Besides, the Heron was long gone from Spalding. "Well," said Ivo, "as Hubert says, we'll have him soon enough; and then we'll have better entertainment than even Wulfric can provide."

Yarmouth.

Hereward found Torfrida in a bare chamber above an inn in the port. He had walked up the stairs meaning to upbraid her, say that he would have been back in Bruges soon, that there was no need for this rashness: but when he saw her he fell into her arms and let her lead him to bed.

They had still hardly spoken by the time they left the inn: but they did not need to. They collected Torfrida's nurse Kolfrosta, who had been sitting downstairs by the parlour fire, and departed. As evening fell, they made their way down to the harbour and Hereward's smack, to catch the last tide.

"A moment, ma'am!" The speaker was a Norman soldier. Hereward's hand hovered by the gap in his shirt where his dagger was concealed: he had not brought Brainbiter.

"What do you want?" said Torfrida coolly.

"Nothing," said the soldier, taken aback. "The end of your gown's trailing in the dirt. You should have your servant there carry it."

"Thank you," she smiled. "Floris – my train." Hereward, avoiding the soldier's face and cursing his distinctive odd eyes, crouched down and lifted the tail of Torfrida's gown out of the mire.

"You are Flemings?" said the soldier.

"Yes," said Torfrida. "I am the sister of Sir Gilbert of Ghent; my brother is in town on business." It was well known that Gilbert had business of varying legality in almost every port on the North Sea. "He has lent me Floris to show me around."

"You'd have been better with a local," said the soldier.

"Ugh, these English!" Torfrida sniffed. "They smell. No, I prefer a Fleming, even if he is careless sometimes. Mind you don't let that train drop again, Floris!"

"You're right enough," said the soldier. "Be careful if you're going down to the harbour; they're a rough lot, those fishermen. But I suppose with a big fellow like that you'll be safe enough."

"Oh, I will," Torfrida assured him. "He knows what Sir Gilbert will do to him if I come to any harm."

Bourne.

"Who goes there?" demanded the sentry.

"Only me," said the newcomer. "Wulfric of Spalding."

"Don't know any Wulfric." He turned and shouted in

the general direction of the Hall: "Anybody know a Wulfric?"

"Tall thin lad, hair like a startled gorse bush?" said Gwynnog.

"That's him."

"It's young Rowena's sweetheart. Let him in." The sentry, who had had his own eye on Hereward's pretty blonde maid-of-all-work, muttered something Wulfric was probably lucky not to hear, and admitted him.

Rowena was in the kitchen, trying to prepare a dinner for the return of Hereward and Torfrida with only the dubious help of Martin Lightfoot. Gwynnog had offered, but Gwynnog had been knighted at Peterborough along with Hereward, and Rowena had too much respect for form to allow a knight to toil in the kitchen: though now she was regretting the Welshman's absence.

"Wulfric!" she exclaimed as the tumbler entered. Ignoring her fussing over the food, Wulfric swept her into his arms; Martin tactfully disappeared. "Why are you here?" asked Rowena, as soon as she could break from Wulfric's kiss.

"Well, there's a fine welcome," he said, mock-indignant.

"Of course I'm glad to see you, silly; but isn't it dangerous? You weren't followed?"

"I know better than to be followed," he said. "Besides, why should they follow Wulfric the Tumbler? It's the Heron they're looking for."

"Shh," said Rowena. "Not even here. And won't the woodcutter miss you?" Thus had Ivo become nicknamed, his soldiers and Norman servants having blabbed among the local people the secret of his ancestors' lowly profession: though few would call him so to his face.

"He's out hunting, with Gilbert and Ogier; they'll be gone for days, probably," said Wulfric. "Plenty of time for us."

"You can't be sure..." said Rowena doubtfully.

"If they do come back it doesn't matter," said Wulfric. "I'll be back in Spalding tomorrow morning – and you're coming with me."

"What do you mean?"

"I want you to marry me, Rowena." Her jaw dropped.

"No, I can't. I can't, Wulfric – not now. It can't work – not while I work for Lord Hereward and you for the woodcutter." Wulfric stepped back from her; she seized his arm. "If you came here – if you joined Lord Hereward –"

Wulfric shook his head.

"I'd lose my information," he said. "Working for Ivo I know exactly what he's up to, and when. The Heron needs that."

"You can still be the Heron fighting for Lord Hereward," Rowena pleaded, but Wulfric insisted:

"If I'd been Lord Hereward's man a week ago, those four men would have died on Ivo's scaffold. And if I become Lord Hereward's man now, there'll be more I can't save, that I could have saved if I'd stayed at Spalding. I'm sorry, Rowena: I can't leave the Keep."

Rowena bowed her head.

"Then I'll have to come back with you," she said simply. "If Lord Hereward will let me."

"You mean it?" exclaimed Wulfric joyfully.

"Of course." And she kissed him again.

Rowena managed, somehow, to cook up some fish and a winter fruits pie to follow, by the time Hereward and Torfrida returned; and even to make enough for Kolfrosta, whom she had not been expecting. The result was that they were well fed and sated when she pushed Wulfric forward to make their request.

Hereward frowned.

"You do know Rowena's hand isn't legally in my gift?" he said. "It's Ogier fitz Ungomar's decision. He's not likely to contest the marriage, but you'll be under Norman law in Spalding, and if somebody did want to contest it – if the priest found out –"

"Father Hugo knows," interrupted Wulfric. "He's agreed to marry us anyway."

"Hugo Ylard?" Hereward's eyebrows rose. "Ivo's own chaplain? It's a trap."

"He doesn't know Rowena works for you," Wulfric clarified. "Just that she's from Bourne and that Sir Ogier hasn't given consent."

"I still don't like it," said Hereward. "We'll miss Rowena here – and I don't like the fact that you work for Ivo."

"It's a living," said Wulfric, shrugging.

"Begging scraps from the invader's table?" scoffed Hereward. "You know what happened to Ivo's last jester."

"Is that a threat, my lord?" asked Wulfric.

"Why do you do it?"

"Spalding is not Bourne," said Wulfric. "Ivo is in our midst whether we like it or not, with a constant guard. We do not have the luxury of resistance."

"The Heron resists," Hereward pointed out.

"The Heron is the Heron. And you are Hereward. It isn't the same for ordinary people, without swords or the skill to use them."

"I am minded to say no."

"Let them go, my lord," said Torfrida suddenly. "They could have eloped; it took courage to ask you honestly. Courage should be rewarded." Hereward, briefly, smiled.

"You're right, of course," he said. "I can't stop them. Well, you have my permission – even my blessing; but also my warning. Do not stay in Spalding. You will not be safe there."

"There is nowhere else, my lord," said Wulfric.

"There is Bourne." Wulfric shook his head.

"If I leave, Ivo will be insulted, and he'll want revenge. My family and friends in Spalding would suffer. I can't do that."

"Then you are an honourable man," conceded Hereward. But his face was grave; and he was gloomy for the rest of the evening.

The Bromeswold.

"Not a stag," insisted Modi. "They belong to the King."

"What difference does it make now?" demanded Finn. "We're under sentence of death already." He crept forward, notching an arrow to his bow. Suddenly, something startled the stag, and it darted away. Finn cursed loudly.

"Who's there?" called a voice from the road.

"It can only be outlaws, my lord," replied another that they knew only too well. It was Hubert: which meant that the first speaker must have been Ivo.

An instant later, the Norman horsemen came crashing through the bushes. They were almost on top of the two poachers when a weighted rope, hurled from out of the trees, entangled the forelegs of Ivo's horse, sending the beast and knight crashing to the ground; they fell right in Hubert's path, compelling him and the men behind him to rein up sharply. By the time Ivo was on his feet, the outlaws were far away, and had left no trail the Normans could follow.

"You were lucky this time – I followed Ivo out of Spalding," the masked man told Finn and Modi. "But I probably won't be there to save you a third time. Take better care. Perhaps you should go to Bourne and join the Lord Hereward. That's what Gils and Witta mean to do."

"We will," said the chastened Finn. "Thank you. Is there any way we can repay you?"

"Stay alive," said the Heron, "and keep plaguing Ivo and the Normans."

"Why don't you come to Bourne yourself?" asked

Modi. The Heron shook his head.

"I work alone," he said. "You can tell Hereward that."

"Alone?" marvelled Hereward. "The arrogance of the man! Well, let him work alone, and die alone, as he surely will. It'll be a waste, but a lesson to the other enemies of William the Bastard: we have to cleave together. We have no other hope."

"Curse the Heron," grated Ivo, taking a swig of Rhenish wine. "He's a worse plague than Hereward Askilsson. At least we know where Hereward is; this Heron might turn up in my bedchamber." He picked up a goose leg and took a large bite. "Wulfric," he said, spraying fat from his mouth, "give us a riddle."

"I saw a creature born before it was conceived," said the tumbler, "and I ate it without eating flesh."

"Born before it was conceived?" echoed Ivo. "How can that be?"

"Aha – I think I have it," said Hubert. "It is the Host, the Body of Christ. Christ was born of a virgin, and the bread is the body without being flesh."

"But Christ is God," objected Father Hugo. "You cannot call the Creator a creature."

"Then the riddle makes no sense," said Hubert. "There's nothing else it can be."

"It makes sense to a man with sense in his head," said Wulfric. He had noticed that Ivo liked it when he cheeked the steward. "Do you not see it, my lord?" Ivo frowned. Something faint was nagging at his mind; he was sure he would recognise the answer when he heard it; but somehow it eluded him.

"An egg," said the priest.

"Of course!" Ivo thumped the table. "Obvious, really."

"Every riddle's obvious when you know the answer," said Hubert sourly. "Another?"

"No," said Ivo. He did not want to take the risk of being outguessed again. "Play for us."

Wulfric chose an old English love song, which he picked out delicately on a rebec, his eyes straying frequently to Rowena. His glances, and her blushing reaction, could not but draw Ivo's eyes thither too: and the knight smiled a wolfish smile. He liked what he saw.

"Who's our minstrel's pretty sweetheart, Hubert?" he asked.

"I don't know, my lord," said the steward. "I haven't seen her before today."

"Wulfric," said Ivo, "you have been ill mannered. You have not introduced us to your lady friend. I'll say nothing about bringing her into the keep without my permission."

"She is my wife, my lord," said Wulfric stiffly.

"Indeed?" Ivo raised a sceptical eyebrow. "You are my bondman. You may not marry unless I say. And who is her lord?"

"She is from the manor of Spalding, lord," said Wulfric. "We were married in King Harold's time."

"I have not seen her," said Ivo. "Hubert has not seen her. You have not mentioned her. We should have noticed one so beautiful, and you should have boasted of her."

"She has been living outside the town, my lord," said Wulfric. "It was a troubled time after the Conquest, and we were afraid for the future. But your benevolence has made Spalding a safe place once again."

"So it has, so it has." Ivo, frankly staring at Rowena, licked his lips. "What is your name, my dear?"

"Rowena, lord," she said. "Ailwin of Fulney's daughter."

"Then Ailwin of Fulney breeds goodly daughters," said Ivo. "A very flower, is she not, Hubert?"

"She is, my lord," agreed the steward.

Their contemplation of Rowena was interrupted by the entry of a soldier.

"What is it?" said Ivo irritably.

"So please you, my lord, we've caught the outlaw Modi." Wulfric glanced anxiously at Rowena; Ivo scowled.

"Take him down to the dungeons; we'll hang him in the morning. No, wait – bring him in. We might as well make it clear that he won't be rescued this time."

Modi was hustled into the room, blinking, confused, and terrified.

"Listen to me," said Ivo, leaning forward. "Your friend the Heron won't save you this time. We're going to hang you from the walls of the tower. Even he can't penetrate Spalding Keep." He paused. "But you can save yourself. All you have to do is tell me the Heron's name."

"I don't know," quavered Modi; "I don't know!"

"Take him away," said Ivo with a wave of the hand.

"What are you doing here?" said Modi suddenly. "She – she's a spy, my lord! That must be how the Heron knows what you do!"

"What are you talking about, man?"

"Spare me, my lord, spare me! That woman – I've seen her in Bourne, in the Lord Toli's time! She worked at the Hall! She must have been sent by Hereward!"

"From Bourne, are you?" said Ivo, looking back to Rowena. He did not seem angry; instead, a smile was playing about his lips.

"It's a lie, my lord," said Rowena hotly.

"It may well be," agreed Ivo. "The ravings of a desperate man. Take him away," he said again to the guard. "And find *her* a comfortable lodging."

"My lord?"

"You have been accused of spying, my dear. It is my duty to investigate, and during that time you must be detained. You need have no fear – I shall personally see that you are kept comfortable." He nodded happily at the thought. "I shall visit you every day. I am sure it will not be for long. And as a mark of my goodwill I shall leave your husband here at liberty. What more can I do?"

Wulfric wished afterwards that he had rushed at Ivo there and then and taken him hostage; but he had been too stunned to think of it. Lying later in the rushes of the hall, ignoring the snoring of the other menials – Loquifer, so rumour said, had had a room of his own, albeit one about the size of a moderately spacious beer barrel – he realised that, free though he might be, he would be under suspicion now. It would not be easy to slip out of the keep by night, or at least not by the gate.

Fortunately, Spalding Keep was no great fortress, and climbing down the walls on a rope might be practical enough: but he had to free Rowena first. He thanked all the saints that Ivo had been too drunk to make any attempt upon her tonight: he had kept the knight up with songs and revelling: but he could not rely on doing the same again.

"I know what you are thinking, and you cannot risk it alone."

Wulfric leapt to his feet, feeling for his dagger; but the speaker laid a hand on his arm and hissed at him to be silent. To his astonishment, it was Father Hugo.

"Why should you help me?" he demanded.

"Because even if you and your wife are spies, I cannot in conscience let her remain at Ivo's mercy," replied the priest. "You know what he is. If she stays here… I may be wrong, I may pay dear for it, but I would rather connive even at treason than…" He could not bring himself to speak the word.

"Do you have a plan?" asked Wulfric eagerly.

"I will serve the guards drugged possets. They will never suspect me." Wulfric frowned.

"But in the morning, they will remember who brought them." Hugo shrugged.

"The wine barrel in the kitchen is four fifths empty," he said. "I've added a flask of poppy straight to that – a full barrel would have needed bushels of the stuff, but as it was I was able to find enough. Anybody could have done as much, and everybody will assume it was you. Especially as I'll drink the longest draught myself and be found sleeping like a baby tomorrow." Wulfric stared at the priest in open-mouthed admiration.

"Tell me," he said, "do you make a habit of organising jailbreaks?"

"I have never done anything against lawful authority before," said Hugo. "I render unto Caesar the things which are Caesar's."

"A pity," said the tumbler. "You have a talent that any thief in Europe might envy."

The plan worked to perfection. While the guards slumped snoring on the ground, Wulfric, stepping gingerly over them, slipped into the cell and hustled the bewildered but ecstatic Rowena out; and soon they were on the road to Bourne. Wulfric did not like to seek Hereward's help after refusing it; but, as Rowena pointed out:

"It was the Heron who insulted him, not Wulfric."

There was, in fact, only one flaw in the plan: those who had already gone to bed when the posset was mixed had not been drugged, and Hubert was an early riser.

"My lord!" he bellowed, hammering on the door of Ivo's chamber.

"What?" croaked Ivo groggily. "God damn you, Hubert, it's scarce light. What in Beelzebub's name do you want?"

"The wench is gone, my lord!"

"What!" That was enough to rouse Ivo, pounding head and all, and have him flinging on clothes and armour in such a hurry that he put on his hauberk back to front, and had to call Hubert in, cursing and spluttering, to help him take it off again.

"The tumbler's gone too, my lord," said Hubert as he

pulled the mailshirt over Ivo's head. "I can't wake the guards: he must have drugged them."

"Bastard English cockroach!" spat Ivo. "I should have spitted him on the spot when that sniveller Modi identified the girl. Rouse the grooms and have them saddle our horses: we're going after them."

"Which way, my lord?"

Ivo sighed. He knew that Hubert thought himself cleverer than his master, but sometimes the steward could be very obtuse.

"Which way? To Bourne, of course, you blockhead! Hereward sent her, Hereward will be waiting for her report."

"But they've run through the night," objected Hubert; "we've no chance of catching them."

"We have, on horseback," said Ivo grimly. "You and I, with the foot soldiers following behind in case there's trouble later."

"Two of us?" Hubert frowned. "In Hereward's territory, with the Heron abroad?"

"This is *my* territory!" bawled Ivo.

"Bourne is Sir Ogier's, actually," Hubert reminded him tactlessly, before ducking out of the room just ahead of a hurled chamber pot.

As the sun cleared the treetops, Wulfric and Rowena, tired and draggled, were limping out of the woods towards Bourne. Rowena had never known an ordeal like it; Wulfric too was flagging. It had rained and their clothes were sodden, clinging clammily to their bodies. The gate was in sight when they heard the sound they dreaded: the thud and splash of a horse's hooves in the mud.

They did not need to speak: after one glance at each other they ran, hand in hand, for the gate, shouting fit to burst their lungs. Out of the woods behind them came Ivo and Hubert; the gates ahead began to creak open as the horsemen neared their prey. Hubert, pulling ahead of his master, reached down to grab at Rowena. In avoiding his hand, she slipped, and fell to her knees in the mud. The horsemen reined in, and Ivo gave a victorious grin as he swung his sword at Wulfric's head.

Quite how the tumbler avoided his blow he never knew: but an instant later Wulfric was standing alongside Ivo, grasping the knight's wrist with his left hand and the blunt upper length of his blade with his right. He gave a sharp twist and disarmed the gasping knight. Ivo kicked him in the chest, and he fell back a step, but did not fall.

"Run!" he shouted to Rowena.

"No," she tried to say, but Wulfric yelled urgently again:

"Run!"

There were men coming out from Bourne, armed men: Wulfric would be safe, surely. Rowena stumbled towards them, while Hubert drew his sword and lunged at the tumbler.

Wulfric parried his blow easily, and then again. The steward's old suspicions flooded back. When the tumbler warded off a third sally, he was sure.

"My lord!" he exclaimed. "This is the Heron!"

"Yes," said Wulfric. "I am the Heron. And I'm not limed yet." At that moment, Ivo's boot connected with the back of his head, and he crumpled and fell like a dead man.

"They dragged him away between their horses," Winter told Hereward. "Faster than we could run, and anyway we had Rowena to see to."

"So he was the Heron, was he?" said Hereward. "So much for working alone."

"So brave a man deserves to be rescued," said Torfrida.

"Brave?" scoffed Hereward. "Foolhardy. And worse than foolhardy. A madman with no thought for his life I can perhaps respect: but he took Rowena into danger. And for that he deserves whatever Ivo does to him." Rowena, huddled miserably by the fire, sobbed loudly.

"You don't mean that," said Torfrida firmly. "And you will rescue him."

"How?" demanded Hereward. "Storm Spalding Keep with bows and billhooks? Drug another barrel of wine when it'll be watched day and night until he's hanged? Or snatch him off the scaffold from under the noses of an army?"

"Fire." The speaker was the tax thief, Finn. "Ivo is having a stone tower built but they've not even finished the foundations. Spalding Keep is made of wood. A fire in the night will sow enough confusion for ten rescues."

"And wake the whole garrison," Hereward pointed out: but those who knew him could already see that the idea appealed to him.

"This won't be an attack, just a small party," said Finn. "In and out. I know the cells, I can lead you straight to them. We'll be gone before the garrison knows we're there."

"And while we're there, I suppose you expect us to save your treacherous friend as well?"

"Modi?" said Finn. "Let him burn."

There were two sentries at the gate towers and two more before the main door of the keep. Finn and Martin shot the first two before they had even seen the attackers approach; each died silently, hit neatly in the throat. Ladders were propped against the gate and the inner sentries were dead before they realised anything had happened to their comrades. Descending swiftly by the sentries' steps, the two archers unbarred the gate and opened it a fraction, just wide enough for Hereward and Winter to slip in. Witta and Gils had volunteered to come, but they were not fighting men by training, and Hereward had decided that four would be enough.

Martin drew two arrows with rags of cloth tied above the barbs, lit them at the guards' brazier, and handed one to

Finn.

"Which window?" he whispered. Finn pointed to the window of the hall where he had been brought before Ivo after his first capture. The two archers took aim, and loosed.

Within moments exclamations could be heard and smoke smelt, but it was only when the window was lit by the rising flames that Hereward and Winter put their shoulders to the door and smashed their way into the Keep. Guided by Finn, the attackers hurried through the already emptied guardroom, ignoring the cries from upstairs, to the studded door of the cell where Ivo Taillebois' prisoners were kept. Martin drew his hand-axe from his belt and struck off the lock.

There was only one prisoner in the cell.

"Modi!" exclaimed Finn. "You treacherous bastard!"

"Where's Wulfric?" hissed Martin, raising the axe.

"I, I don't know," bleated Modi. "They said something about taking him upstairs, but they were outside – I couldn't hear them properly. Please let me go."

"Let you go?" said Finn incredulously. "It's thanks to you the Heron's going to hang, and you expect us to let you go?"

"But they'll kill me!" sobbed Modi.

"No more than you deserve."

"Well, well," said a familiar voice from the door of the guardroom. "Hereward himself. Throw down your weapons: you'll get a quick death and your followers can live." Behind Hubert were half a dozen soldiers, and there was no other way out.

"If you want our weapons," said Hereward, "you'll have to take them from us."

Hubert's sword was already in his hand. He lunged forward, striking at Hereward's head; the Englishman parried, and punched the steward with his left hand, knocking him off his feet. As the other soldiers surged into the room, Martin sliced through Modi's bonds and pressed a knife into his hand.

"You want to go free?" he said. "Earn it."

Two men attacked Hereward, standing in the centre of the guardroom; the other four made for the cell. Winter, standing outside the door, engaged one of them; another turned aside to strike at him but was brought down by a sudden belly-thrust from Finn. A third made it into the cell before Martin cut him down. The fourth fell back: there were now three armed men in the cell, and he did not feel like attempting it alone. He turned to join the attack on Hereward. Hubert stirred and groaned.

Seeing that the Normans were not blocking the door, Martin was the first to rush out of the cell. The man who had just turned back from the door spun round again just in time to parry an axe-blow that would have split his head to the chin. With all four of the Normans who were still on their feet now engaged in fighting, Finn had time to nock an arrow to his bow, and shot one of Hereward's assailants; the man fell, writhing and screaming. A second arrow ended his misery. Hereward ran the other through the chest before he had recovered from the shock.

Suddenly, Modi rushed from the cell, ducking between Martin and Hereward, and leapt onto the back of Hubert, who had been crawling out of the guardroom, unnoticed by the rest of the attackers. He raised his knife.

"No!" shouted Hereward. "We need him alive!" Modi lowered the knife slowly, and placed it against Hubert's throat.

"Tell them to surrender," he said.

"Go to hell," spat the steward. Finn calmly loosed a third arrow, killing Martin's opponent. The man fighting Winter, seeing that he was now alone against four men, dropped his sword and raised his hands. Winter knocked him out with one blow.

"Now," said Hereward, "you, steward, will take us to the Heron."

"I'm not going up there," said Hubert. "In a fire? It's insanity."

"Where is he?"

"On the roof!"

Wulfric's guards had been asleep when the fire started. They had little enough to do: the Heron was loaded with chains and lashed to a pole in the centre of the roof. Only now, with the building blazing beneath them, had they been startled into life.

"What'll we do?" gibbered Hob.

"We'll have to get out," said Dickon. "Leave the prisoner."

"But Lord Ivo -"

"Lord Ivo wants him dead, doesn't he? Come on." Dickon hurried down the ladder which connected the roof of the keep with the top floor. It gave way beneath his feet, and he crashed through onto burning planking below; as he struggled to rise, gasping with pain, Hereward's sword pinned him to the floor.

"The ladder's gone," exclaimed Finn.

"Is there another guard up there?" shouted Hereward. Hob hesitated. "Wulfric, are you alone?"

"No," shouted the tumbler. "There's one more."

"Then listen to me, Norman," Hereward called back. "There's only one way to get off that roof alive. Unchain Wulfric and use his chains to climb down."

"You'll kill me," said Hob.

"We won't kill you. You'll have to take your chances with the fire, but that'll kill us all if you don't do as we say."

"Do it," ordered Hubert, watching the approaching flames nervously.

"Well?" said Wulfric. "Do as he says." His hands trembling, Hob began to unfasten Wulfric's chains.

That they all got out of the keep alive was little short of a miracle; but by that point the building had been evacuated. All the survivors were gathered in the courtyard. As Hereward and his men edged out, Ivo swore loudly, and yelled to his men:

"Attack them!"

"I have your steward, Ivo," warned Hereward. "Make a move and he dies." The soldiers hesitated.

"What are you waiting for?" shouted Ivo. "Attack!" One moved forward, thrusting a spear towards Martin, in a clumsy attempt to free Hubert from the Irishman's grip. Martin hurled the steward forward, so that he was almost spitted on the spear himself; as it was he was badly gashed, and fell howling to the ground.

Now that there was no hostage, the Normans moved forward with more confidence: but the gate was still open and only a few yards away. The first two to charge at Hereward were picked off by Finn as the intruders moved towards it. Cursing their incompetence, Ivo snatched up a crossbow himself. It had belonged to one of the fallen sentries, and was already primed. Ivo Taillebois was not the best of marksmen: but the range was short. He shot Finn in the chest, and the archer fell in the mud, gasping, spluttering, red bubbles oozing from his mouth. Modi stared wildly at Ivo.

"God damn you, woodcutter!" he screamed. "God damn you!" Shrieking an incomprehensible war-cry, he launched himself at the knight. Within twenty heartbeats he had been cut to pieces; the bloody mess that remained was scarcely recognisable as a human body. But the other four were gone.

"Spalding Keep is a shell," said Winter. "But Ivo will rebuild it."

"And the people of Spalding will pay for it," said Wulfric. "And they no longer have the Heron to protect them."

"And Hubert's recovering," added Martin. "I should

have killed him when I had the chance."

"Two men died to save me," said Wulfric. "Two men for one, and I can't even be the man you came to save any more. The Heron's nothing if his enemies know who he is."

"We didn't go to save the Heron," said Hereward. "We went to save Wulfric of Spalding, Rowena's husband. A good man and a brave man, and one we need at Bourne. Finn and Modi are beyond their enemies' reach now. The rest of us must keep on fighting."

"Until when?" demanded Wulfric. "Until the last Norman is dead? Until they pack their bags and go home? We'll be fighting till Doomsday."

"Some day there'll be no more need to fight," said Rowena. "We'll know that day when it comes because it will be the most joyous we have ever seen. But until then, there's nothing else we can do but pray, and hope."

"And when we cannot hope?"

"Then," said Hereward heavily, "it will be time to die. But that day has not come yet."

Chapter 5: *The Treasure of St Edmund*

Hoxne, 870.

"Enough!" Prince Ivar held up his hand. The whoops of his men died down, and they lowered their cudgels. "Is he alive?" asked the prince. The prisoner moaned. "Good. Get water, wake him up. Spread his arms and lash them to the tree. He can die the same death as the god he loves so much."

Ivar's orders were hastily followed, and the Saxon king strung from the branches by his wrists.

"Do... your... worst," he croaked. "I... will... die... in... Christ."

"Hypocrites," said Ivar. "All of you. Christians! You call your milksop god a god of peace but it didn't stop you murdering my father, did it?"

"That... was... Aelle," wheezed the king. "Not... I."

"And the good Christian King Aelle will die for it," said Ivar grimly. "But today is not Aelle's day, it is yours. And you have still a chance to save your life." Some of the Danes muttered angrily at that. This was not like their prince.

"How?"

Ivar smirked. So, the Saxon wanted to live. He would have him yet.

"Yield yourself and your kingdom to me," said the Dane. "Pledge fealty to me as High King of England, seal the bargain with a joint sacrifice to Odin, and you may reign once again as King of East Anglia, master within your domain. I will require tribute, of course, and men for my campaigns: but you'll be alive and your people will not be harried. Refuse and this whole kingdom will pay for your pride."

"Rot... in... hell."

Ivar scowled disgustedly.

"Give him a few hours to think about it," he told his captain. "If he's alive at dusk and still says no, the archers can use him for target practice."

Spalding, April, 1068.

"The Saxons found King Edmund's body, but not his head," said the scop. The whole feast hall listened raptly. The hiring of this English bard was one of Sir Ivo Taillebois' most popular decisions since he had arrived at Spalding. "The Danes had cut it off and hurled it into the forest, so that he should never be buried whole. His friends were in despair, and they shouted out 'Sire, sire, where are you?' And a voice from the forest answered 'Here, here.' And so they followed the voice, hacking their way through bramble and thorn, until at last they found the King's head. It was clasped between the paws of a wolf, as grey as steel and as big as a bull: but the wolf had not harmed the head, and when they came to claim it the beast neither fought nor fled, but surrendered the head and meekly followed them, tame as a lapdog.

"They buried the King in a secret place, and when it was done the wolf turned and went back into the forest. Years passed. The Danes were defeated, and King Edmund was declared a saint. A great shrine was built, and men were sent to retrieve his body from the secret place and bring it for reburial. When they dug it out of the ground, they found that the King looked no worse than the day he died."

"With his head cut off?" said Ivo sceptically.

"His head", said the scop, "was miraculously reattached, and the marks of the arrows gone. The only scar on his body was a red line around his neck where that wound had healed. They carried his body in pomp to the shrine, and reinterred it there: and the wolf that had guarded his head came out of the forest and followed them, and watched the second funeral as it had the first."

"And just how long do wolves live?" asked Hubert.

"This was no ordinary wolf," insisted the scop testily.

"But there is another story."

"Which is?"

"I have heard it said that the body in the shrine is not King Edmund's."

"If it was fresh and had a head," the steward pointed out, "anybody might have guessed that."

"The people still feared the Danes might return. As they did, indeed, some years later. So an unknown man was buried in the shrine and the King's body hidden in an underground chamber – and with it, a fabulous treasure."

Ivo sat up at that.

"Treasure?" he said. "I don't suppose you heard what it was? Or where this hidden chamber might be?" The scop shrugged.

"A pile of plate and jewels, some say. Others say golden statues of the twelve apostles; or that he was armed in silver from crown to toe. And the very gates of his castle are said to have been of gold, and to be buried with him. As for where... if I knew that, my friends, I'd be sitting in a greater hall than this, and I would be lord there. Suffolk is riddled with quarries and earthworks, to say nothing of the ones that have fallen in; they say there are secret tunnels leading for miles between some of the old monasteries there."

Ivo turned to Hubert.

"If I had this treasure," he said, "I could rebuild Spalding Keep so magnificently that even King William would envy me, instead of living in this Saxon hovel." The former lord of Spalding's mead hall was, in fact, spacious, warm, and less smoky than such buildings tended to be: but Ivo missed his bailey. Building on the stone tower, which he had already commissioned before the wooden one was burnt, was proceeding, but not nearly fast enough for his liking; and his former keep itself consisted of a few blackened timbers.

"It's a children's tale," replied the steward. "If Edmund was ever found, he's in that shrine, with his head still off and his flesh as rotten as any other dead man's, and if he had any treasure then Danes and monks between them have had it years ago. There's no secret tomb. Things like that don't happen." Some of the Englishmen present crossed themselves. To question St Edmund was, in Anglian eyes, something closely akin to blasphemy.

"I'm not so sure," said Ivo. He sounded almost thoughtful, something the steward had never heard before. "It might be worth taking a look at the chalk quarries."

Bourne.

"*... et lux perpetua luceat ei,*" intoned Father Wulfwine. "*Requiescat in pace.*"

"Amen." The congregation crossed themselves as old Osred was lowered into the ground, and Winter took up the first handful of soil and threw it down upon his father.

The priest at Bourne had died in the winter. Pressure had been placed on the Bishop to appoint a Norman in his place: but the local people, convinced that the newcomer was a spy, had barred the doors of the church and pelted him with filth until he fled. An attempt by the Bishop's soldiers to punish the peasants' insolence had been met by Hereward and the men he called his housecarles, the outlaws and renegades to whom he had given shelter on condition that they serve him as household troops and rob only Normans. The Bishop's men had soon taken to their heels, and since then Wulfwine had served the spiritual needs of Bourne on his occasional visits.

After the funeral, Hereward and Torfrida invited the priest to dine at Bourne Hall and tell them all the news from Ely. He gladly accepted, and, over a cup of good ale and a pot of stewed cheese, imparted all the woes of Abbot Thurstan with Norman impositions, and in particular his disputes with Ivo Taillebois.

"But Ivo's out of the abbey's way for the moment, at

any rate," he added.

"How so?" asked Hereward, leaning forward. Any absence on Ivo's part was good news for the men of Bourne.

"He's gone off into Suffolk on a wild goose chase – hunting the secret grave of St Edmund. You remember the story?"

"Vaguely," admitted Hereward. "But surely there's nothing in it. Edmund's in his tomb at Bury."

"Maybe," said Wulfwine. "Maybe not. After all, he *was* buried secretly at first. And the story of his wounds disappearing is… dubious. Though of course all things are possible to God," he added.

"But why would Ivo look for this tomb, if it does exist?" asked Torfrida. "I've never heard that he was a religious man."

"Two reasons," said Wulfwine. "Firstly, the shrine at Bury is a very holy place for the local people. If Ivo could prove it was not the true resting place of the saint, then that would be one more symbol of old England struck down, one more victory for the Normans. Also, the scops and skalds say that there is a great treasure hidden in the tomb. Ivo is a greedy man: he wouldn't be able to resist that, especially now that he has a castle to rebuild." The priest gave a half-smile to Hereward. Officially his attack on Spalding Keep had been condemned as an act of rebellion; in fact there was hardly an English heart that had not been gladdened by it.

"And you think there might really be a secret tomb?" said Hereward, frowning. Wulfwine shrugged.

"Your uncle Brand would know best," he said. "He has studied the local saints all his life. But it hardly matters; Ivo won't find anything. If the King was hidden in a quarry, a trench or anything else, it would have to be one that was disused already – and that was two hundred years since. It will have fallen in long ago."

"If St Edmund is hidden there," said Hereward slowly, swirling his ale in the cup, "Ivo *must* not find him."

"What shall we do?" asked Torfrida.

"I will go to Peterborough," said Hereward. "I'll learn what Brand knows; and if the saint is in the quarries we will put his body and his treasure beyond Ivo's reach."

"It will be a dangerous journey," warned Wulfwine. "And probably a wasted one."

"Nobody will trouble four pilgrims on their way to Bury St Edmunds," said Hereward. "I'll take Martin, Wulfric and Winter, and we'll go on foot."

"Winter?" said Torfrida. "He's just lost his father."

"All the more reason he shouldn't be sitting at home."

"With respect, my lord," Martin spoke up, "have you not forgotten Ogier the Breton? Queen Mathilde gave Bourne to him; now that spring is here he may come to take it any day. If he comes when we are gone –"

"The Lady Torfrida will be here," replied Hereward. "The defence of Bourne is in her hands."

"There are a dozen tunnels leading off this digging alone," said Hubert. "And how many more there must be, God knows."

Ivo surveyed the dry dirty-white walls of the quarry, pitted with holes as if a horde of giant water rats had made their nests there, and swore under his breath.

"Well then," he said, "you had better get on with it."

"It'll take years!" said the steward angrily. "Are we going to comb every chalk pit and farm ditch in Suffolk? In God's name, my lord, we need to know where to start looking."

"I shall offer a reward for information," said Ivo calmly. "In the meantime, you and these idle soldiers will earn your keep." Hubert gritted his teeth, but said nothing.

Peterborough.

"My lord abbot."

"What is it?" said Brand irritably. He had been reading a new life of St Dunstan and had fallen into a light doze; he did not appreciate being found asleep, let alone wakened.

"Pilgrims, my lord, who demand to speak with you. They would not be denied."

"It had better be important."

"Is that a loving uncle's welcome?" said Hereward, pushing into the abbot's cell and sweeping the broad-brimmed hat from his head.

"Hereward!" exclaimed the abbot. "God guard you, lad, what are you doing here?"

"What I told the gatekeeper," said Hereward. "My companions and I are on our way to the tomb of St Edmund."

Brand's eyes narrowed.

"What's your business there?" he asked.

And so Hereward explained about the rumours of a secret burial site, and the Norman expedition to find it. Brand frowned and stroked his beard.

"I know the rumours, of course," he mused. "There was a book in the library – our catalogue is in a poor state, but I might be able to find it… Come with me."

And he strode forth from the cell with such a determined pace that the younger man was hard pressed to keep up with him.

"It's in one of the old local chronicles," said Brand. "The main text simply records the King's death at the hands of the pagans, and that his body was later moved to the shrine, but one of the copyists has scribbled another story in the margins – there's no knowing when, but when I first came here over thirty years ago I asked the old librarian how old it was, and he said it had been there when he was a novice – that must be another forty or fifty years…" Monks looked up as abbot and pilgrim swept past them, and some muttered to each other as they recognised Hereward's blond hair and famous odd eyes.

The librarian pressed himself forward ingratiatingly to ask what his lord required, but Brand ignored him and went straight to the shelf where last he had seen the chronicle.

"Here it is," he declared. "Now, let me see, St Edmund... that was in 870, wasn't it? 868, 869, 870 – here we are." There was little illumination to the chronicle text, only thickly written black script: but to the large initial E of "Edmundus", a crude drawing of the King pierced with Danish arrows had been added – and, in tiny red lettering crammed into the margin, one word running into the next and onto the line below, so narrow was the space, there was the note for which the abbot had been searching.

"What does it say?" said Hereward, straining his eyes. He could read a little, but the mess of crushed letters in the margin of the chronicle made no sense to him – though he could see that it was in English, not the Latin of the main text.

"'This is false,' read Brand. 'The King was buried in the third passage of seven, under the chapel of St Sebastian, and lies there still, watched by a golden guard.' The statues of the apostles, perhaps. But I know no chapel to St Sebastian in those parts."

"Might it have been destroyed by the Danes?" asked Hereward.

"It's possible," agreed Brand. "Some were. But he was never a popular saint with the Saxons – it seems strange that there would be a chapel dedicated to him. Appropriate, of course, though, since he and Edmund died the same way." He snapped his fingers suddenly. "A Roman chapel! That's it, of course! It wasn't Danes who destroyed it, but Saxons!"

"Would it still be standing?" said Hereward.

"After the English became Christians some of the Roman chapels were rebuilt and rededicated," said Brand. "Maybe this one has a new patron saint, but the monk who wrote this used the older name as a sort of cloak – the rest of his directions aren't exactly clear, after all. 'The third passage of seven' could mean anything. But how would a man writing after St Edmund's death know whose chapel it had been five hundred years before?"

"An image of some sort," guessed Hereward. "A statue or a painting."

"Or a mosaic," breathed Brand. "You have it, Hereward, you have it! There's a Roman mosaic of St Sebastian in the chapel of St Seaxburga at Thingoe, and a chalk quarry not a hundred yards away."

"And seven tunnels leading off the quarry, I'll wager," said Hereward. Brand laid a hand on his arm.

"If you find the tomb," he said, "the saint must be laid to rest where the Normans will never find him."

"Don't worry about that," Hereward assured him.

"And the treasure, too," insisted Brand. "It is sanctified." Hereward grimaced.

"St Edmund fought for England's freedom when he was alive," he said. "He can spare some gold to pay for the same fight now he's dead."

"You'd sell the statues?" faltered the abbot.

"If I can find a buyer," said Hereward, shrugging. "More likely I'll have to melt them down."

"Melt them down!" exclaimed Brand. "I cannot allow it. I, I will buy them for Peterborough – we have some funds still –"

"And how would they bring you in any revenue if you can't display them without the Normans learning where they came from?" demanded Hereward. "You'd have to hide them in the vaults where they'd do no good to anybody."

"Then I'll find you a buyer," said Brand firmly. "A foreign abbey, in Flanders or Germany – anything rather than destroy them."

"Remember," said Hereward, "we don't even know yet if these twelve statues exist."

Brand offered the pilgrims a meal and a bed for the night, but Hereward declined: it was not safe for the monks to be found sheltering outlaws. He did accept bread and cheese for the journey, and the four set out, leaving behind the flat plain for the rolling green land of Suffolk.

"Two days, my lord," said Hubert through gritted teeth. "Two days already we have been searching these tunnels and we have nothing but bumped heads and scraped knees to show for it. We're no nearer finding this Saxon saint, if he was ever here."

"It's not my fault nobody's come forward," Ivo spat back. "Damn all tight-mouthed peasants! I swear they know where the real tomb is. I should have put them to the rack instead of trying to sweeten them."

"These serfs aren't yours, my lord," the steward reminded him. "Their own lords will hardly take kindly to your offering them money – they'll never allow you to torture them."

A rider came cantering up the path. He wore a particoloured tunic in red and yellow, and a Phrygian cap; he looked more like a jester than a messenger. But he had a shield slung over his back and a sword at his side.

"My lord!" he exclaimed. "My lord Ivo Taillebois!"

"Yes?" snapped Ivo. "Who wants him?"

"My name is Drogo fitz Dudo, my lord," replied the messenger. "I was appointed by the Bishop to serve as a guard at the Abbey of Peterborough."

"I want your message, not your life history!" growled the knight.

"Prior Herluin sends his compliments to your lordship, and bade me tell you that the traitor Hereward Askilsson left Peterborough yesterday, making for Thingoe."

"For Thingoe?" echoed Ivo. "Where is that?"

"Very near here, my lord," said Hubert. "A little outside Bury St Edmunds."

"And what's Hereward Askilsson doing in Suffolk?" Ivo spat on the ground after naming the man who had become his nemesis.

"The Prior heard Abbot Brand mention the resting place of St Edmund, and the chapel of St Seaxburga in Thingoe. He knows no more, but he felt it his duty as a loyal subject of King William to inform your lordship."

"Indeed," said Ivo. "The Prior's loyalty is much to be commended." He turned excitedly to his steward. "Do you see, Hubert?" he exclaimed. "Edmund is buried in this chapel! Hereward is on his way there, but he must think I'm still blundering around in the quarries! We'll kill two birds with one stone – find Edmund, and take Hereward!" Hubert, who had grasped all of this some seconds ahead of his master, nodded. "Men!" Ivo said loudly. His soldiers, who had been enjoying a welcome break from searching the crumbling and dangerous tunnels, looked wearily up. "Our quest is almost at an end," he declaimed. "We will find our prize at Thimboe!"

"Thingoe," Hubert corrected him. Ivo scowled.

"Thingoe!" he repeated. "So take up your tools, and make ready to march!"

"There should be seven tunnels," said Hereward. "I see only five."

"No, my lord," said Martin. "See there, and there – the tumbled-in areas – the rocks have blocked the mouths of the tunnels, but you can make out where they were."

"So if that blocked tunnel is the first, counting from the left, then *that* is the third."

"If they did count from the left," Winter pointed out.

"Well, if we find nothing we can explore the third tunnel from the right," said Hereward. "But we'll start here. Light the torches."

The priest at Thingoe was a sparse-haired old man whose outsized head sat uneasily atop a thin neck. He looked like an elderly bird beginning to lose its feathers, an impression furthered by his clucking and hand-flapping as Ivo and Hubert pushed past him into the chapel.

"My lords!" he cried. The men at arms trooped after them, tramping across the worn old mosaic of St Sebastian. One of the tiles cracked loudly. "If I had had warning of your coming – what can I do to help your lordships?"

"Do you have a crypt here?" asked Hubert.

"There's a vault under the floor, but it hasn't been used –"

"Show us."

"Very good, my lord – but all these soldiers –"

"They are coming down with us," said Hubert firmly. The priest made unhappy noises.

"They are carrying digging tools," he whined.

"I know that," said Ivo. "It's none of your business."

"I hope your lordship does not intend – anything, ah, anything ill-advised." The pitch of the priest's voice was rising with his agitation.

"Father," said Ivo, "I will do as I like. If I find what I think you are concealing here then it won't matter what desecrations you accuse me of, no Norman bishop will listen."

"We are on King William's business," put in Hubert, "in a manner of speaking. Business that will give him cause for gratitude, anyway. And the Church blesses King William and curses his enemies. Remember that." The priest shrugged, bit his lip, and led the Normans down the stair and into the dripping vault.

"Torches," Ivo commanded. The brands were lit, with some difficulty in the dank air, and flickered palely into uncertain life. Crumbling old sarcophagi standing around, with images of fighting men and fabulous beasts carved in relief upon them, were dimly illuminated. "Open them," ordered Ivo.

"My lord!" The priest's voice had risen to a squeak.

"If you wish to preserve the other tombs you need

only tell us which is the right one," said Hubert.

"I, I don't know what you mean," the priest managed to say.

"Who is buried here?" said Ivo impatiently.

"The slabs in the walls mark Roman tombs," said the priest as calmly as possible, indicating a row of flat square grey stones bearing no adornment but their Latin inscriptions. "These sarcophagi are Saxon, but they are very old – the crypt hasn't been used in two hundred years –"

"Open them all," interrupted Ivo. His men muttered among themselves; one made the sign of the cross. "Get on with it!" the baron exclaimed. A couple of soldiers stepped forward, placed the blades of their shovels under the lid of the nearest sarcophagus, and pushed.

"The golden gates of St Edmund," breathed Hereward.

"Not much gold on them," Martin pointed out. The gates partially blocking their path, though their rusted-through hinges were decorated in filigree, were made of oak. They did not appear to be attached to any posts.

"At least it shows there's some truth in the legend," Hereward said. "And we're in the right tunnel."

"Now all we have to do is get past them."

Hereward, holding up his torch with his left hand, reached out and gingerly took hold of the great iron ring that hung before his face. When no disaster followed, he gave it a gentle tug. The nails, all but made of rust, snapped, and he was left holding the ring. For a long moment, there was silence; then, with a hideous grating noise, the unsupported gates began to slide down the wall of the tunnel, finally collapsing in a cloud of chalk dust. The intruders stood stock still, terrified that the tunnel would collapse – but when the dust had settled, all was still sound. Hereward stepped forward onto the fallen gates, holding his torch before him: and the others followed.

"Nothing," said Hubert. "Perhaps he's under the floor."

"It's solid rock," Ivo pointed out. "Nobody's dug into it since Adam."

"Behind a wall, then. Behind one of these Roman slabs."

"Then find out which one."

"But my lord," said one of the soldiers, "if we damage the walls, we could bring down the vault."

"They were dug into to make these tombs and nothing came down," said Hubert. "It'll be safe enough."

Even without his torch, Hereward would have felt by the change in the air that he had stepped into a chamber, wider and taller than the tunnel. It was hewn out of the soft rock, dug in a hurry to judge from the roughness of the walls and floor; only at the end opposite the tunnel was there a manmade wall, built in some grey stone that was not local. But it was not that that caught Hereward's eye: it was the yellow glint in the far corner of the chamber. Bringing his torch round, he saw standing there an angel. Naively shaped, with raised hands and round eyes, about half the size of a man, its curled hair and patterned Greek supertunic marked it as the work of an earlier age: but what was truly astonishing was the material. It appeared to be fashioned entirely from gold.

Only after all four of the pilgrims, having filed after Hereward into the chamber, had gazed for some minutes on the statue did they see what lay at its feet. Uncoffined, on a wooden pallet, its few clothes rotted through, there was a human skeleton: and the third bone of the neck had been neatly sliced through, the skull lying on its side roughly near the body, appearing to stare at the four men who had disturbed its rest. All four crossed themselves as devoutly as any hermit: they were in the presence of the true body of St

Edmund, king and martyr.

To carry out the pallet and corpse was an easy enough task: the fleshless saint was not heavy, and Winter and Wulfric lifted him easily and bore him out of the chamber. But the angel was another matter.

"We could fashion some kind of a sling," mused Hereward. "Some contraption of rope and broadcloth. Or a sledge. Between the four of us we should be able to move it."

"But then who will carry the body of the saint?" asked Martin. "And besides that, do we have the time? The Normans could be searching for us even now."

"Why should they look here?" shrugged Hereward, unconcerned. Martin said nothing, but pointed to the grey stone wall. Hereward looked, and listened. Something struck the wall heavily on the other side; dry crumbling mortar fell from it and rattled on the floor. Another blow fell, and this time a stone moved.

"Somebody *is* looking here."

Hereward did not hesitate: throwing down his torch, he reached forward with both hands, grabbed the angel, and hoisted it onto his shoulders. It was much lighter than he had feared. Crouching as low as he dared, he set off along the tunnel; Martin, drawing his sword, backed after him.

With every blow, the chamber shook, and dust fell from the ceiling. At last, the great Roman tombstone crashed down out of the wall, and lay split into three on the floor of the chamber: and as it fell, every crack and every loose rock in the tunnel was shaken. By the time Ivo and his men stepped through into the chamber, the way to the quarry was hidden behind a ton of fallen chalk.

"Yes, my lord Ivo," said the English cleric, "this is the treasure of St Edmund." He whipped the cloth off his cart, and even Ivo could not suppress a gasp. Guards and builders, working on his new stone keep, craned their necks to see what had been wheeled into the courtyard, and not a few whistled in surprise. The golden angel lying there must be worth – no, Ivo could not even think of a sum.

"How did you come by this?" demanded Hubert.

"I am the deacon of Bury," replied the Englishman. "The outlaw Hereward left the statue in my care while he went north with the bones – but I know my duty. King William is the Lord's Anointed and as a good Christian I must be his loyal subject."

"No doubt you will want a reward for your loyalty," Hubert remarked. The deacon bowed his head.

"You shall be well paid, I assure you," promised Ivo. "I didn't catch your name?"

"Leofric, my lord," said the deacon. "I was named for the late Earl of Mercia: my father was one of his housecarles."

"Earl Leofric was Hereward's uncle, no?"

"By marriage," the deacon assented. "That is why the wolfshead trusted me."

"They call you Leofric the Black, don't they?" said Hubert. The deacon nodded, and stroked his smooth sable hair. "The Saxons will say you've earned that name today."

"My conscience is clear, my lord."

"And soon your purse will be full." Leofric smiled, licked his lips, and bowed once again.

St Edmund was buried secretly beneath the Abbey of Peterborough two nights later. The four pilgrims, still in their disguise, Abbot Brand and his secretary Brother Benedict – who had been christened Cuthred, but had taken the name of the saint when he became a monk – were the only people present: Prior Herluin had not been informed.

"Was there no golden guard, then?" asked Brand, disappointed. "Or have you already melted it down?"

"There was one statue," said Hereward curtly. "Ivo has it." The Abbot sighed.

"Then this is only half a victory," he said. "Oh, I don't blame you, Hereward, you had to save your men, and above even them the body of the saint. But the treasure of St Edmund should be in English hands."

"The golden guard wasn't the treasure of St Edmund, father," said Martin, grinning.

"I don't understand."

"We have the treasure – *and* the money Ivo paid for the statue. It's on its way to Bourne now; Black Leofric will be safe there from any vengeance once Ivo learns the truth."

"The statue was hollow," Hereward explained. "It was a reliquary – huge and costly but a reliquary nonetheless. It was made to hold this." He took from his scrip a small box. Made of red gold and studded with sparkling gems, it was shaped like a tiny church with a high roof and pointed steeple. Hereward opened it: inside was a tiny sliver of wood with a rust-coloured stain at one end of it. The Abbot drew a sharp breath.

"Is this -?"

"A fragment of the True Cross, stained with the blood of Christ," said Hereward. "Sent here by the Emperor Constantine when St Sebastian's chapel was first founded."

"Is it real?" asked the secretary. Brand peered at the box.

"This is very ancient," he said. "Not as far back as Constantine's time, but the inscription says it was made to replace an older reliquary – and the chapel was Roman. Of course, that is still three hundred years after Christ. But St Edmund believed in it. This is his treasure. It has been saved from the new invaders as it was once saved from the Danes: maybe that is chance, maybe a sign of the favour of God; we cannot know." He looked up, into his nephew's eyes. "But this I know," he said. "If Ivo had produced the saint's body to show that the shrine at Bury was false, it might have broken the spirit of our people. You have spared us that."

"So the pilgrims at Bury go on praying to a lie," said Benedict.

"Not a lie," said Brand gently. "Faith is faith, and St

Edmund is in Heaven and hears their prayers, wherever his body lies. He has worked incontrovertible miracles at Bury." Martin, who considered the "miracles" highly contestable, bit his lip, but did not contradict the old man. "He will continue to do so," Brand went on, "and perhaps here too, if God wills it."

 Hereward bowed his head.
 "Amen," he said.

Chapter 6: *Martin Lightfoot*

Waterford, 1044.

The boy shrank back into the corner, his arm across his eyes; but the bearded man reached down, cuffed him across the head, and dragged him to his feet.

"Watch," he commanded. Still covering his face, the child shook his head. "Watch!" bellowed the man. "You'll see how disobedience is paid in my house!" The child peered fearfully through his fingers as the dark-haired woman, tearful, pale, her iron collar wounding her neck, but her eyes showing something as yet unbroken, was dragged forward by her bound hands. The bearded man glanced upwards at the roof-beam; taking his meaning, the woman's captors slung the rope which bound her over the beam, and pulled until her arms were stretched above her head and she was forced to stand on tiptoe. The boy half-swallowed a sob.

"Give me the rods," said the man. "I'll flog the bitch myself. I want to make sure she and her brat never forget this."

Bourne, May, 1068.

"It's true," said Winter excitedly. "Harold's sons have landed in the west with an army from Ireland. Half the country's ablaze." Hereward sipped thoughtfully at his ale.

"Well?" said Wulfric. "Will we join with them?"

"We have a rightful King," said Hereward, setting down his cup. "Edgar the Atheling was recognised as heir by the Witan. The House of Godwin were usurpers who terrorised King Edward, murdered Prince Alfred, and ended up throwing the whole country away while they fought among themselves. Harold's sons are the fruit of a rotten tree."

"The Witan also recognised King William," Martin pointed out. "So did Prince Edgar. Besides, he's in Scotland and Harold's sons are in England. Has Wild Edric joined them?"

"That's what they say," said Winter.

Edric of Shrewsbury had been in rebellion since the Conquest. Tidings came from time to time of his doings in the Marches – a castle burnt in Herefordshire, a Norman town raided in Shropshire; supported by Welsh and English alike, he had made the West all but uninhabitable for the invaders. When Normans spoke of him, it was in hushed tones, making furtive signs against the evil eye: Norman mothers told their children he was an ogre who drank human blood, and even grown men half believed it. Hereward had always rather envied the western thane: his own reputation was not nearly so fearsome.

"What about Ednoth of Bristol?" he asked. Winter shrugged.

"I heard nothing about him," he said. "Does it matter?"

"Yes." Hereward nodded. "Ednoth carries respect in the West. He was a good servant of King Edward and always just to the common people. By all accounts he doesn't care for the House of Godwin, and he certainly won't take kindly to them bringing in a foreign army. If he sides with the Normans then many will follow him."

"Perhaps", suggested Winter, "this is the best opportunity yet to press our campaign here. If King William summons his knights away to fight the sons of Harold then the eastern cities will be undefended. Lincoln. Cambridge. Norwich." Hereward shook his head.

"With a band of outlaws?" he said. "It's all we can do to defend Bourne. We're not an army. Most of the men have never even seen battle." He looked over at his wife. "What do you think, Torfrida?"

"I'm sorry," said Torfrida, "I wasn't able to concentrate... I feel a little -"

Suddenly, she lurched to her feet and out of the door, collapsing onto her knees in the yard outside, spluttering and retching.

"Torfrida!" exclaimed Hereward.

The men rushed out: but ahead of them all, hobbling on her stick at amazing speed, grey gown and mantle flapping, was old Kolfrosta. They had not even seen her in the hall. She bent over her mistress, and muttered a few words in a language not even the well travelled Hereward recognised, though he guessed it must be Lapp; then she looked up, into his face. He realised suddenly that he had never looked Kolfrosta squarely in the eyes before. They were black, but bright and sharp.

"There is nothing to fear," she said, sounding faintly amused. "My lady is with child: that is all."

"With child?" echoed Hereward. "With child!" The second time it was a joyful exclamation. Taking Torfrida tenderly by the arm, he helped her gently to her feet. "Torfrida, is this true?"

She nodded, beginning to look stronger as the blood returned to her face.

"I want to lie in at St Omer," she said.

Hereward did not reply until she was sitting down again and a cup of small ale had been brought and heated with a poker – no strong drink, he decreed, in her condition: though Gwynnog shook his head and muttered that small ale was good for no one. But when Torfrida had taken a couple of sips, he ventured to say:

"St Omer? Are you sure?"

"The women of my lady's house have always returned home to bear their children," said Kolfrosta. "As is right."

"But they married their neighbours in Artois," Hereward pointed out. "We have a sea between us and St

Omer, and there is a war afoot. It is dangerous to travel, and I cannot leave England."

"You are not needed," said Kolfrosta simply. She was not trying to insult Hereward: merely stating a fact. "As long as I am there to open the locks and unloose the knots that the child may not be stayed by witchery, none other need be by. I delivered the Lady Torfrida alone, and alone I shall deliver her child." It was her longest speech in weeks.

Hereward opened his mouth to protest again, but Torfrida laid a finger to his lips.

"Brunman of Skirbeck can carry us to Antwerp, and Count Baldwin will give us safe conduct," she said. "It is safer that I should be out of England if there is to be a war here – and better that I should leave sooner, rather than travel when I am far gone."

"How soon must you travel?" asked Hereward. Torfrida's eyes flickered to Kolfrosta.

"Two months, no later," declared the nurse.

"The war in the west likely won't be over before the autumn," Martin pointed out. "If we go there we will not be back in two months; and if we do not, in two months the war may come here."

Hereward nodded heavily.

"The war is here already," he said. He took Torfrida's face between his hands. "But if I go to the west, I will bid you farewell first. I will see you aboard the *Gannet* before I take one step towards the Marches, and in the spring I will be there to see you home again with our child."

"'From Godwin Haroldsson of the House of Godwin, by law King of England, and from Diarmait mac Mael, by God's Grace King of Dublin, to Hereward, Lord of Ware and Steward of Bourne, greeting.

"'Inasmuch...'" Leofric put down the letter. "It's a summons," he said. "In the name of God, the Witan and the so-called King Godwin, calling you to come to Bristol with all your power."

Hereward, who was brushing Swallow's shining coat, looked up. "Power?" he said. "I've barely half a dozen men that I really trust." Something struck him. "Bristol? So Ednoth has joined them?"

The deacon scanned the letter.

"It says nothing of him here," he said.

"Well, with or without his help, they must have taken the city," mused Hereward. "And the King of Dublin has a formidable army."

"Which he surely needs to defend Dublin," replied Martin. "Unless Norsemen and Gaels have started to agree, and the wolf and the fox will be friends sooner."

"Stranger tales have been proved true," said Hereward, moving round to the other side of Swallow's stall. "Harold had friends in Ireland among chiefs of both races; that's why his sons fled there. To bring down fat Norman rams it might be worth the wolf and the fox hunting together."

"You're not meaning to go?" asked Martin. Hereward stroked his chin.

"It may be that I can do more good in the west than here," he said. "As you said, Edgar is hiding in Scotland while Godwin is fighting for the throne. And with Edric, Diarmait, and maybe Ednoth as well, he really does have a chance." He sighed. "I don't know. I'll call a meeting of the men; they all deserve a say."

The meeting was decisive, and Hereward rode with Torfrida to Skirbeck the next day. It was a tearful parting, the first time he had wept since his brother's funeral; nor did his spirits lift in the days following, on the road westwards with his motley little force. Half his men he had left at Bourne, under Winter's command, with Wulfric as his lieutenant. That had caused some murmurings: the tumbler was their finest swordsman, and men muttered that he was needed in the west – better to leave that Welsh cripple, he would be a liability in battle, and was he not Winter's oldest friend? But Hereward would hear none of this. Wulfric's place, he insisted, was with Rowena: and with half of Wild Edric's men being Welsh, Gwynnog would be a useful man to have by his side in the rebel camp, an interpreter and perhaps a gatherer of information.

The roads of central England were all but deserted. Certainly hardly a Norman was seen; they rode through royal forests without the sight, let alone the challenge, of a verderer. Even the birds seemed hushed. An easy journey they had of it, and made Bristol inside a week.

The rebel camp was pitched outside the city, hastily erected wooden huts clustering against the walls and around the grand tents of the leading men, Godwin, Diarmait and Edric. Over Godwin's tent stood the standard of Wessex, not a flag but a dragon cast in silvered bronze, the white dragon of which the Welsh bards said Merlin had prophesied. For his brothers Edmund and Magnus, there were no separate tents: they slept alongside Godwin, their swords within reach. The sons of Harold were distrustful men.

Only a few weeks previously, they had been entrenched in the south-west, in fortified Exeter. King William himself had come that time, rooted them out and sacked the city: and when they fled to Ireland he had thought the matter over and returned to London. Now they were back, with an army in the thousands, and they would not be so easily dealt with.

Before he had eaten or washed, Hereward, with Martin and Gwynnog in tow, marched up to Godwin's tent and announced himself.

"And who are these with you?" asked the sentry.

"Sir Gwynnog ap Sion, and my squire, Martin Lightfoot."

"*Sir* Gwynnog?" The sentry raised an eyebrow. "A Welsh knight?"

"Yes," said Hereward. "He was knighted by Wulfwine of Ely, a worthy priest, in the form prescribed by the late King Edward – as was I. To doubt his knighthood is to doubt mine. I do not recommend it."

"Hereward, Lord of Ware; Sir Gwynnog ap Sion; and Martin Lightfoot, esquire," the sentry announced, not altogether managing not to sound sarcastic: and the three were admitted.

There were four men in the tent. One, wearing a heavily embroidered dark green tunic, a gold circlet and a luxuriant moustache, was reclining on a large cushion, drinking mead, while a youth dressed in the characteristic short tunic of Ireland played softly on a clarsach and the man in the circlet waved his fingers more or less in time with the music. The third and fourth wore similar rich tunics to the first, but in red and blue respectively: the one in red was refilling a jug from the mead barrel set against the hinder wall of the tent, while the one in blue sat at a desk, poring over a map.

"Hereward, my dear fellow." Like the sentry, the man in the circlet spoke the purer Saxon English of the south, rather than the Anglo-Norse that Hereward and his men were used to in Lincolnshire.

"My lord Godwin," said Hereward, surprised. "Is King Diarmait not here?"

"He's in his own tent, no doubt, with his captains – and Edric is in his," said the man in the blue tunic. "I am the Earl Edmund, by the way, and this is the Earl Magnus." Earls already, with the kingdom unconquered: and just whose earldoms would they be taking, when there were dispossessed English earls enough waiting to have theirs back? "How many men have you brought?"

"Forty," said Hereward. "It was all that could be spared from the defence of Bourne. I fear not many of them have been soldiers, though I've been doing my best to train them."

"All are welcome," said Godwin breezily. "Have a drink." Hereward shook his head.

"I don't care for mead, my lord," he said. "I prefer ale. But what is the disposition of the enemy?" Godwin shrugged.

"My intelligence is that they should have arrived yesterday at Gloucester. No doubt Lord Edric has a more recent report."

"Then why have you not had it?"

Godwin sat up, angry at last.

"Do you think I haven't asked?" he snapped. "If Edric is a stiff-necked savage, can I help that? If Diarmait refuses to make him yield up what he knows, can I help that? If you think they should be communicating intelligence to me, tell them! Maybe they'll listen to you; I'm only the King." Magnus laid a calming hand on his brother's shoulder.

"Will you come outside?" said Edmund quietly to Hereward.

Outside the tent, the new-made earl sighed.

"I am sorry you had to see that," he said in a low voice. "Diarmait and his captains do not take us seriously; they have pushed us to the margins of this campaign and Godwin seeks refuge in drink and music. It is not always enough. I suppose after we lost Exeter Diarmait does not think us competent to have a say in the running of the army."

"Then what makes him think your brother is fit to be a king?" demanded Hereward fiercely.

"Honour," said Edmund simply. "Diarmait swore a blood oath to my father. Godwin *is* Father's heir. And he is not a fool; he is not normally as you saw him. I truly believe he will be a good king." He paused. "But if you still want to make that happen, I suggest you speak to King Diarmait. That's his tent – with the eight sentries." He grimaced; only two guarded the tent of the self-styled King of England.

Edmund disappeared abruptly back into his brother's tent. Martin whistled.

"Have we ridden across England to make *that* a

king?" he said. "I'm sorry I ever advised you to come here. Better the boy Edgar than this drunken fool." Everybody drank, and it was a strange warrior who did not get drunk of an evening if he had no battle on the morrow: but for a leader to be drunk in his tent in the middle of the day was an ill sight.

"His brother believes in him," said Hereward doubtfully. "If he's been frozen out of his own war it's no wonder he's in a poor state. Anyway, we are here now and so is this army. One way or another there will be a battle – tomorrow, probably, if the Normans were in Gloucester yesterday – and this is our best hope of freeing England."

"Should I go with you to see King Diarmait?" asked Gwynnog. "I speak no Irish and precious little Norse."

"Yes," said Hereward. "You're a knight, and here as my lieutenant – it might be taken as an insult if you weren't there, at least for the first meeting."

In Diarmait's tent too there was a harper and a barrel of mead: but otherwise the atmosphere was entirely different. Chain mail was more in evidence than velvet, and at the centre of the pavilion was a table with a map of western England and the Welsh Marches spread out on it. Around this were gathered three men. The only one without armour was tall and gaunt, with a dark grey beard in plaits reaching almost to his waist, and a gold torque about his neck – evidently the King of Dublin. To his right stood a slight but wiry man, grizzled and fierce-looking, with a short-hafted axe stuck into his belt. Martin narrowed his eyes as soon as he saw this character, and appeared to study him intently. The object of his scrutiny was quite oblivious to him. To Diarmait's left stood a slightly younger man, perhaps forty, wrapped in a squirrel-skin cloak, his shaggy and unkempt hair streaked light and dark – perhaps a trick of nature, perhaps merely dirty.

These three looked up as Hereward and his friends were announced.

"My lord Hereward," said Diarmait warmly. "Welcome to our council." Though a Gael, he spoke excellent Norse. The man in the squirrel-skins squinted suspiciously, clearly only half understanding what was said; Gwynnog caught barely a word, but both Hereward and Martin were fluent in the language. Diarmait gestured towards the skin-wearer. "This is the Lord Edric of Shrewsbury; and this man perhaps you know?" Hereward shook his head. He would have remembered the man on Diarmait's right, as a beast remembers a predator: everything about him felt dangerous. "He is Thord Gunnlaugsson, my chief captain in this expedition." Martin bit his lip. "He was formerly in the service of Prince Sitric of Waterford; I understand you know the Prince."

"I do, my lord," said Hereward, "but I did not meet the lord Thord while I was in Waterford." No doubt Thord had been pillaging and ravaging in Munster somewhere. Hereward knew the Norse warlords of Ireland and their bloodthirsty habits.

"Well, you know one another now," said Diarmait. "How many men have you brought?"

"Forty, my lord."

Diarmait chewed his hairy lip.

"We could have done with more," he said. "Oh, I am sure you raised every man you could; but Ednoth the Staller and Count Brian de Penthièvre are at Gloucester with at least four thousand, maybe five. Including Edric's men, we haven't even three: and forty will make little difference."

"So Ednoth has chosen the Norman side?" said Hereward.

"Alas, yes. We could not persuade him otherwise."

"And he has taken his cavalry with him? As well as the horse the Normans already have?"

"Horsemen are our weakness," confessed Diarmait. "The Lord Edric has some two hundred irregular cavalry, but what they can do against knights in open field, we do not know. I have none to speak of. We must ensure that we are the ones to choose the site of battle, that we can make their knights a liability instead of an asset."

"If we could lure them into the Haywood," said Edric, "it would not matter if they were ten thousand, against my men." Though he spoke Norse haltingly, and with a thick Mercian Saxon accent, the palpable confidence behind his words – and the bass timbre of his voice – inspired respect.

"That we cannot do." This was Thord, speaking for the first time. "They would simply cut off the roads and leave us in the forest to starve. We must draw them into the hills."

"But all the hills near here are gentle," objected Edric. "They would be no obstacle to cavalry – unless we could withdraw west onto the moors. The hills are steeper there."

"It would be the same as in the forest," said Thord impatiently. "They would have no reason to pursue us."

Hereward, wondering what he had got his men into, looked round at Martin: only to see that he was still staring at Thord, and the look in his eyes was unmistakeable. It was one Hereward had seen before, usually on the battlefield, but never in the eyes of the usually good-humoured Martin: unadulterated hatred.

"The fair-haired man does feats of arms," chanted the harper,

> "And many a scar is on his skin.
> The light of a warrior is on his brow:
> There gather all the virtues.
> In his eyes are seven pupils apiece,
> Bright as jewels fit for a hero.
> Unsheathed is his sword, and red is his mantle,
> And his visage beautiful.
> The women are astounded:
> The lad with the comely face
> In battle will look fierce as a firedrake."

Gloucester

Brian de Penthièvre mopped his brow. He was not sure if the weather had taken a hot turn or if he was falling ill.

"Hereward of Ware passed this way yesterday with forty men," said Ednoth. "By now he will be with the rebels."

"You are certain that your informants in Bristol can be trusted?" asked the Count. Ednoth nodded.

"They love me and they do not love the House of Godwin. Many in England were glad to see Harold fall." He stopped there, but it did not sound like the end of the sentence.

"But?" prompted Brian.

"I said no such thing, my lord."

"But you meant it. They were glad to see Harold fall, *but* sorry to see how William has ruled since, and the older ones speak of how different it was in King Canute's day, he may have been a foreigner but he left Englishmen in their right positions, yes?" Ednoth inclined his head and said nothing. Brian sighed. "I don't blame them. I advised from the first that Canute's example should be followed: keep the old structure and governing class. But William had promised his knights plunder, baronies and earldoms. If some around him had had their way there wouldn't be a native earl, thane or sheriff, bishop or abbot left in England. Fools. How do you rule a country where the machinery of rule has been destroyed?" Ednoth, once again, did not judge that a reply was needed. "So instead of the support of men like Edric and Hereward – men whose fathers served Canute happily enough – we have their hatred. We've turned a generation against the Norman race: not that they care to distinguish Norman from Breton or Fleming." Count Brian, like a third of William's original army, was himself a Breton born. "And good men like you and Archbishop Eldred, who try to keep the peace, are labelled traitors." He sighed again.

"Such is the nature of conquest, my lord," said

Ednoth. "Every change of dynasty brings disorder, and as a sheriff my first duty is to preserve order. That's why I fought for Harold against William and that's why I will fight for William against all his enemies now that he is King."

"Well, it's done now, and we must face the consequences. First of which is this rebellion. Did this Hereward bring cavalry?"

"No, my lord. There were but three horses among the forty. I have told you, my lord, before Edric of Shrewsbury sat his foresters on their Welsh ponies mine was the only force of native cavalry in England – an innovation of King Edward; he had seen in Normandy what mounted soldiers could do. But even in his day more than half my men were Normans. A horse is transport to most Englishmen, not a weapon."

"That, at least, is good," said Brian. "And we still have the advantage of numbers. But it will not do to wait. There are English thanes who have not taken sides yet; there are Welsh princelings who may be marching against us even now. Do you think it would be practical to march through the night?"

"A dawn attack?" mused Ednoth. "Yes, if we put out enough guards to the van and the flanks. We mustn't take the risk of ambush."

"Oh, I agree. But if we can take the rebels by surprise, perhaps we can end this quickly, and without too much loss of life."

Loss, at least, of Norman life.

Hereward tore hungrily at a haunch of lamb. His stomach had been rumbling all the time he was in Diarmait's tent. When he had swallowed enough to calm it, he turned to Martin.

"Who is Thord Gunnlaugsson?" he said bluntly.

Martin's face did not flicker.

"King Diarmait's general," he answered.

"Come, Martin, I could see you knew him, even if he didn't recognise you. I know you were born in Waterford. What is there between you and Thord?"

"Whatever is between us, I would keep it there, my lord."

"If that is your wish," said Hereward. They fell silent, and continued eating. After a few minutes, a man joined them by the campfire: and when Hereward looked up, he saw that it was Thord. Martin stared into the fire and ignored the Norseman.

"My lord Hereward," said Thord. "Do you look forward to the battle?"

"To be frank, sir, I do not," said Hereward. "We are outnumbered and we appear to have at least three sets of leaders pulling in different directions. It's no way to run an army."

"I'd agree with you if that were so," said Thord; "but it only appears so. Godwin and his brothers count for nothing in the field, and Edric for very little – he has only two hundred men. This is King Diarmait's army, and below him, I lead it. In one direction, and that is against the heart of the enemy. Edric may talk of hiding in moors and forests, and there in front of the King I cannot call it a coward's counsel: but that is what it is. The Norse of Ireland do not flee. My father fought the Gaels at Clontarf; I fought the Scots at Deerness; I will fight the Normans where God pleases. And if we fall, we will be welcome in Valhalla." Hereward raised an eyebrow at the mix of Christian piety and pagan sentiment, but said nothing: such was common enough, and he had been guilty of it himself in the past. Thord stood, clapped him on the shoulder, and strode off.

"He killed my mother," said Martin quietly. Hereward stared at him. "She was a slave in his house; her name was Eithne and she was very beautiful as I first remember her; I saw that beauty fade day by day. By the time I was seven I'd watched her age twenty years. Thord was a brutal master. One day a thrall whose hand had been mauled by one of his hounds killed the creature for revenge: Thord had him thrown into the kennels for the other hounds to eat. But Mother stayed out of his way when she could, until the night he tripped over me in the feast hall. I kept a pet mouse, and it had got loose: I went in there to make sure the dogs didn't get it, I got under Thord's feet, and he kicked me across the room. When Mother saw that she walked up to him and slapped his face." Martin, who had not lifted his eyes from the fire all this time, turned and looked into Hereward's face. "He beat her to death," he said simply. "I was made to watch. I would have run away that night, but I got no chance. Besides, that was the year of the great hunger; if I'd made it out of Waterford I'd either have starved or been eaten by the poor folk in the hills. When I was ten I did escape. I lived as a beggar and a thief for years, before I met you in York. When we were in Waterford half my soul shuddered every day at the thought of meeting him, and the other half longed for the chance of vengeance. But that time Heaven did not send him to me. Now it has. I would have killed him on the spot when we walked into Diarmait's tent, and damn what became of me afterwards: but we can't fight this war without him. So I must smile and serve beside him, for the greater good." He fingered the blade of the short-handled axe at his belt. "The greater good."

There was nothing Hereward could say. He placed a hand on Martin's shoulder, and left it there: and both looked back into the fire. They sat there until it burned low; and they heard King Diarmait's bard singing.

> "Lo, here is a willow wand.
> What tidings does it bear for us?
> What meaning is hidden here?
> Who laid it down, and were they few or many?
> What doom will it bring on the army that passes it?
> Answer, o wise men, why was it left here?

A hero set it down.
Quickly did he cut it.
Soldiers he baffles,
Chiefs and retainers he entraps,
And he set the wand here with one hand."

Dawn.

It was only when the sun peered over the hills that the lookouts sighted the Norman spearpoints. At once they clapped their horns to their lips to rouse the camp; Thord, on his feet in seconds and struggling into his armour, snapped furious orders at the guards.

"Out, you maggots!" he roared. "Form up before the gate!"

"But we'll leave the walls unmanned," protested one. Thord punched him on the jaw and he fell senseless.

"There's a whole army to man the walls if you've got the guts to buy them the time!" he declared to the rest. "Defend that gate and stop the enemy's advance!"

"That's our captain you just knocked out," said one man. Thord looked at him dangerously, then declared:

"Then I'll lead you, you bunch of poltroons! Follow me!"

And so, as the Normans broke into a trot, Thord Gunnlaugsson led the night guard of the rebels out at the gate of their camp. They were at the end of a shift, tired and hungry, half of them still busy putting their helmets on or lacing up their hauberks: against them were Ednoth's cavalry, already levelling lances. There was no contest. They rode easily across the chaotic guards as they were forming up, and on to the gate, which was not yet fully closed. Behind them, survivors staggered uselessly away, while blood soaked into the dusty earth.

Hereward, woken by the first horn, was by this time

armed, and rousing his men. There seemed to be no central command, but he would at least form them into some sort of shape to beat a retreat, surely the only thing that could now be done. Already the Normans were in the camp; men were dying in their beds. The handful of Godwin loyalists who had followed Harold's sons from Exeter to Dublin were gathering around the white dragon tent, to sell their lives dearly in defence of their prince; Diarmait and his bodyguards were forming a tight knot at the centre of the camp; and Edric – where was Edric?

Suddenly, out of nowhere as it seemed, there appeared an extraordinary sight. A bare handful of horsemen in patched clothes and furs – far from Edric's two hundred; probably not even twenty – charged towards the now dispersing ranks of the Norman cavalry, whooping and hollering. And at their head, his squirrel-skin cloak flapping open and revealing a blood-red tunic over a dull, tarnished hauberk that must have been older than its wearer, was Edric of Shrewsbury, unhelmeted, swinging his sword, and with a mad light in his eyes. They locked onto those of the Sheriff of Bristol, and he shrieked in an otherworldly voice the single word: "Traitor!"

The Normans had begun to break ranks as they entered the camp, hunting down easy kills. Now Edric and his men ploughed through them as easily as they themselves had through Thord's phalanx at the gate. With every blow Edric cut down another man, until at last he arrived in front of Ednoth. In a low hiss, he repeated: "Traitor". He raised his sword, and drove the point under the chin of the Staller and through his skull.

But there was no other counter-attack. By now the Norman infantry were surrounding the eastern side of the camp, and de Penthièvre's standard was at the gate.

"Form up to retreat!" bawled Hereward. "Everybody! Form up and fall back fighting!"

With no orders coming from any other quarter, men

rallied to Hereward's voice. Several of those from around Godwin's tent threw themselves into the front of the fighting, taking down Normans with them as they fell; the sons of Harold themselves, with their Irish harper and a handful of guards, ended up in the rearguard along with Diarmait and his chosen men, and they fell back foot by foot, yielding ground but no space to attack, until at last they backed out of the camp and abandoned it, and those still in it, to the Normans.

Exmoor.

"Higg. Gils. Witta. Eomer. Snell." The names of the dead thudded down one by one as Gwynnog recited them. "And Eadulf won't walk again if he lives the night; we had to half carry him most of the way here. Half the rest of our men are wounded."

"Edric and his men have disappeared," put in Edmund. "Methelgar here is the only one with us out of two hundred." He gestured at the man in the black woollen cloak, so far silent, who had joined the leaders of the rebellion in their conference by the main fire of their makeshift camp.

"Edric was surrounded by Norman cavalry after he killed Ednoth," said Hereward. "I saw him. He couldn't have survived."

"You don't know Edric," said Methelgar. "If he is dead indeed, then God rest him. He bought us all our lives by what he did: without Ednoth the horsemen had no head. But I'll not believe it until I see his body."

"Have we enough men to strike again if we rejoin King Diarmait?" demanded Godwin. Edmund was right: his brother was a different man sober: but it was a little late for that. Hereward gave a hollow laugh.

"Against Bristol, invested and fortified?" he said. "No. Half the army must have died in that camp. If King Diarmait keeps the meeting – if he isn't halfway back to Dublin already – it'll only be to pick up those who have to fly back with him."

"He won't break our meeting," insisted Godwin doggedly. "He gave me his word."

"And so far his word has been good. You'd better pray that it continues so, for we've no other ships than his."

"Lord Hereward is right," said Edmund quickly, before Godwin could retort. "We have no choice but to return to Ireland, at least for the moment. Next year, perhaps, we can try again. But what of you, Lord Hereward? Will you come with us?"

"No." Hereward shook his head. "I can't abandon my men, nor yet lead them into exile. It's my duty to take them back to Bourne."

"Back to Bourne?" echoed Edmund. "Across two hundred miles of Norman territory?"

"We made it to Bristol. We'll make it back. There are enough places to hide; we're only forty –" Hereward corrected himself – "thirty-five men." Thirty-four by morning, he thought.

Out in the darkness, an owl hooted three times.

"Approach, friend," Edmund called out.

The scout came into the firelight. He was spattered with mud – the hot weather had broken in the afternoon, a heavy shower of rain leaving the ground sodden – and somewhat out of breath.

"What's the news?"

"The Count has invested Bristol," he said. "He's making as much as he can of Ednoth's death – the heroic Sheriff defending his city from savage Irish invaders." There were growls from around the fire. "There's no word of Edric, or nothing reliable; some of the Normans say they saw him fall, but there's no body." Methelgar smiled grimly. "But Thord Gunnlaugsson is dead. They're displaying his body in the marketplace: his skull was split by a blow from behind.

The Normans are loving that: they say either he was a coward who turned his back on the enemy, or our army was so riven with treachery that one of us slew him." The growls got louder.

"That camp was chaos," said Edmund. "It was easy for the Normans to get around a man on all sides. I'm sure there were a hundred men with wounds behind: it didn't take cowardice or treachery to put them there."

"But Thord didn't die in the camp," Magnus pointed out. Men looked round in surprise: the third son of Harold did not speak often. "He was out before the gate with the guards, remember? The Normans didn't get behind them until after they were all dead."

"Not all," said Hereward. "Some fled; some were left wounded on the ground. But it's not impossible some came back into the camp to carry on fighting."

"That would have been like Thord," said Godwin; and Magnus had to concede that it would.

"If Edric is alive," said Methelgar, "he will return to Haywood. I must rejoin him there."

"We'll come with you," said Hereward. "If we can get past Bristol and Gloucester, Haywood will be the perfect place to hide up until the Normans forget about us."

"And we will go to the meeting place and wait for Diarmait," said Godwin.

Edmund suddenly threw back his head, and began to chant.

"So quoth the thinker in his mind," he recited,
"Sitting asunder from counsel.
Well bides he who holds troth,
Nor never shall a berserker reckon
The grief of his breast in haste,
Unless he knows the cure before:
A prince must act bravely.
Well bides it with him who seeks mercy,
Balm from the Father in Heaven:

There, for us, stands the only fastness."

"There, for us, stands the only fastness," repeated a soft voice from outside the ring of firelight: and Hereward recognised it as Martin's.

At dawn, though they had hardly eaten in two nights and a day, Godwin and his retinue left the encampment on the moor for Ilfracombe, to meet King Diarmait's ships – if they came. None chose to remain; only Methelgar and the men from Bourne were left. Methelgar went out with Martin to chase the wild sheep, and they brought back enough to provide the men with some form of breakfast, a relief after a cold and hungry night.

"What do we do now?" Gwynnog asked Hereward.

"First we must bury Eadulf," said Hereward heavily. The wounded man's groans and cries had kept men awake half the night, but in the second watch had grown fainter, and by dawn he had given up the ghost. "Then we must find a way past Bristol, so that we can get into the Forest of Dean and through it to Haywood. There we may meet with Edric: and from there we can plan our return to Bourne."

While Edric's grave was being hacked from the rocky hillside, Hereward went up to Martin.

"You have your wish," he said. "At whatever Norman soldier's hands it might be, your mother is avenged."

"It was after the camp had fallen," said Martin, not looking at Hereward. "We were retreating through the western fence and Thord came out from among the tents. He was covered in blood and raving, shouting that we should fight on, charge the Normans again; but there was nobody to hear him. I was the last man in the camp at that end of the line. He shouted 'Follow me!' and turned to charge back in. He shouldn't have shown me his back." He paused. "I feel no guilt, no shame," he said. "Nor peace neither. Nothing good or bad. Yet I have committed the worst crime in the world." Another pause. "I have killed my father."

Chapter 7: *The Wild Huntsman*

Berrington, June, 1068.

Gwyn dropped his ball. Something was wrong. His mother looked up from washing her husband's mud-stained cloak: the child seemed afraid.

"What is it, bach?" she called. Gwyn didn't move; but his face crumpled up and he began to cry. His mother rushed out and gathered him into her arms. "There, there, Gwyn bach, there's nothing –" She stopped. There was something; she could hear it now. The thunder of approaching hooves. For a long moment the sound hung in the air, slowly getting louder: then, with what felt like a blow to the stomach, she realised what it was.

"The Wild Hunt!" she shouted. Instantly, the hamlet was thrown into pandemonium. Men and women ran hither and yon, scooping up children and animals, hurrying them inside, everybody shouting, some, even grown men, weeping as loudly as Gwyn.

The door of the hall was flung open, and Sir Roland marched out in full armour, with his men behind him. For the first time, the locals were glad to see their Norman overlord.

"Have no fear!" he barked. "You are under my protection – no demon of the woods will enter Berrington!" Drawing his sword, he motioned his men forward. In good order, the Norman line began to march – just as the Wild Hunt came over the rise.

They were an extraordinary sight. They rode on small horses and ponies, for the most part, though the villagers' fear swelled these to the size of bulls. Men with their faces painted white, wrapped in the skins of wolves and great dogs, the upper jaws of the dead beasts forming hideous hoods over their heads, brandished darts, spears, axes: and at their head, in a tunic the dark green of forest shadows, rode the Huntsman. His cloak, too, was made from the skin of a beast: no wolf or hound this, but a gigantic stag. The creature's skull formed a half-mask over his face, his eyes gleaming through its long sockets below mighty thirteen-point antlers; and the skin below was stained, not the ghostly white of his followers, but black as soot. In his right hand he bore aloft a broadsword almost as long as a man: to wield it one-handed, his strength must have been something superhuman.

The Hunt outnumbered the Norman footsoldiers by ten to one. As the Huntsman and those around him smashed into the front line of the defenders, the rest surged round to the sides, surrounding the square. A pair of chickens, running squawking from the noise of battle, were crushed beneath their hooves. In minutes it was all over, and the Huntsman held up Sir Roland's head by the hair, a ghastly, gore-dripping monstrosity.

"People of Berrington," he declaimed. "Your oppressor Roland fitz Ademar is dead. But it does not please us that we have had to free you without your help. Word has reached us that you pay your taxes to these thieves willingly; that you have given up your arms; even that women in Berrington have consorted with the invaders. This day we will spare your lives: but we will expect to find you grateful. If we have cause to call on your help and do not get it, you will suffer."

He threw back his arm, and hurled the head into the air. It arced over the nearest hut, bounced off the roof of the one behind it, and fell in the road that ran through the centre of Berrington. His followers gathered up the bodies of their two comrades who had fallen – a small price for eleven Normans – set them on their horses, and wheeled to ride away. Within a hundred heartbeats they were gone beyond sight or sound.

Slowly, the people of Berrington began to come out of their houses; nobody spoke, and only the fierce keening of a woman who had lost a Norman sweetheart broke the silence. None comforted her, or even looked in her direction. They had no desire to earn the wrath of the Huntsman.

Haywood.

"There's been another Wild Hunt attack," Methelgar reported. "At Berrington. No peasants were killed this time, just the local knight and ten Norman soldiers."

"The second in a week," mused Hereward. Since he and his men had set up camp in the depths of Haywood, where they lived on King William's deer, they had heard many rumours from the local charcoal-burners about the Wild Hunt, and one or two of Hereward's own men even claimed to have seen the Huntsman and his Wish Hounds slip silently through the forest. The most persistent belief was that the Norman invasion had stirred up the old spirits of the land, and the Huntsman had arisen again to drive out the interlopers. Hereward was sceptical of this: but men had certainly died at the hands of the Hunt. It was something more than legend. "Who leads this Wild Hunt?"

"A man with the head of a stag, they say, and with eyes like coals of fire. He rides a vast horse with eight legs, and carries a brand as big as a tree." Methelgar curled his lip. He had little faith in the accounts of the peasants.

"But who was said to lead it of old?"

Methelgar shrugged.

"The Welsh say it is the King of the Dwarves; the Cornish, that it is their old hero Arthur." Hereward remembered dimly the tales of Arthur: to the Cornish especially, but to the Welsh also and even to some Saxons in these western parts, he was little less than a second Messiah, who would one day return to deliver them from their tribulations. "In the north they used to say Woden was the Huntsman; in the south, that it was a forest spirit called

Herne. The Scots say it is the Devil himself."

Hereward made the sign of the cross.

"And who do you think leads it now?"

Methelgar answered without hesitating.

"Edric," he said. "I know him and I know his work. He always did take the old legends to heart; and he always had an eye for the best way to strike fear into the souls of his enemies. Well, he's certainly achieved that."

"Then he is alive," said Hereward softly.

"I never doubted it," said Methelgar.

"If it is Edric, where will he be encamped?"

"Within Haywood, probably. Or over the border in Wales, but I think we'd have heard if any of the princes had granted him open protection. This is where we had our main camp before the rebellion, but he always had other hiding holes. He must be somewhere further north, perhaps a day's walk from here; no Norman will ever find him unless they raze the whole forest to the ground, but perhaps I could."

"He seems to have taken care not to find us," mused Hereward. "Perhaps he doesn't want our help."

"More likely he doesn't want his secret broadcast," said Methelgar. "Better that the ignorant should go on believing he is a god of the woods. But if we go to him, that will be a different matter."

"Hmm." Hereward stroked his chin. He had three weeks' growth of beard; he had had no chance to shave since the battle. Most of his men were similarly unkempt. "Is there anything you know, about Edric or the legend of the Hunt, that might help us?"

"It's nearly Midsummer," said Methelgar. "In these parts they say that the power of the Hunt is at its height in the last three days and nights before St John's Day. He'll be planning something special for then."

"What?"

Methelgar shrugged.

"Who knows? This Roland of Berrington who was

killed yesterday had a brother, Geoffrey fitz Ademar, lord of Ullingswick. He'll want revenge: he may even be planning an expedition into the forest: maybe Edric will strike against him. But he might have something more spectacular in mind. Hereford, perhaps."

"Hereford?" echoed Hereward incredulously. "A fortified city?"

"It's the last thing the Normans will expect," Methelgar pointed out. "The garrison there is small enough, and the gates are open by day. With speed and surprise he could do a lot of damage there. Or in Shrewsbury; it's farther from Haywood but it's his own city. It eats his soul that the invaders sit in his hall." Hereward found it hard to believe that any sane man could plot something so foolhardy, but he did not argue; Methelgar knew Edric better than he did.

"So, if we are to find him, it must be by three days before Midsummer," he said.

Ullingswick

Geoffrey fitz Ademar covered his mouth. He did not want to appear weak or squeamish before his men.

"Do we know -" he began to say, but it was no good. He turned aside suddenly and let fly a stream of vomit. As he coughed up the last of his dinner, he looked up anxiously: the eyes of all were on him, but he did not see in any of them the contempt he had feared.

"Do we know", he managed to say, "who they were?"

The carter who had brought the corpses into his courtyard nodded.

"Egfrith and Ingwy," he said. "I'll swear they were English." When a murdered body turned up, it was assumed to be a Norman assassinated by local insurgents unless credible witnesses could be found to swear the contrary: and communities were heavily fined for such deaths.

The man and woman on the cart had been dead for two or three days. They were beginning to stink, and the flies were gathering, but that was not what had made the lord of Ullingswick retch. The tongues of the dead couple had been torn out by the roots and nailed to their chests: and from the quantity of blood dribbled down the front of their clothes, it must have been done while they were still alive.

"What does it mean?" demanded Geoffrey. "In God's name, what does it mean?"

"It's the Huntsman's warning," said the carter. Several of the Normans crossed themselves. "Had these two given you any information, Sir Geoffrey, anything at all?"

"That's not your business," snapped the knight.

"Maybe not," agreed the carter. "But the Huntsman thinks they did. This is the fate of informers. Plenty of people saw me bring the bodies here, and then there are the boys who found them: you may find it difficult to gather intelligence after this. They'll all have understood: and nobody wants to cross the Huntsman."

"Who is he?" said the Norman. The carter laughed softly.

"Oho, no, you'll not get anything out of me. For one thing I know nothing; for another I'm attached to my tongue."

"There are other parts which could become detached from those who do not aid me," said the knight. He never had much stomach for torture, but his orders were to use all necessary means to put down rebellion wherever he found it. Furthermore, he had Roland's death to avenge: and, squeamish or not, there was nothing he would stop at when the fight was for his family. If he had to crucify children to catch this Huntsman, he felt right now that he could do it.

"Cut off what you like, you can't get more from me than I know, and that's no more than you do," said the carter. "I can tell you who they *say* he is. My granny was Welsh, and she told me the story of King Herla. But if that's the truth it'll do you no more good than if you were to try to hunt down the Man in the Moon."

"Come inside," said Geoffrey. "Friend. And tell me about King Herla."

"Herla was a petty king of the Britons in these parts, before the days of Arthur," said the carter, and took a sip of mead. "While hunting one day he met the King of the Dwarves, a little pygmy fellow with cloven hooves and a great beard, thick as a hedge and red as hellfire, riding on a goat: and he invited the little king and his train to his wedding. Did I mention he was to be married the week after?"

"No," said Sir Geoffrey. "Who was his bride?"

"It doesn't matter, she's not important. For after the wedding the dwarf told Herla that he himself was to be wed a year from that day, and bade him attend with his companions in the Otherworld." Geoffrey chewed his lip. He was aware that the Welsh bards sang of a fairy realm that was not Earth, nor Heaven, nor Hell, but it sounded heretical to him. "King Herla kept the appointment. He and his closest attendants went to the Dwarf King's palace, ate of his meats, drank of his wine, and danced with the little women of the Otherworld; and after three days they made to ride back to their own land. The Dwarf King gave them a gift before they departed: a hound which rode on Herla's saddle with him, now in his arms, now draped over the neck of his horse: and he gave him also a warning: 'Let the hound be the first to set foot on mortal soil.'

"When they came to their own lands they seemed different. A field which had grazed cattle when they left was golden with wheat, and where barley had grown there were cattle. New walls had been built, and there were long houses where they remembered round ones. One of Herla's companions said 'That should be old Blodwen's house: I'll ask her what's afoot': and he leapt lightly down from his horse.

"The moment his feet touched the ground, he staggered, and clutched the bridle. Herla started forward and looked into his friend's face, and saw the skin grow grey and withered in an instant, and the light fade from the eyes. The man collapsed and in minutes he was nothing but a pile of bones and hair in rotting rags.

"Out of old Blodwen's house there came a man, startled by the noise outside. When he saw the dead skeleton on the ground, he crossed himself. 'Who are you?' he demanded of Herla: but as he spoke English, a language the king had never heard before, he was met with a blank stare. He repeated the question in Welsh.

"'I am Herla, your king,' Herla replied. 'Who are you, that show me no respect, speak in foreign tongues and have come out of Blodwen's house? Where is the old woman?'

"'I know no Blodwen,' said the Saxon. 'I am Gurth and this is my house, and Offa is my king. You're on the wrong side of the Dyke, Welshman, and King Herla has been dead these three hundred years. Take your jokes home before I set my dogs loose.'

"So King Herla rode away, with the Dwarf King's hound still in his lap. And until the hound chooses to get down, neither he nor any of his men may leave their saddles, or they will crumble to dust and bone like the man who died outside Gurth's hut. Another three hundred years have passed since that day, and he rides still."

"So Herla wore no antlers," said the knight. "And his men no wolfskins, nor had he any hounds when he returned from the Otherworld save the one which rode on his horse with him. And this Huntsman who plagues us now carries no dog in his lap. What makes men think he is the same?"

The carter shrugged.

"Who knows?" he said. "They say the High King of the Otherworld was followed by Wish Hounds. But then, I've seen a painting of Arthur as a dwarf on a goat's back, like the king in the Herla story – and the Cornish say that Arthur is the Huntsman, riding aimlessly until the time comes for the Britons to reclaim this island and drive Saxon, Dane, Norman and Scot alike into the sea, when he will be King again. Some say the Huntsman's quarry are elves escaped from the Otherworld, or souls escaped from Hell; others that the Wish Hounds themselves are the damned."

"And what do you believe?" asked Geoffrey. "Nobody can hear us here, I swear."

"Can you swear that the Huntsman cannot hear us?" retorted the carter. "They say that if God has ears everywhere the Devil has but one ear less."

"Is Edric of Shrewsbury the Huntsman?" pressed the knight. The carter lowered his eyes, and was silent a long while; when he did answer his voice was smaller than before, and his fear palpable.

"If it is any mortal man, it must be Edric," he said. "But better it should be the Devil. I fear him less."

"They have been here."
"I see nothing," said Hereward.
"Nor I," added Gwynnog.
"Nor are you meant to," said Methelgar. "But they cannot pass and leave no trail, nor set straight every blade of grass they bend. The camp of the Wish Hounds cannot be far; much further and we'll be out the north side of the wood."

"You won't be going much further."

The voice came from a bush that had looked far too dense to hide any man. Yet out of it there now stepped a Wish Hound, in full wolfskin and whiteface, bow in hand, arrow strung. Hereward started: he had never seen the like before. Looking again, he realised with surprise that the paint and furs hid a youth, perhaps sixteen or seventeen years old: but the boy's eyes betrayed no fear or doubt. A second Wish Hound, an older man, appeared at the other side of the road.

"Methelgar," he said.

"Bana," said Methelgar calmly. "And Ailnoth." He acknowledged the boy. "This is Lord Hereward of Ware."

"I know who he is," said Bana. "I saw him in the Irishman's camp." He spat on the ground.

"He wishes to speak with the Lord Edric."

Bana grinned, baring his yellow teeth.

"I'm sure he does," he said. "Well then, he'd better follow me."

The clearing was hidden from casual sight. Banks of earth between the trees were covered with brambles, holly and other greenery, in which there was only one opening, so that the great circle carved out of Haywood formed a kind of living fortress. At the back of it, past the huts where the Wish Hounds and their few womenfolk lived, and the rather better appointed buildings where they stabled their horses, three saplings had been lashed together with ropes of ivy, and branches and bones fixed between and before them to form a double throne: and there sat the Huntsman and his lady.

The lady's face was not painted entirely, like those of her husband and his followers. Instead it was marked with patterns in a startling blue, a spiral on the left cheek, three stripes like claw marks on the right, and a star upon her forehead: between these marks, dark eyes stared out unblinking. Her hair appeared black in the shadow, but when sunlight fell on it shades of red and even gold shimmered in and out of view, as if it were all colours at once; she wore no veil or mantle, but let it hang free over her shoulders. Her kirtle was blood-red and her supertunic grass-green, and she wore a narrow silver torque about her neck.

This was the sight that greeted Hereward, Gwynnog and Methelgar when they were ushered into the presence of the Huntsman.

"Hereward," said Edric softly.

"My lord Edric." Hereward inclined his head.

"Where are your men? How many did you lose at

Bristol?"

"Six. The rest are at your old camp to the south, under the command of Martin Lightfoot."

"You should have brought them here."

"I wished to see for myself the camp of the Wild Huntsman before I raised a noise by bringing thirty-four men tramping through the woods."

"And what do you think now that you have seen it?" asked Edric.

"It is most impressive," Hereward admitted. "I would not have seen it from outside unless I had come very close, and then no doubt I would have been spitted on an arrow. But you have little room for more men here. And, forgive me – this mummery –" He gestured at the antlers Edric still wore.

"This is necessary," said Edric. "I am no longer only Edric of Shrewsbury. I am Herne, I am Arthur, I am Woden. I am the Lord of the Wildwood and my Rhiannon is its Queen." He laid a hand on his wife's arm. "She is born of elfin blood, you know. The line of the fair folk descends through her to my son." He indicated Ailnoth, who bowed. Hereward and Gwynnog glanced at Methelgar, but if he was surprised he showed no sign of it. Edric touched the gilded hilt of his sword. "She brought me this," he said. "Lightning. An elfin blade."

"You have, ah, managed to hurt our enemies," said Hereward hastily.

"I have."

"I ask that I may ride with you when next you go forth against them."

Edric smiled and licked his teeth.

"You want to become a Wish Hound?"

Hereward shook his head.

"My duty is to lead my men back to Bourne," he said. "I cannot stay in Haywood. But I would ride at least once with the Wild Hunt."

"No man rides with the Wild Hunt unless he is

prepared to become one of us," said Edric. "If you still wish to leave Haywood afterwards, then you may: and you will be the first Wish Hound who ever left my camp." He turned to Methelgar. "And what of you, my friend?" he said. "Will you join the Wild Hunt?"

Methelgar broke into a smile for the first time since Hereward had known him.

"Try and stop me," he said.

Edric's eyes went next to Gwynnog: in answer, the Welshman held up the stump of his arm.

"Then Hereward and Methelgar shall undergo the tests," said Edric; "and after that will come initiation."

He turned and nodded to Bana. There was a patch of grass by the Wish Hound's feet; he bent down and put his hand to the edge of it. Hereward, looking more closely, realised that the grass was growing on top of a wicker roundel like a training shield. Bana lifted it and exposed beneath a pit, some two feet across and three feet deep, with a puddle of dirty water at the bottom of it.

"Who will be tested first?" said Edric.

"I will," said Hereward.

"Then lay aside your cloak, your sword and your shield, and step into the pit." Hereward did as he was told. The cold water seeped into his shoes and the bottom of his hose. The lip of the pit was above his waist. "Arm him," said Edric. Bana handed down to Hereward a wooden cudgel and a small targe of the Irish style; it had been somewhat battered, especially around the edges. "When I give the word," said Edric, "three men with sticks will attack you. They have a hundred heartbeats to land a blow. If they fail, you are fit to be a Wish Hound." It seemed a strangely irrelevant test for men who fought almost entirely on horseback: but every warrior needed speed and coordination. Hereward gripped his wooden weapons and gritted his teeth. "Now!"

The first blow came from behind. Hereward sensed it rather than hearing it, and raised the cudgel above his head, blocking it just in time. As another man came from his left, he drove the targe forward to take the force of the second stick. His right side was now exposed, and the third man drove a sweeping sideways blow towards his body: but he whirled the cudgel forward and down, snapping the Wish Hound's stick. Edric laughed and clapped his hands; the man with the broken stick snarled like the dog he was dressed as.

The other two did not let up in their attack, and soon Hereward's arms and shoulders were beginning to ache with effort. Surely a hundred heartbeats must have passed by now? It felt more like a hundred hours. But still the wooden whirligig went on, *thwack, thwack, thwack,* every second more exhausting than the last.

"A hit!" exclaimed one of the Wish Hounds. Hereward wheezed. Surely after all this he had not been defeated? Just in time, he saw the other driving a blow down towards his head, and blocked it. Evidently the appeal did not mean any break in the test.

"I did not see it," said Edric. "Rhiannon?" The lady shook her head. "No hit. And I believe that is time." He rose from his throne, and all the Wish Hounds bowed their heads. Striding forward, he extended his right arm to Hereward, clasped him by the elbow, and helped him to clamber out of the pit. Hereward lent on his cudgel, feeling twice his age; and Edric slapped him on the back. "Welcome, brother," he said. "When Methelgar has passed the test, you will become Wish Hounds together."

The test appeared very different when watched from a safe distance. Hereward had to bite his tongue a few times to stop himself calling out warnings to Methelgar, but the Marcher clearly did not need them: probably he had trained in similar fashion when serving with Edric before. And, of course, he knew his attackers, knew their style, and could perhaps more easily predict who would strike where. Nevertheless, he was as weary as Hereward when he was finally hauled from the pit and pronounced worthy to become a Wish Hound.

"Which of my Hounds will blood these men?" asked Edric. Bana stepped forward, holding out his right hand.

"That will I," he said. Edric, grasping Bana's wrist in his left hand, drew his dagger with the right, and slid it quickly across the ball of the other man's thumb. There was a second's pause before the blood welled up out of the cut. Edric released Bana's hand. Stepping up to Hereward, the Wish Hound placed his wounded digit gently against the other man's forehead, then drew it down along his nose and across his lips, leaving a line of glistening blood. He then did the same to Methelgar. Two Hounds stepped forward and draped wolf pelts around their shoulders.

"You bear now the mark of the Huntsman," Edric intoned, his voice seeming deeper than before. "You are one with the wolfhound, and the wolves you shall hunt are the enemies of the people. The forest is your kingdom. The Huntsman is your lord. Whom do you serve?"

"The Huntsman," they replied in unison. Hereward blinked: he had heard his own voice say that, but had not been aware of uttering it. Gwynnog was frowning, surprised.

"Good," purred Edric. "Rhiannon, let us have a song."

Moving for the first time, the lady rose from her throne, hair and kirtle shimmering: and she began to sing, softly at first, then louder, her voice low and haunting. She sang in Welsh: Hereward did not know the language, but he dimly remembered his Cornish, and this was not dissimilar; as the song went on, it grew easier to understand. Gwynnog, son of Welsh parents, and Methelgar, bred in the Marches like most of the Wish Hounds, understood every word.

> "Not of mother and father
> Did my Creator fashion me:
> Of ninefold faculties,
> Of the fruit of fruits,
> Of the fruit of the eldest god,

> Of the primrose and the hillside flower,
> Of blossom high and low,
> Of earth and the flower of the nettle,
> Of the foam of the ninth wave.
> I was enchanted by King Math
> Before I became deathless;
> I was enchanted by Gwydion,
> The cleanser of the Britons.
> I have travelled far and wide:
> I have laid my head on a hundred islands:
> I have dined in a hundred castles.
> O wise and learned men,
> Declare it to Arthur:
> What is older than I?
> One is come who has seen the Flood,
> Who has witnessed the Crucifixion,
> And who sees the doom to come."

"Her real name is Goda," Methelgar told Hereward over a supper of hare stew. "She's half Welsh and half Norse-Irish: her father was a pirate from Dublin and her mother a princess from one of the tiny petty kingdoms on the west coast. He calls her Rhiannon after some old Welsh tale. She's a strange one, but that makes them well matched."

"Whatever you say about her," said Bana seriously, "the Lady Rhiannon does have power. She knows the arts to kill and to heal; I have seen her raise a mist to hide our numbers; her predictions are never wrong. The elves of wood and hill speak to her, and when she speaks back they listen." Hereward raised a sceptical eyebrow, but did not argue.

"While we're speaking of real names, Bana," he said, "what's yours? No mother ever called her child 'Killer'."

"You haven't met my mother," said Bana with a smile. "Bana's the only name I've ever had." He slurped down the last of his stew and smacked his lips.

"When is Lord Edric going to tell us his plans?" asked Methelgar. "Midsummer's Eve is only two days away now. He used to take his officers into his confidence about strategy."

Bana guffawed.

"Strategy?" he said. "We ride when the Huntsman gives the word and go where he leads us. We kill until he tells us to stop and then ride home. That is our strategy. And there is no officer among the Wish Hounds. Would you tell your dogs where you meant to course a stag a week before the hunt? What need, so long as you're there to direct them?"

"But what if Edric should be killed?" asked Hereward, frowning.

"He is the Huntsman," said Bana simply. "They cannot harm him. That is not his wyrd. And Wyrd is set fast."

"And yet she goes ever as she will," murmured Hereward.

"Lord Hereward?" He looked up. The boy Ailnoth was standing a little way off, eyes lowered, twisting his hands.

"Yes?" said Hereward, giving what he hoped was an encouraging smile.

"Is it true that you once killed forty Normans single-handed?"

"Four*teen*," said Hereward. "And they were drunk and taken by surprise. I'm sure your father has done greater deeds."

"Oh, he is the Huntsman," said Ailnoth dismissively, as if it was pointless to compare Edric with a mere mortal. "Is it true you sacked a Norman castle with two followers and rescued all the prisoners?"

"Four followers, one prisoner, and a kindly wind to fan the flames," said Hereward.

"And that you killed a giant in Cornwall?"

"Well, it depends what you call a giant," said Hereward good-naturedly. "He was a big fellow but no more than human."

"I'll tell you this, though," interrupted Bana. "If we don't hit Ullingswick before June is out, I don't know the Huntsman." *The Huntsman* again. Hereward realised he had not heard one of the Wish Hounds save Methelgar and himself call Edric by name since he had reached their camp.

"My Wish Hounds!" All turned to face the throne. Edric was standing before it, hands upraised. "The Lady Rhiannon has cast the runes," he declaimed. "Tomorrow is auspicious. We will ride forth and bring destruction to our enemies. Sleep well and be ready."

"Tomorrow?" echoed Gwynnog. "Have we miscounted? That is *four* days before Midsummer, no?"

Hereward nodded.

"He's clever," he said. "The Normans will have been studying the legend to see what they can learn of him. They'll be expecting him the next day but not tomorrow. They'll be caught by surprise." He set down his bowl, and wiped his mouth. "I only wish he'd tell some of us his plans."

"Don't worry," said Bana. "After breakfast you'll be ready to follow the Huntsman into the mouth of Hell."

Breakfast was rye bread, coarse and dry and stale but plentiful: these Wish Hounds had fuller bellies than Hereward's men to the south, or the serfs in the villages. Dunked in the morning ale to soften, it was not too unpalatable. Noticing a patch of mould, Hereward drew his dagger and began to scrape it off.

"No point," said Bana. "The mould's baked into it. It's crazy bread." Hereward flung the loaf away as if it had stung his hand.

"Crazy bread?" he exclaimed. "Before a battle? Have you lost your wits?"

"That's the idea," Bana grinned. "It's not the peasant stuff: this is the Lady Rhiannon's recipe. You'll fight like a demon after this."

Hereward had never been driven to crazy bread by hunger, though he had tried it out of curiosity in his youth. It was made by the country serfs out of the last rotten scrapings of the old year's flour, sometimes mixed with wild poppy or even fly mushroom, and set aside until the last lean weeks before harvest, by which time poor men's stores were exhausted and there was nothing else to eat. It did little to satisfy hunger, but the wild visions it induced took their minds off their suffering until better fare could be found. It was the food of desperation.

"If I'm fighting I want my wits about me," Hereward insisted. "Gwynnog! Methelgar! It's crazy bread; don't eat it." The other two had begun on their loaves, but quickly threw them away at Hereward's warning.

"Your loss," Bana shrugged. "If you'd rather go into battle on empty stomachs that's your choice. But remember a full belly is three fourths of most men's courage."

Gwynnog found some stew at the bottom of an unwashed cauldron. It was cold and congealed, but they forced it down. They were still scraping the last of the solidified fat from the bottom when Edric came out of his hut, in full painted and antlered finery, straightened up, and boomed a single word:

"Ullingswick."

Geoffrey fitz Ademar had also risen early. His worried wife found him pacing back and forth outside the stables, and asked tenderly what was wrong.

"The Wild Hunt will ride tomorrow," he said. "Their camp in Haywood will be unprotected. I mean to find it and destroy it – but I don't know where they're going. If anybody knows, they're too afraid to speak. What if this Huntsman has the same plan as I? What if he strikes Ullingswick while I'm sacking his camp?" He sighed. "Or I may meet them on the forest paths. They outnumber my men ten to one, and they know the territory: we wouldn't stand a chance. If I could only have summoned the garrison from Hereford I'd have gone into the woods today, and taken them at their rest: but I can't do that without an army."

"You should wait," she said. "You'll have nothing to be lord of if you don't protect the people of Ullingswick. Stay here and defend the village."

"While the Huntsman keeps on slaughtering every Norman and English collaborator in the shire?" said Geoffrey bitterly.

"Until St John's Day, at least," said his wife. "That's when it ends, isn't it? If these are mortal men, that's when they'll retire to their camp, tired and sated like wolves that have taken a fat ram. And that gives you time to send for help from Hereford – it's still four days away. But don't leave us before then. The people here need your help. Think of Giles and Hilda with their baby – do you think the Huntsman will spare an English mother with a Norman's child? And Father Wibert, a Norman priest in an English benefice? Can you honestly leave them unprotected?"

"You're right, of course," said Geoffrey. "Maybe I'm letting what he did to Roland cloud my mind. But I'll tell you this: come St John's Day I'll have the Huntsman if I have to burn down the forest to find him." And he took her in his arms.

The same arrow killed them both. Geoffrey died instantly; the lady lasted a few seconds, pinned to her husband, gurgling blood onto his dead face.

The soldiers tried to mass for defence, but running as they were from every part of the hall complex, some half asleep, they were easily picked off one by one as the Wish Hounds streamed into the village. Giles, coming out of his wife's hut, had his skull cloven before he could get his helmet on.

"That's where the whore Hilda lives," rasped Edric. "Burn it." A brand was tossed onto the roof of the hut, and within moments it was aflame. Choking and coughing, a young woman stumbled out, clutching a baby to her chest. They did not get far. Bana, his eyes gleaming, charged them down, and before the woman even saw him approach she and her child together were trampled under his horse's hooves; wheeling round, he planted a spear in her back, finishing the grisly job.

"Stop!" roared Hereward, too late. "We came to kill Normans, not women and children! Edric, call your men off!"

"That brat was a Norman," snapped the Huntsman. "And the woman was a traitor who slept with the enemy. We are here to destroy Ullingswick." Other huts were already burning as he spoke. A woman ran screaming out of one with her hair on fire. The acrid reek stung Hereward's nostrils. "Those who collaborate with the invaders must be taught a lesson. If the ordinary people think the fight can be left up to us while they serve two masters then the Normans will never be driven out."

"I'll have no part in murder!" bellowed Hereward.

"What sort of a soldier are you?" sneered Edric. A half-dressed man at arms lunged up at him, and he cut off the man's head, almost casually, without looking away from Hereward. "In Scotland, in Flanders, can you honestly say you never killed some poor unarmoured peasant who got in the way of a charge? That you never hurt a woman or a priest? Wasn't your first deed when you came back to England to kill a jester? This is war, and war is murder."

"We have to be better than they are," insisted Hereward. "If we wipe out whole villages then what's the difference between us and William the Bastard? If we don't show justice what are we fighting for?"

"This is justice," said Edric levelly. There was, Hereward noticed, none of the wildness of the Wish Hounds in the Huntsman's eyes: he had eaten no crazy bread. This was Edric thinking clearly. "Now, will you fight?"

"No."

"You cannot help these traitors," said Edric. "If you

oppose us you will be dead before you can draw breath. You are a mighty warrior and with your men from the southern camp our force would be irresistible. Stay with us. Embrace your wyrd."

"No!" shouted Hereward. Behind Edric, he saw Ailnoth ride down a priest and drive his sword through the old man's brain.

"Then you are no longer a Wish Hound," spat Edric. "Leave us now and count yourself lucky I spare your craven life." Hereward said nothing, but turned and rode for Haywood without looking back. He expected to feel an arrow between his shoulder-blades any minute, but none came. Behind him, Ullingswick burned, and the screams of the dying tore the air.

"Lord Hereward!" The voice was Methelgar's. He was galloping up to draw alongside Hereward, his white face paint now marred with soot and spatters of blood.

"I'm not going back to that!" Hereward yelled over his shoulder.

"No more am I!" Methelgar called back. "Edric is mad! Take me with you."

At the Wish Hounds' camp, they told Gwynnog quickly what had happened. They had nothing to pack but what they wore, so they set out south at once. The women peered out of the huts and whispered, but nobody made any move to stop them: and soon they were on their way.

Suddenly, as if she had sprouted from the ground, Rhiannon was standing in their path, arms held aloft.

"Go your ways, Hereward of Ware," she said in heavily accented English. "You must fight in your own way and in your own land, and leave the West to the Huntsman: but remember that you have eaten his salt and worn his colours, for he will not forget." And, as suddenly as she had appeared, she was gone.

The journey back across England was slower and

more wearing than the ride from Bourne to Bristol. They were forced to travel largely by night and to keep off the roads by day; Norman patrols were everywhere. After some two weeks of this they entered the Bromeswold and struck north towards Bourne.

Suddenly, Martin held up his hand.

"Did you hear that?" he asked. Silence fell. A bird twittered. "There it is again," he said. "That's a signal." The men's hands went to their weapons. Whoever was hiding among trees and whistling like birds would not be a Norman, but not all outlaws had rallied to Hereward at Bourne: there were some who preferred to lurk in the woods or the fens and rob indiscriminately. They might be a threat even to an armed troop.

"Lord Hereward," called a voice from deep in the bushes ahead of them.

"Who is there?" asked Hereward, gripping the hilt of Brainbiter.

"A friend you ought to know." And Wulfric stepped out into the path.

"Wulfric!" exclaimed Hereward. "What are you doing here?"

"We've posted men by every road for weeks now, in case you should return without being warned," said Wulfric. "Bourne has fallen."

"Fallen!" Hereward looked for a moment as if the news was about to fell him. He tottered on his feet; it was some moments before he could compose himself enough to ask: "What of Winter and the men? And Rowena? Are you camped in the forest? How many survived?"

"Rowena is safe," said Wulfric, "and Winter. Ogier the Breton came by night with twice our numbers; there was nothing we could do. We got eighteen of our men out, and most of the freemen and their families came with us. Abbot Thurstan has given us land on the Isle of Ely and opened the monks' stores to us; the Normans can't come there without an army. Half the freemen have never been so far from Bourne before. But Ogier has the Hall."

"Eighteen," murmured Hereward. "Eighteen out of forty! I should never have gone to the west. I have murdered them."

"I have murdered them," he repeated.

"No," said Lysir. "Ogier has done that." The two were sitting alone together amid the reeds at the edge of the Isle of Ely; Hereward knew better than to ask how the one-eyed man had crossed the fens. Over the trees to the west, the sun was sinking.

"It's the same thing," said Hereward bitterly. "I abandoned my people to follow that preening sot Godwin in a war we were doomed to lose, and I knew it from the start. How am I better than Edric?" He sighed. "And the Wild Huntsman is a mad Marcher who kills his own people. What future can there be for England?"

"Edric is not the Wild Huntsman," said Lysir. Hereward looked up.

"You don't mean you believe in the real Huntsman? Hunting souls with a flying horse and red-eared hounds?" For a moment, his old mad thought that Lysir might truly be Woden flared up: was he speaking to the Wild Huntsman even now?

"The Wild Huntsman is neither man nor spirit," said Lysir. "He is *fear*. And the Hunt is with both Edric and you, because your enemies fear you."

"Ha!" snorted Hereward. "Then he's with King William as well. More people fear him than either of us." But Lysir shook his head.

"No," he said. "They fear William as they fear any man stronger than themselves. But for you they feel another kind of fear: as if you were a ghost, or a dragon. Or a god."

Chapter 8: *The Giants of the Fens*

Ely, July, 1068.

Martin threw aside the chicken bone he had been sucking on. The monastery cat sniffed at it, turned up its nose and stalked off.

"Dry," he said. "How much food do we have left?"

"Not enough to get us to harvest," said Father Wulfwine. "There was enough in the barns to feed the monks and their tenants, but with all these new mouths – and more arriving every day -"

"I am sorry we are such a burden," said Hereward.

"Lammas is only a week away," said Wulfwine. "In less than a month our stores will be full again. Over short periods, men can live on very little, if they need to. But your men need their strength in case they come up against the Normans; and there are nursing mothers and small children among the incomers. The game you bring in from the forests helps, but if we're to last until the harvest is in we must buy food from outside."

"Travelling to the towns is dangerous," said Hereward. "And we have little money."

"Then we'll steal it," said Martin. "The Norman landlords are already sending out their stewards to collect the Lammastide rents. We have enough sympathisers to find out where they'll be going on which days, especially in Spalding and Bourne. Ivo and Ogier can pay for our keep: it's only fair, considering it's their fault we're here."

"What does the Church think of that suggestion, Father?" Hereward cocked an eyebrow at the priest.

"What you take from those two is no theft, it's a fine," said Wulfwine. "But remember that their tenants need to eat too. You should return at least some of the money to the villages."

"We won't let them starve," Hereward promised. "But keep an eye on that cat of yours. If one of my hungry men eats it while I'm out hunting rent collectors, we'll end up gathering in the harvest just to feed the mice."

Fulney.

"We have no more, my lord, I swear. Neither grain nor coin."

Hubert curled his lip.

"You can pay in kind, can't you?" he said. "You keep pigs; a couple of them ought to make up the shortfall."

"Then what will we eat when winter comes, my lord?" demanded the Saxon priest.

Hubert shrugged. He disliked Father Putta's reasonableness. In other villages people had either stood back, sad-eyed and silent, or screamed and sworn at him, promising the vengeance of God. Neither was any real trouble, except one of the latter who had tried to leap onto his wagon and throw the bags of coin back to the people. He had not lasted long. But then, most of the other villages had not had their own priests. These places were not like Spalding, which might be small but was a true town, with all the major professions gathered together: the spiritual needs of the villages were generally met by priests from the city minsters, who travelled out only on the high feasts to say Mass for the deprived peasantry. Priests were freeborn, often highborn, and few of them chose to live among serfs: those who did tended to be hereditary pastors, some of whose families had played the same role in the same village for other gods, before there was an England. The Church was beginning to mutter about celibacy, but rural priests with wives, and sons who expected to succeed them, were not uncommon. But very occasionally one came across the awkward types, men who valued their pastoral duties above ambition or comfort: and they could be relied on to make trouble. This cleric whom the people of Fulney had apparently chosen as their spokesman argued calmly and rationally, and in almost decent Norman French, at that. It was not something the steward had been prepared for.

Putta repeated the question.

"What will we eat?"

"That's your business," said Hubert. "Grub for roots or go fishing in the river. My lord Ivo will have what is owed."

"We are forbidden to fish, my lord," said the priest.

"Then you should have told your flock to control their lusts and not breed so many children!" expostulated the steward. He turned to one of his soldiers. "Take the two fattest pigs from the herd on the green there. Cut their throats and sling them in the wagon."

"Sir." The soldier nodded and drew his sword. A frightened child in the small crowd that had gathered behind Father Putta whimpered.

"What are you staring at?" Hubert barked irritably at the crowd. "Get back to work."

The soldier never reached the herd of pigs. A stone struck his helmet with a dull clang and knocked him off his feet. As his three colleagues turned in the direction it had come from, one of them was struck in the face with a wooden cudgel, and went down like a sack of grain; the cudgel whirled round to catch the second on the side of his head with his sword still halfway out of its sheath.

The man who wielded the cudgel was the biggest Hubert had ever seen. More than six and a half feet tall and nearly three across the shoulders, he seemed ready to burst out of his brown worsted tunic: and, worse, he was about to board the wagon. Hubert raised his whip, unsure whether he was about to goad the horses on or to strike the interloping giant: but he never got the chance. Instead of boarding it, the huge Saxon seized the vehicle by the near side wheel, and, with a grunt, hefted it up onto its side just as the fourth soldier came running at him, so that the falling bags of coin and last year's grain knocked the Norman to the ground. Hubert, sent flying from his seat, sprawled beside him.

The people let out a cheer: but none moved to help the newcomer. Hubert was already struggling back to his feet while the giant freed the horse from the wagon; and the soldier hit with a stone, though looking a little dizzy, was also up and armed. The giant had lost the advantage of surprise, and now had only a cudgel and main strength against two trained swordsmen in hauberks and helms.

As the giant slapped the horse's rump to send it on its way, Hubert caught at the beast's bridle.

"Ah-ah," he said, waving his sword at the Englishman. "No you don't."

"Yes he does," said Hereward. Hubert looked up in the direction of the forest: the old enemy was there, standing before the row of trees, with Brainbiter in his hand, and nine men. Four of them had bows, every one with an arrow nocked and drawn and aimed at him. The steward knew when he was beaten. He lowered his sword. "Take your horse," Hereward went on, "and as many of your men as can stand, and get back to Spalding as fast as your legs will carry you." Scowling, Hubert sheathed his sword, and motioned to the soldier to do likewise. The man who had been hit by the tumbling bags got painfully to his feet, and the three of them trudged out of Fulney, leaving the wagon, the rents and their unconscious comrades behind them.

"My lord Hereward," said Father Putta, bowing.

"There's no need for that," said Hereward. "I'm no thane – I'm a wolfshead, remember? I was banished by King Edward and my father's manors are vacant until a true king says otherwise. But who's this?" He indicated the giant. "One of your flock? I didn't know you bred them this big in Fulney."

"My name's Hiccafrith," said the big man, colouring.

"I come from Wisbech."

"You're a good few miles from home, then," Hereward remarked. "Did you come here planning to get yourself killed, or were you just passing through and took on five armed men on a whim?"

"I came to see Ebba," he said, going an even deeper red. A girl at the front of the crowd clapped her hand to her mouth, and Hiccafrith lowered his eyes. "I often come fowling on this side of the Fens, there's less chance of being seen by somebody who knows me; and I met Ebba, and -" He tailed off. Hereward smiled. "But I wasn't in trouble," said Hiccafrith doggedly. "I'd have beaten them. I was doing alright. I've already taken down one of these bastard stewards." Ebba's mouth dropped open and the admiration on her face gave way to something like worship.

"Don't tell me where," advised Hereward. "You've already said enough to hang yourself five times over." One of the stunned soldiers stirred; Hereward kicked him in the jaw and his eyes rolled upwards again. "Well, you've saved us a bit of trouble," he remarked. "I wonder why Ivo let Hubert out with such a small escort? They're getting careless. Anyway, you're assured of a welcome at Ely any time you want to join us – you and Ebba, and if Father Putta here won't marry you, we can find a priest who will." He looked at Putta. "I wouldn't blame you," he said. "Ivo will never give his permission and without it you'd be robbing him of a serf; he could get you fined or even kicked out of your benefice for that, and no doubt they'd send a Norman to replace you."

"I'm not an outlaw," said Hiccafrith, raising his chin.

"You are now," Hereward pointed out. "Hubert Gervase knows what you look like, everybody here knows who you are, and you say this isn't even the first time you've done this."

"Nobody in Cambridgeshire knows," Hiccafrith pointed out. "I'll be safe back in Wisbech."

"For how long?"

"Until I'm not safe any more."

"Well," said Hereward, "what about the swag?"

"The what?"

"This, the money. You wouldn't have lived to finish your little robbery without us so it seems fair enough that we get a share. How much do you think is reasonable?"

"This?" Hiccafrith looked horrified. "This belongs to the people of Fulney."

"Very commendable," said Hereward. "But they can spare a little. We have food for one more day on Ely, two at the most. The people rely on us to fight the Normans for them; they can hardly let us go hungry."

"Begging your pardon, my lord," said Father Putta tentatively, "but we've been saving all the food for the children and the sick here for five days now, save a few handfuls of lentils. We're already starving." Hereward looked around the crowd. There was hardly a face whose cheeks were not hollow.

"And you weren't here to fight the Normans when they came," added Hiccafrith accusingly. "If it hadn't been for me they'd have been back in Spalding with the rent by now."

"You think charging in single-handed with a rock and a piece of wood is the way to fight them?" scoffed Hereward. "We saved your life. How many English lives have we saved here in the past?" He eyed Hiccafrith's large frame sardonically. "You don't look as if you've been going short of food yourself. Why don't you give up some to help the hungry?"

"Things haven't been so hard in Wisbech," said Hiccafrith defensively. "And I told you, I poach fowl off the marshes. I haven't been to Fulney in a month, I didn't know how bad it had got here." The crowd was muttering, and most of them seemed to be on the big serf's side.

"There's money and grain here from all over the manor of Spalding," Martin pointed out. "The people of Fulney can keep what they gave, and there'll still be enough to feed us."

"And what about the other villages?" said Hiccafrith doggedly.

"We can't help everybody," snapped Hereward. "But we'll save more by working together than by fighting amongst ourselves. Come to Ely: I'll not make the offer again."

"I'm not a rebel," insisted the big man. "My quarrel's with these barons and stewards, not King William."

"Don't you see it's the same thing?" exclaimed Hereward; but Hiccafrith shook his great shaggy head.

"Take what you need," he said. "I can't stop you. But if one soul starves in Fulney I'll know it isn't Ivo Taillebois who's to blame."

Hereward looked again at the sad, subdued faces behind Father Putta.

"Not one will," he swore.

"No, my lord," said Hubert, rubbing the back of his head where it had hit the ground as he fell from the wagon, "the big man attacked alone, I don't think he was with Hereward."

"Of course he was with Hereward," said Ivo irritably. "He just arrived a little early. Even a giant doesn't attack five armed men alone."

"Remember the Heron, my lord," said Hubert.

"What of him? One of Hereward's men, just like this one."

"But he fought alone. When he rescued those men from the gallows, he fought alone."

"Wulfric is an expert swordsman, not a lout with a club," said Ivo, getting up and pacing along the hall, kicking rushes away to either side. A dog yelped and ran for cover as his foot connected with its nether parts. "I can't conceive how you let yourself be bested by this English pig. Blood and bones! Do I have to do everything myself? No, he's with

Hereward. And now, so is my money." He stroked his chin. "This makes three attacks," he went on. "I got word today of another on the Cambridge side of Deeping Level. Father Hugo!" The priest coughed, and produced the letter.

"It was near where last week's attack took place," he said. "And both speak of giants."

"God's teeth, he must be recruiting an army of the bastards," muttered Ivo. "Where this side of Hell is he getting them?" He turned to the steward. "What did your giant look like?" he asked. "Other than big."

"Ruddy face, brown hair, bearded," said Hubert. "But that describes half the serfs on this manor. It's his size that marks him out." A thought occurred to him. "If the other attacks were in Cambridgeshire, Fulney's a little out of their way, isn't it?" Ivo cuffed him round the head, and he winced.

"They came to Fulney to spite me," he said. "This is Hereward, remember? He hates me like damnation, so he steals from my manor, practically within sight of Spalding. Well, I'm not going to let him win this time. Isn't he content with burning down my keep and humiliating me in front of my own serfs? He'll not keep my money. I want it back!" The last word jarred painfully through Hubert's skull. The steward paused before speaking.

"*If* Hereward has taken your money, my lord," he began.

"If!" snorted Ivo.

"If he has taken your money, it will be on the Isle of Ely. It's surrounded by the marshes; we could never bring a big enough force there to take it."

"I want my money!" repeated Ivo. "Don't tell me what we can't do – do it!"

"We can't," said Hubert, as patiently as he could, "but there may be some who can."

"Who?"

"The Gyrvians."

"The Gyrvians?" echoed Ivo uncomprehendingly.

"Surely they're a bogey story, to scare naughty children."

"No, my lord, they're real, though they're not trolls as some would have it, nor even a different race – they do have customs of their own, but most of them are Saxons or Danes by birth. They live on the islands in the wilder parts of the Fens, off what they can poach and plunder. Strictly speaking every fowler and turf-cutter out there can be called a Gyrvian, but what most men mean when they use that name is the outlaws. They're broken men, the desperate ones, the ones even Hereward wouldn't take. They know no law of God nor man. Mostly they keep to themselves because they don't like attention: but when they need food and can't get it in the Fens they'll attack a native village. A remote one, usually, so that nobody will hear of it for a few weeks, even months. I've met survivors; there aren't many, and none with all their limbs. They say if the livestock in a raided village aren't enough to feed the band then the Gyrvians roast the bodies of the dead and eat them. They have a leader: nobody seems to know his real name, or if they did they were too afraid to tell, but he calls himself Grendel." Ivo showed no sign of recognition.

"After a monster in a Saxon legend, my lord," Father Hugo put in helpfully.

"This Grendel and his men know the marshes better than anyone – better than the monks or Hereward's outlaws, I'll be bound. If anyone can get to Ely, they can: and if anyone can take back our money – your money, sorry – from Hereward, it's Grendel." Hubert paused. "Of course, he'll want a cut."

"Give him one shilling in the pound," said Ivo.

"I think four might be more appropriate. Or… even five." Hubert ducked instinctively, but although Ivo's hand convulsed, he didn't throw anything.

"Whatever it takes," he said quietly. "Find this Grendel and hire him; and tell him his reward will be doubled if he brings me Hereward's head."

"What if this Grendel fails to penetrate Ely?" asked

Hugo. "He'll still want to be paid."

"So will I," said Ivo. "Tell him if he can't get the money from Ely he is to take it where he can."

"But, my lord," objected the priest, "that's as good as giving him licence to raid other manors, perhaps murder other barons' rent collectors for their takings!"

"I'm not telling him to do that," said Ivo. "How he interprets his orders is his own affair. All I want is my due, and I mean to get it."

Even under threat of torture, nobody in the manor of Spalding knew where Grendel was to be found. But once the news was abroad that the baron's steward was looking for the Gyrvians, it was not long before the Gyrvians found him.

He was riding near the edge of the marsh when he was hailed: "Good morning, my lord!" He looked around, but saw no one. The land was as flat as the water, they could not be hiding. Then, when he set his eyes back on the path before him, there was a man in his way. And not a man Hubert would have thought he could have missed: he was as tall as Hiccafrith. *He must be recruiting an army...* Did Hereward really have a troop of giants? Hubert felt for his sword.

"Don't be foolish, my lord," said the big man. Hubert narrowed his eyes, and looked the newcomer up and down. He would be a handsome fellow with a short Norman haircut and shave, instead of that mass of hair and the scratchy beard that hid his square chin; and his tunic, though worn, patched and dirty, had clearly once been very rich. There were the remains of gold braid on the sleeves and hem, and, though large, it was a little too tight on his massive chest: stolen, no doubt.

"Who are you?" Hubert demanded.

"I come from Grendel," said the giant. "Our boat is waiting."

"My horse..."

"Your horse will find its own way back to Spalding,

my lord," the giant assured him. "Grendel's invitations are always accepted." He fixed his eye upon the steward's: and Hubert found himself dismounting, slapping his horse's rump and watching it canter off before he was fully aware of what he was doing.

The giant parted the reeds and revealed a punt, the normal mode of travel in the Fens, lying waiting in the muddy water: and Hubert stepped into it without argument. An instant later, the pole connected with the back of his head, and he measured his length on the floor of the boat, dead to the world. Starkad the Gyrvian stepped onto the platform, braced the pole against the bed of the marsh, and set out for the island of his tribe.

There were two people in the world who remembered Grendel's real name, and the Gyrvian chief himself was not one of them. He had been Grendel since childhood. Starkad, however, remembered Geirrod: his brother.

They were twins, Geirrod the elder by a few minutes. The cruel had always joked – though seldom to the brothers' faces once they were big enough to fight back, which was early – that Geirrod was Nature's failed attempt and Starkad the perfected article. They shared their vast frames, thick black hair and deep green eyes: but the elder brother was crooked of back, face and tongue, his nose flattened and squint as if badly broken, his mouth turned downward and never quite closed, his skin blotched, and his speech so thick that only Starkad and their mother could fully understand him. Once he grew old enough, he wore his beard full to cover what he could of his face, but it could not conceal everything. They had taken to the marshes a few years after their father's execution, and quickly made themselves leaders of the Gyrvians: but Grendel was always the master and Starkad the lieutenant. Starkad himself would have it no other way. He had, after all, everything he wanted – even women, a pleasure denied his brother. Every female on the island competed to share Starkad's bed; Grendel slept alone.

Some of their followers had questioned who was truly in charge: all but the simplest of their orders, after all, had to be relayed through the younger twin: but these days such whisperings were kept well out of the brothers' hearing. Once it had been proposed to Starkad that he should take over the leadership of the Gyrvians. Starkad held down the man who had spoken of such treachery, and then and there created a blood eagle, flaying open his ribcage and tearing out his lungs.

"Wake up, Master Hubert." Dirty water was dashed in the steward's face. He stirred, and found himself looking up at a ring of grinning faces, grimy and scarred. He was horrified to notice women among the Gyrvians: like the men, they were all stuck about with weapons until they could carry no more. Glancing to one side, he saw a wagon with a broken axle half sunk into the mud. For a moment he wondered if it was his own: were these creatures in league with Hereward? Or had they already robbed the rebel? He was hauled to his feet and propped before Grendel and Starkad: the steward was a tall man, but the Gyrvian brothers altogether dwarfed him. He felt as if he was shrinking under their gaze.

"Wha' goo ya wa'?" gurgled Grendel. Hubert wondered if he was still unconscious: this monstrous being, its language as deformed as its looks, could not be human, could not be real. This was a nightmare.

"Grendel asks what you seek here in our Fens," said Starkad evenly. It was several seconds before Hubert felt strong enough to respond.

"My, ah, the lord Ivo Taillebois…" he began.

And he explained the situation and Ivo's offer. The Gyrvians sat around in silence until he had finished: then, suddenly, burst into hoots of laughter.

"Five shillings in the pound?" said Starkad. "If we're to get this money from Hereward what stops us keeping it all?"

"Naturally my lord Ivo does not expect you to recover

it unaided," said Hubert. "He is willing to lend as many soldiers as you may ask for."

"And when these soldiers know the way to our island, how are we ever supposed to feel safe here again?" demanded the outlaw.

"You may meet them wherever you choose," said Hubert defensively. "And they will be placed under the command of whatever leader you choose from your own number." He paused. "My lord Ivo cannot, of course, offer pardon from your outlawry," he said carefully. "But he does have influence. The Sheriff of Lincoln is his friend -"

"This is the shrievalty of Cambridge, not Lincoln," Starkad interrupted.

"All good servants of the Crown will be glad to see Hereward discomfited," asserted Hubert. "If you can bring in his head I think you can be sure of a pardon for all." The cackling was not so loud this time, but again the Gyrvians were laughing at him.

"What should we do with a pardon?" said Starkad. Hubert gestured at the camp around him. It was filthy and falling down; half the Gyrvians were obviously diseased; flies and worms were everywhere.

"Surely," he said, "you can't be content to live like this?"

"And how is life in the villages better?" pressed the outlaw. "At least here we do not starve. We can always take what we need somewhere."

Grendel leaned towards his brother, and made another strange series of noises, in which Hubert thought he caught the name "Hereward". Starkad looked round, a new light in his eyes.

"Tell me, steward," he said, "and do not lie: who were this Hereward's parents?" Hubert was surprised. He had thought Hereward's family was known throughout these lands, and in any case he could not see why the Gyrvians should care about noble genealogies.

"His father was Askil Tokason, Lord of Ware," he said. "His mother is Edith, sister to the Countess Godiva." Starkad made a sudden hissing noise, and Hubert became aware that the ring of Gyrvians appeared to have shrunk back from him, as if he had spoken something they feared.

"The House of Mercia," said Starkad softly. "Leofric."

"Yes," said Hubert, confused, "the Earl Leofric was his uncle by marriage." Grendel uttered a deep growl, then pointed at Hubert, and nodded his head. The steward stiffened, struggling not to show his fear.

"We will do as the lord Ivo has asked."

The other Gyrvians knew nothing of why their masters' demeanour changed whenever the name of the late earl was spoken: though they knew enough to be afraid. But Arngrim of Brampton had died for the theft of a sheep, swearing to the end that it was not his doing. The sheep had come from the estates of Askil of Ware; the lord who had passed sentence was Leofric of Mercia; and the sons of Arngrim, watching their father convulse on the gallows as life was choked from him, had sworn vengeance on the families of both.

And now they were to be paid to take it.

Hereward slammed the hilt of his knife against the refectory table, and swore loudly.

"Why can he not see the greater picture?" he demanded. Wulfwine handed him a cup of wine.

"This Hiccafrith is a serf," he said. "He has grown up in places like Fulney. Those are his people. Of course his concern is for them."

"Are they not my people?" said Hereward.

"Not in the same way," said the priest bluntly. "You are the son of a thane; you have never been unfree."

"You think a few days without food gives them the right to lecture me about hardship?" said Hereward. "How far have they had to march in steel hauberks without eating or drinking? How many nights have they had to sleep in a rain-washed trench, or chained to a wall in a tyrant prince's dungeon? I've been an outlaw nearly half my life. An exile, a mercenary. And now I live like a fox hunted from earth to earth, for the sake of their freedom. Is this gratitude?"

Wulfwine paused before replying. It was months since he had heard Hereward speak for so long at once.

"They have never had freedom," he said. "Other than the priest, how many freemen do you think there are in a place like Fulney? It's a serf village. They've never been welcomed at princes' courts, never travelled over the sea or even out of this county, never had the choice of what to eat or what to wear today. They live and die to serve a master – Norman or English, a master is a master. Ivo is crueller than most, but not every Norman will be worse than the man who came before. Some may be better."

"Then why fight them?" retorted Hereward. "William may rule better than Harold. It doesn't make him any less a thief."

"Hundreds of thanes have lost their lands. Tens of thousands of freemen and women have become little better than serfs. Villages have been razed to make hunting grounds for the barons. The law has been trampled under William's iron boot. It is worth fighting to set that right," said Wulfwine patiently. "But those who were serfs before the Conquest can be forgiven if they think they have nothing to gain from our struggle."

Before Hereward could reply, they heard a horn wound somewhere outside the monastery. Hereward jumped to his feet.

"What is it?" asked Wulfwine.

"The island is under attack!"

As Hereward ran out by the postern gate, a Gyrvian axe swung past his head, missing it by a thumb's breadth. The man wielding it lost his balance and stumbled, and

Brainbiter came up into his guts before he could regain his footing.

There were a dozen bodies on the ground outside, mostly Gyrvians, but including two of Hereward's men and one monk. The skirmish seemed already to be almost over; Hereward saw Martin shoot down a fleeing bandit, but there were no more on this side of the monastery. Winter was leaning on his sword nearby, out of breath.

"Gyrvians," he exclaimed. "What are they doing here?"

"They must be after our food," said Martin. "They came in a fleet of little boats, stretched right along this shore."

"They haven't got to the barns?" said Hereward urgently.

"I don't know," said Martin. "Winter and I have been pinned down defending the postern. But just now there was a cry like a hawk in pain, and they fell back. We saw some take to their boats."

Hereward saw no more living Gyrvians that day. It was some time before the defenders could be gathered together, for they were strung out in small groups, none sure that the invaders had gone: but once they were, before even letting them gather up the dead for burial, Hereward asked the question whose answer he so dreaded.

"Yes," said Methelgar, who was nursing a nasty gash to his shoulder. "Four of them got to the barns and broke down the door. I killed three but the fourth got away with two sacks of grain – a great tall fellow with black hair, swung 'em up as light as pillows."

"Two sacks," said Martin. "Well, that's not much."

"It's more than we can be sure of doing without," said Hereward. "What if more men join us here? What if the villagers run short and look to us for help? What if the Gyrvians come back?"

"After losing twenty men?" said Methelgar.

"How many would Edric have to lose to decide a hold

was not worth attacking twice?"

"If he lost the whole Wild Hunt he'd ride back alone the next day with his sword in his hand," the Marcher admitted. "But Edric's Edric. These are just savages, surely?"

"Savages who don't stop," said Winter. "Hereward's right: we know too well round here what the Gyrvians are capable of. They'd been quiet for a year or so, but they always come back worse than before. And after today, they'll want revenge."

"It may not be worth their while to raid the barns again, after giving twenty lives for two sacks of grain," said Hereward, "but they're more than capable of burning them down just to watch us starve. We can't share the Fens with such men. We have to find their base and destroy it."

"And who can do that?" said Martin. "Nobody's seen the Gyrvians' island and lived. The monks here know the Fens so well they could walk from Cambridge to Spalding in the dark, and they don't know where it is."

"There are poachers who go fowling on the Fens," said Hereward. "Some of them may have seen something. Somebody *must* have."

"That man in Fulney," volunteered Wulfric suddenly. "The big one – Hiccafrith. He goes fowling, and he's crossed the Fens from one side to the other more than once. Handy in a fight, too."

"Yes," agreed Martin. "If anyone'll know the way, it'll be Hiccafrith." Hereward frowned.

"I'll not be beholden to him," he muttered. Martin leant forward, gripped him by the shoulder, and spoke quietly, so that only Winter and Wulfric, sitting either side of Hereward, could hear.

"You will," he said. "You said yourself, we need that grain. I'm not going to starve for the sake of your pride nor let these people go hungry neither. We'll ask Hiccafrith's help, and if we have to we'll beg for it."

Wisbech was practically an island itself, an isolated little town in the Fens, marshland creeping up to the edge of its fields. Around the actual houses was a high fence, something Hereward had seen in the borders of Scotland and Flanders, but hardly the norm in England for a settlement of this size. He soon found Hiccafrith, tending sheep on the common.

"If you've come from Ely, you must have passed close by the island," said the giant. "It's not far from here; that's why we have a palisade round the town. We still have to pay blackmail to them. They're worse than the Normans."

Hereward blinked. He had expected argument, or at least some mention of their quarrel at Fulney: but the moment he had announced the reason for his presence in Wisbech, the big serf had snapped into businesslike planning, sounding more like a general than a peasant and not once questioning the idea of attacking the Gyrvians' island.

"How many are they?" asked Hereward. Hiccafrith shrugged.

"It's hard to tell. I don't think anybody's seen more than about thirty at a time."

"There were more than that at Ely," said Martin. "We killed twenty and as many again must have escaped. And they won't have left their own island unguarded."

"Do you know anything of a giant with black hair among them?" pressed Hereward.

"If he had a face like Lucifer's after he hit the ground falling from Heaven, it was Grendel; otherwise it may have been his brother. They're the leaders. I've heard they can rip men's heads off with their bare hands."

"Foes worth the fighting, then," remarked Hereward, fingering the pommel of Brainbiter, and remembering Gartnait Ironhook and Holbert of Guines. There was something grimly satisfying about bringing down men far larger than himself. He wondered for an idle moment what it would be like to fight Hiccafrith: but he doubted if he could bring passion to it. He needed to oppose wrath to wrath, malice to malice: his own soul in combat reflected his opponent's. The big serf might irk Hereward but he was simply too pleasant to rouse his true fury.

"Will you attack tonight or stay here?" asked Hiccafrith. "If you have more of your men they may have to sleep outside, but my mother could open her hut -"

"No need," said Hereward, smiling. "Martin and I came alone, to fetch you back to Ely. We'll put out for the island tomorrow with all the men we can muster; and you'll show us the way."

"But it'll be dark before we can reach Ely now," objected Hiccafrith.

"Just as well you know the Fens so well, then," said Hereward. "We'll be there by the second watch. You have somebody you can leave in charge of the sheep?"

"Yes." Of course he did, or he could not have spent his evenings fowling on the Fens or dallying with Ebba.

"Good. We've no time to lose."

A low mist hung over the Fens the next morning. Hereward declared it perfect.

"It'll cover an attack well enough," agreed Martin dubiously; "but if this island is so well hidden, can we reach it in the mist?"

"I can find it," said Hiccafrith. "I've grown up in its shadow. Getting there will be the easy part; but they'll have sentries on every corner of the island."

"Our bowmen will go with you in the first boats," said Hereward. "Every sentry will be picked off as they come into sight. It won't buy us much time but it should be enough to make a landfall before the enemy is roused."

And so it proved. By the time the mist began to disperse, Hiccafrith and Martin were ashore, Winter and Wulfric clambering from the boat behind them over a Gyrvian corpse, and the rest of the flotilla within yards. By the time sleep was shaken off the camp, half a dozen Gyrvians were dead and forty invaders were on the island.

When the Gyrvians began to fight back, though, Hereward's men felt it. Archers, darters and slingers lined the rough fence that guarded the camp, pelting the attackers with poisoned missiles. Most glanced off helmets or were taken on bucklers, but some found their marks, and the screams were horrible.

In their drowsy state, however, and with their sentries dead, the Gyrvians had not thought to bar the gate to the camp. It was Hiccafrith who saw this first, and roared "The gate!", gesturing with the axe Hereward had given him: he would have been happier with his cudgel, but had been told that it was not worth carrying anything against the Gyrvians that would not kill with one blow. Hereward's men, well breakfasted and clear-headed, saw his meaning before the still fuddled islanders, and it was a matter of a few heartbeats before they rushed the gate and bore it down.

Once they were within, however, the Gyrvians swarmed round them like flies. Martin was wounded in the forearm, and had to fight one-handed while he sucked the venom from the wound; Hereward found himself fighting three men at once – no, two men and a woman, her teeth filed to animalistic points which she gnashed fiercely at him. Starkad's sword whirled in a double circle and two of Hereward's men fell before they could raise a hand: then Grendel appeared.

The fighting around him seemed to still as men looked up at this demonic figure; to Hereward's men he looked as if he had risen through the waters of the Fen from the depths of Hell. In his hand he bore an iron mace that no normal man could have wielded: one foolhardy soul, rushing at him with his swordarm forward, had his skull smashed to pulp like a rotten apple. Even his own people drew back from him: there was a fury on the huge man different from anything they had seen before. He was about to avenge his father's murder.

As he moved towards Hereward, Hiccafrith stepped into the way. Grendel did not even waste his mace on the serf, but thrust him aside with his left arm, casting him against the broken, half-sunk cart, which the Gyrvians had taken from a Cambridgeshire steward only a week before Hiccafrith himself had done the same thing at Fulney. As his massive weight struck the waggon, the already cracked axle snapped in two, and the nearside wheel fell. It would have crushed Hiccafrith's leg if he had not caught it, but he moved as fast as a cat, and braced his hands against the rim. The wheel stopped: and Hiccafrith, slowly forcing it upwards, began to clamber back onto his feet.

Grendel saw none of this: he was closing on Hereward, his mace raised once again. The first, and last, he knew of Hiccafrith was when the wheel collided with his left temple. With a noise that was half groan and half sigh, the monstrous Gyrvian fell to his knees, then after a long second kneeling before Hereward collapsed sideways, the side of his head broken and bloody.

"Geirrod!" screamed Starkad, rushing to his brother's side. Geirrod reached feebly up, and Starkad clasped his hand. Nobody but he understood the last words of the Gyrvian chief: the usual thickness of his speech was overlaid with the wheeze of death: but Starkad heard him.

"Look after Mother."

Without their Grendel, the Gyrvians were soon scattered. Starkad disappeared, none could tell where. More food was recovered from their hoard than ever the people of Ely had lost: and not only food, but silver and gold, crosses and pyxes, coins dating back to King Alfred's days and beyond. The Gyrvian menace was a very ancient one, and there would be rejoicing all around the Fens that it was gone; even Normans would be grateful to Hereward and Hiccafrith. But the serf still would not join the rebels.

"We work differently," he said. "Your cause and mine

may overlap but they en't the same. I'll work with you when that's what the people round here need, but I can't say more than that."

Hereward grasped him warmly by the hand.

"That will be enough for me," he said. "Lucky are the people, to have a champion like Hiccafrith of Wisbech."

Chapter 9: *Brainbiter*

Gweek, 1061.

"Gentlemen, the toast is Hannibal, Lord of the Hundred of Marazion – and my future son-in-law!"

Thirty horns of mead were raised and thirty heads thrown back. Much of the drink spilled: horns were difficult to drink from at the best of times, and most of the warriors were already intoxicated. Hannibal, a pale, stern-faced, soldierly man with straight black hair, long moustaches, and a thin gold torque about his neck, bowed to Lord Aleph and to his daughter Gwendolen. She swallowed hard and avoided the two men's eyes.

Aleph took his daughter's hand and placed it in Hannibal's: and from his sleeve he drew a cloth of white samite, which he wrapped around their wrists, binding the two of them together.

"Thus are the houses of Gweek and Marazion linked forever," he declared; "and thus will the pride of Cornwall be restored. Merlin has foretold that the seed of the White Dragon shall be rooted out; that those who live as beasts in the forest groves shall hunt within the walled cities of their enemies; that Britain shall be Britain again, as if Roman and Saxon had never been. Today we plant the seed of that future! Cornwall will be a kingdom once again!"

The Cornishmen cheered to the echo. It appeared to have slipped the Lord Aleph's mind that his own champion was English; but Hereward, who was used to Cornish boasts and the extraordinary faith his employer's people placed in a long dead wizard, bowed his head and said nothing. He doubted if any more would come of it this time than on the last half dozen occasions; and if it did, if King Edward lost Cornwall and a few English thanes lost the lands their fathers had stolen, why should he care? If Aleph became a king, so much the greater would be his servant's prestige.

But yet he was worried. Not for King Edward or the thanes of Cornwall, perhaps: but he could see as well as any man the look on Gwendolen's face. And he could not help but remember how much happier she had looked in the company of the Prince of Waterford.

Spalding, August, 1068.

"And so the Sword of Tiw passed out of mortal knowledge once again, and the curse with it. Let us pray that it is never found."

Ivo yawned loudly. This was the first time he had admitted Aldwine the Scop to his hall since the affair of St Edmund's treasure: but that time Aldwine had put him on the track of gold, even if he had not managed to break the people's faith in their saint. This time he had not pointed the way to any loot. He had told a dull and repetitive story about a magic sword: if it existed it must be in Denmark or Sweden somewhere, and in any case it hardly sounded worth the finding, so many curses hedged it round. Ivo lacked the patience to listen to stories for their own sake, although he knew that those of his soldiers who understood the native tongue enjoyed the scop's tales.

"Magic swords," he scoffed. "Prophecies and dragons and dead thanes rising from their tombs! Have you nothing but fairy tales?"

"Strange things happened in the heathen days," said Aldwine. "And not all the old powers are dead. There are still such swords, even if they are not quite so powerful as Tiw's."

"Name one," Ivo challenged him.

"Brainbiter," replied the scop unhesitatingly. "Hereward's sword."

Ivo raised his eyebrows.

"And what are its powers?" he asked.

"That I do not know, my lord," said the scop. "Some say that while he carries it he shall never be defeated, others merely that he shall not be killed. Others say that it is a talisman to summon a familiar demon that fights beside him. But it was forged by trolls in the lands beyond the northern ice, and it was from a giant that Hereward captured it – in Cornwall, which all men know is a land crawling with elves and ogres. How without such a blade could he have defeated the Gyrvians, when everyone knows their skin is of iron?" Hubert grimaced at that, remembering the reality. But several of the soldiers crossed themselves, and one whispered to his neighbour:

"That's why we've never captured him."

"Silence!" barked Ivo. "This is all lies, English lies to make us afraid."

"But if the people believe it..." said Hubert pointedly. Understanding spread slowly over Ivo's face.

"The sword doesn't need to be magic to be the secret of his power," he said. Hubert nodded. "And if we take it from him, they'll see he's not invincible after all. And if it *is* magic, then we'll be its masters!" Hubert smiled; he was not used to his lord catching on so quickly. "Fetch me Hamo fitz Hamelyn," he ordered. The steward bowed, and oiled out of the room.

"Will you have another tale, my lord?" asked Aldwine. Ivo threw a cup at him, but this time he aimed to miss: he was in a good mood.

"Martin Lightfoot?" Martin, who had been burnishing Hereward's shield, looked up sharply. He knew the woman who had spoken by sight only: the Lady Gwendolen's servant, La-... Lamorna, that was it.

"Yes," he said guardedly. "What do you want?"

"My mistress would speak with you."

"With me?" he echoed. This made no sense. He had never seen Gwendolen so much as look in his direction.

"She cannot with propriety entertain your master in her chamber, even with me present."

"Whereas I am so far beneath her that suspicion is unthinkable?" said Martin, understanding. Lamorna bowed her head. "The Lord Hereward is not my master," he added. "I follow him because I choose to. So she has a message for the Lord Hereward: why can you not carry it? Or give it to me now? She trusts you, surely?"

"But the Lord Hereward might not trust me," said Lamorna simply. "You will follow me."

"And if we are seen?"

"Then the Princess has sent to ask the return of her favour, which it is improper for the champion to wear now that she is betrothed to another man. The Lord Hereward was abed so you deliver it for him."

So now Gwendolen was "the Princess". Aleph had already crowned himself King of Cornwall in his mind, and it seemed the fantasy was infectious. Well, good luck to him. Martin had little love for the English thanes of Cornwall: they reminded him too strongly of the Norse lords of Ireland: and better that Hereward should serve a king, as he had in Scotland, than a profligate hundred-lord living on hopes and close to bankrupting his small estate.

Gwendolen had a small house of her own a little way outside her father's mead hall. Lamorna led Martin quickly across the yard, unchallenged by the sentries, and admitted him: the shuttered house looked dark from without, but the lamps were lit, and the lady was standing by the far wall, still in the shimmering azure dress and gold circlet she had worn at the feast.

"You are the Lord Hereward's serving man?" she said softly. Martin bit his lip.

"I flatter myself that I am the Lord Hereward's friend," he said.

"So much the better," said Gwendolen. "I believe you and he served in Scotland alongside Prince Sitric of

Waterford?"

"That is so, my lady." Martin had joined the young prince's train in Dublin hoping for a chance of revenge on Thord Gunnlaugsson, but Thord had not been there. Sitric had turned out to be on his way to York to aid his kinsman the Earl Siward in his war against Macbeth: and in York, Martin had met the newly banished Hereward. When Sitric had returned to Ireland after the war he had left Martin behind, and he had kept company with Hereward ever since.

"I saw how glad they were to meet again when Prince Sitric visited my father." Gwendolen paused. "Martin, I do not wish to marry Hannibal of Marazion." Her voice remained quiet and low: she spoke only a little faster than before.

"Your ladyship would prefer to marry the Prince," supplied Martin.

"Is it so obvious?"

"Well, I hardly think I'm the only one to have guessed it. But if he feels the same there should be no problem: your father can hardly prefer a thane over a man who will be a king one day. And if he does not feel so, then, forgive me, lady, but you were best to put him from your mind."

"You do not know my father," said Gwendolen, shaking her head sadly. "He will always prefer a Cornishman over a foreigner, and one of ancient lineage over a family as young as Sitric's." Sitric's family had ruled Waterford for over a century and claimed to have been earls in Norway before that, but that made them infants in the eyes of blood-proud nations like the Cornish and the Welsh, who reckoned their genealogies back through Arthur, Cymbeline and Lear to before the fall of Troy. "Besides, this marriage is crucial to his mad scheme to expel the English from Cornwall. Even apart from my happiness, it must be stopped for that reason alone. Such a war would be insanity and could only end in the destruction of the Cornish people." The irony was not lost on Gwendolen that it was only thanks to English rule that her father was able to treat her so: Cornish law in the old days had protected the right of a woman to choose her own husband.

"Would the Prince accept you without a dowry?" It was blunt, but it was not Martin's way to shirk questions that needed to be asked.

"Yes," said Gwendolen decisively. "He has promised me as much. But, in any case, once we were married I believe my father would accept it." Aleph's ability to accept what he could not change was far from apparent to Martin, but his daughter presumably knew him best. And she did not strike him as a fool: if she believed Sitric's promise, he must have been at the least very convincing.

"So your ladyship wishes that the Lord Hereward and myself should help you to escape from Gweek?" said Martin.

"If you would!" Gwendolen looked beseechingly at him. "But you must be careful. Hannibal's champion, Gartnait Ironhook, has the eyes of an eagle. If my feelings for Sitric are known then he will surely be watching me; and no doubt he will have seen you come here." Martin silently cursed her for saying nothing before, and himself for not thinking of Gartnait. He restrained himself from asking what was in this for Hereward or himself, but he would certainly put that question to Hereward when he passed on the Princess' message.

"I will communicate this to the Lord Hereward," he said coolly. "More than that I cannot promise."

Ely.

The Lammas fires were lit and the harvest had begun, and hunger was at last banished from Hereward's camp. Indeed, the rebels fed better than the people in the villages: and they needed their strength. After what had happened at Bristol Hereward was determined to be ready for the next blow against the Normans, and had begun to train his men to fight as a unit. As a youth he had played at being a warrior king and had called his friends his housecarles: now he meant to make true housecarles out of these peasants, a finer guard than ever followed King Harold. Every day he had them training with axe, bow and spear, drilling and rehearsing the formation of a shield wall. Swords, helms and hauberks were more problematic: with little iron and few men trained to work it, they had to rely on what could be captured from unwary Norman patrols.

Occasionally runaways, both serfs and free, would join them: especially now that the Gyrvians were defeated, there was no other recourse for outlaws save to take to the woods or marshes alone. That with Hereward they were required to be soldiers and not thieves did not suit all of them, but they had little choice.

The boy from Spalding, however, was not typical. For one thing, he was expensively dressed, and nobody on Ely had seen him before. For another, although his English was impeccable, he was no Saxon.

"My name is Hamo," he told Hereward when he was brought before him. "I'm a Breton, from Dol. I served the Baron Ivo Taillebois as a cup-bearer until I ran away."

Hereward looked him up and down. He was perhaps sixteen or seventeen, dark, scrawny, bright-eyed, and wore his embroidered tunic carelessly, managing to make the rich garment look slovenly.

"Were you a slave?" he said. Hamo spat.

"No," he said, "but nobody seems to have told Ivo that. I spilt his wine and he had me flogged. That's why I'm here."

"Take off your tunic," ordered Hereward.

"My tunic?"

"You say you were flogged. I want to see if you're telling the truth. Take off your tunic."

The lad shrugged, and pulled his tunic over his head,

turning and presenting his thin, bony back to Hereward. It was indeed criscrossed with weals, red and recent. He had been whipped very viciously.

"Who did this to you?"

"Hubert Gervase, the steward," said Hamo. "The baron would have done it himself, but he's lazy and hasn't as steady a hand as Hubert."

"Well, you're safe from them here," Hereward promised. He turned to Winter. "What say you – shall we take the lad into our band?" Winter frowned.

"There'll be ill feeling about letting in a Breton," he said. "Half the people here are here because of Ogier fitz Ungomar; they love his people no more than the Normans."

"The boy's a victim of the same enemies who've dispossessed us all," said Hereward. "I'd take even a Norman if he proved his goodwill."

"If you think he has proven it, then let him stay," agreed Winter.

"There is little harm he can do to us if he is not taken into our counsel," said Hereward. "Ivo already knows the lie of the island, and he has not the strength to assault it. And perhaps he can bring some new songs and stories to the campfire. The Bretons have always been fine storytellers."

"Oh, I have a few tales," agreed Hamo. "New ones and old. But I'd love to hear of your adventures."

"It has been a while since you last played the scop," Winter reminded Hereward.

"I told how I came to own Swallow only last week," said Hereward defensively.

"We'd heard that one before. And it's Martin's tale, not yours." Hereward had done little to acquire his beloved mare: it was Martin who had concocted the story that she was a wizard's wife trapped in enchanted shape, and thus scared the Frisian horse-thief who'd taken her from Count Baldwin's herd into abandoning her; and when Hereward's old stallion Fafner had been slain in battle, the Count had bestowed

Swallow on his champion.

"What about how you came by your sword, Brainbiter?" Hamo piped up. "I hear there's a fine tale behind that."

"Do you, now?" said Hereward, smiling. "And who tells you so?"

"Aldwine the Scop. He entertains the baron sometimes."

Hereward stroked his chin.

"Well," he said, "if your head's already filled with Aldwine's version then the truth may be a disappointment. But I'll tell it nonetheless."

Gartnait of Cardoness had not been so massively built as Grendel or Hiccafrith. He was a tall man, but no giant, nor indeed heavily made: enemies tended to underestimate his strength until they saw him wield his sword. He could twirl Brainbiter in one hand as if it had been a knife, and fight for hours untired. One-handed, indeed, was how he had to fight, for his left hand was at the bottom of Lough Laoigh in Ulster, and in its place he bore the iron hook that had given him his byname, and on which many an unfortunate had since been skewered. Unable to hold a shield, he had devised a steel sleeve which he wore clamped around his left forearm in battle, so thick that blows as heavy as that which had cost him his hand rebounded off it. His forbidding appearance was topped off by a mass of thick, coarse, tangled red hair and a beard that hung to his breastbone: from somewhere within this mane, like a hunting wolf peering from the undergrowth at a hare, two perpetually narrowed, unblinking bright blue eyes regarded the world with suspicion and hostility.

He spoke little Cornish and less English, preferring to converse, when he spoke at all, in the mix of Gaelic and Norse favoured in his native Galloway. Martin, who had grown up speaking both tongues, and Hereward, who knew Norse and had learnt some Gaelic in Scotland, had tried to make conversation with Gartnait in his own language, but their overtures had been met with grunts and they had given up the effort.

Gartnait's loyalty to his ring-giver was absolute. If released from Hannibal's service, he would seek another lord and not care who: but while he served the Lord of Marazion he would pledge to him his life and soul, as he had to the earl in whose service he had sacrificed his hand. His lord's engagement, and anything that might threaten it, were therefore his concern: and he did not trust women. He could not watch the Lady Gwendolen at all hours, but he kept his eyes open when he could: and he had seen Martin Lightfoot visit the lady by night.

A scandal would embarrass his master: better that the Irishman should simply die. But then there would be the vengeance of Hereward to contend with: he might accuse Gartnait publicly, and the scandal would be unaverted. Now, if Hereward were to die first, would any listen to what Martin might say? They might: the risk was less, but still present: but if an excuse could be found for a duel, then Gartnait was confident that he could kill Hereward openly, in fair fight, and none could call him murderer. Martin might try to avenge his friend secretly, with a dagger in the night, but Gartnait had seen off assassins before. Yes, a quarrel must be fastened on Hereward. Killing Aleph's champion would also show the Lord of Gweek and his friends who the true commander of this alliance was: and many of the Cornish warriors might be glad to rid their company of a Saxon, one of the enemy's people. Gartnait stroked his beard with his hook, and smiled. It remained only to find the grounds for the quarrel.

"All the black rocks of Brittany hidden? A likely story."

"It is true," insisted Hamo. "Aurelius is a kinsman of mine. I saw his lord return after Hastings. I had the whole story from Aurelius' own lips."

"A spring tide, nothing more," said Martin. "The wizard knew when it was coming and that Sir Arviragus would return at the right time of year; it was a lucky coincidence that he got back on the very day."

"True or not, it's the best tale I've heard in a good while," said Wulfric. "Now, Hereward, you promised to tell us how you came by Brainbiter." The people gathered round the fire leaned forward expectantly; the orange light flickered on their faces.

"Martin and I were in Cornwall," Hereward began, "serving the Lord of the Hundred of Gweek. It was about this time of the year; the Lammas Fires had been lit, though the custom is different in Cornwall – they burn bundles of herbs in the fires in honour of the strange saints of those parts. They have hundreds, with names I can't begin to pronounce. But I fell afoul of a Scottish mercenary…"

"I warned you not to trust an Englishman!" exclaimed Hannibal. "Of course he sides with his own blood. The saints help us if the Saxon thanes already know our plans."

The two hundred-lords and the one-handed champion were the only men still awake in the mead hall; the torches were burning low and the warriors on the benches were too drunk to wake.

"You are certain?" said Aleph, troubled. "You saw Hereward converse in secret with the Lord of Morwenstow's steward?" Gartnait nodded. "There can be no mistake?" He shook his head, still silent. "All the same," said Aleph doubtfully, "it could have been something innocent. Two fellow countrymen in a strange land…"

"It's treachery," declared Hannibal impatiently, thumping the table. A man at the far end, his head jolted by the blow, groaned but did not stir. "Deceit is meat and drink to the Saxons. This Hereward will be the death of our enterprise if we do not put him out of the way."

"I have always found Hereward trustworthy," said Aleph. "But will you accuse him publicly?"

"It is Gartnait who makes the accusation," said Hannibal, "but if it needs my backing I will give it, and challenge Hereward to prove his innocence in trial by combat. Gartnait is ready to fight him. God will show which side has the truth of it."

"The ordeal by battle is custom, but not law," Aleph pointed out. "This is Cornwall, not Normandy. What if Hereward refuses it? He has every right to choose the manner of his trial."

"When once the idea is broached he'll be too vain to refuse it," insisted Hannibal. "Besides, if you were the Saxon, wouldn't you rather trust your safety to your own right arm than to a court of Cornishmen? He'll fight; and Gartnait will gut him, and our problem will be solved." Gartnait fingered the hilt of Brainbiter. The sword had never yet failed him; he only wished he had had it at Lough Laoigh. He had no doubt that then he would have kept his hand.

"Very well," sighed Aleph, twisting his cup in his hands. "It is a pity; he has been a good champion. I will be sorry to lose him. But so it must be."

At Ely, seven years later, another group of warriors was also lapsing into sleep. Hereward had not had a chance to finish his story, but he was not sorry: he didn't like to talk at length, and now his throat was dry and the ale was not helping, he might have to resort to water. He had drawn Brainbiter and held it before him to illustrate his story: now he planted it in the ground and set off in search of a drink. Hamo fitz Hamelyn opened his eyes. The sword was unguarded. He sat up, propping himself on his elbow.

"Still awake?"

He blinked, and Martin came into focus. With the fire between them, Hamo had not seen the watchful Irishman. He yawned and smiled.

"Barely," he said. "I think I'll just sleep here."
"Pleasant dreams."

"It is a lie!" declared Gwendolen fiercely. "A wicked, odious lie. Lord Hereward is loyal to you, Father, and if Hannibal says otherwise –"

"It is not for you to question the Lord Hannibal," said Aleph crisply. "If he is wrong to place his faith in Gartnait then God will show us so and Hereward will win the duel."

"You really believe that?"

"It is what we are taught," said Aleph, as firmly as he could. "And if it is only skill that decides the matter, why shouldn't Hereward win? He may not have Gartnait's reach, but he's broader built; he's never lost a fight before; and he has both his hands."

"But -"

"Hush, child, they're taking their places."

A square piece of ground before Aleph's hall had been fenced in for the fight, with two gates, and on one side high benches under an awning for Aleph, Gwendolen and their noble guests. Hannibal had not yet joined them: he was down by Gartnait's gate, placing Brainbiter in his champion's hand and saying something encouraging to him, while Hereward entered opposite, handing his cloak to Martin. The two foes wore light helms, but no mail; Hereward carried a small buckler, while Gartnait had his iron sleeve and his hook. A priest sidled between fence and bench and confirmed that both combatants had confessed their sins and received absolution.

"Gartnait of Cardoness," said Aleph loudly, "you have accused Hereward Askilsson of conspiring with our enemy the Saxon Lord of Morwenstow. Do you still maintain that accusation?" Gartnait nodded silently. "And Hereward Askilsson, how do you answer this?"

"I deny it utterly," declared Hereward, "and am ready to prove my innocence upon his body."

"So be it," said Aleph. "At my signal, the combatants will engage. The fight will be until the death or surrender of one or other of the combatants, or until I order that it should cease. May God defend the right." And he raised his hand.

Gartnait struck instantly, but Hereward sidestepped deftly and Brainbiter bit into the turf. Hereward struck at it with his own blade, and Gartnait staggered slightly from the impact: but at the same time, he swiped sideways with his hook. Hereward had to jump backwards to avoid the cruel claw, and this gave the Gallovidian time to regain his balance.

Gartnait's next blow struck resoundingly against Hereward's buckler, jarring both men's arms. Holding the great blade back, Hereward essayed a thrust of his own: but Gartnait caught the blade with his hook and forced it down, placing a foot on it. Hereward was forced into a crouching position: then Gartnait suddenly pushed forward. Hereward lost his footing and his grip on the hilt at once, and fell backwards against the fence, unarmed. He rolled aside as Brainbiter cleaved through the timbers of the fence, and a frightened spectator who had come too close yelped out a loud curse; as Hereward tried to get back to his feet, Gartnait was already raising Brainbiter again.

Down it came, this time not against the flat but against the edge of the buckler, and split it so far that the blade was a hair's breadth from Hereward's knuckles. Seeing his chance, Hereward hurled himself backwards again, heaving on the buckler with all his weight, which despite the height difference was greater than Gartnait's: and the sword came out of the Scotsman's hand.

The crowd gasped and Gartnait uttered a wordless roar; Gwendolen and Lamorna started to their feet. Hereward flung his useless buckler aside, dashing it against the fence to loosen the embedded sword; his own dropped blade, his enemy had already retrieved. As Hereward made to pick up Brainbiter, he dodged a blow from the sword, but was unprepared for Gartnait's second attack: the hook tore into his arm and he could not suppress a howl of pain. Gartnait laughed into his beard and raised Hereward's sword to finish the job: but at that moment, Hereward's free hand found the hilt of Brainbiter. He struck half-blindly upwards, and buried the blade in Gartnait's grinning face.

Gushing hot blood, the Gallovidian's body toppled forward on top of Hereward; and, with that dead weight on top of him and gore filling his eyes and nose, and still the searing pain in his arm, he gave up consciousness. He only dimly heard the beginning of the cheers – and boos.

"He's won! He's won!" exclaimed Gwendolen delightedly, and most of the locals were almost as pleased: for though the folk of Gweek had no great love for the English, the champion of Marazion had not made himself popular during his stay there, and they were not sorry to see their own lord's champion slay the outsider. Even Aleph could not help but feel gratified. The men of Marazion, however, were less than happy, and Hannibal was muttering darkly to the other Cornish nobles: and Martin, even as he heaved Ironhook's body off Hereward and all but sobbed with the relief of finding his companion still breathing, yet kept half an eye on them. He trusted the master no more than the man, and did not believe that they were safe yet.

There were night guards posted, but the Isle of Ely was large, and Hereward's men could not surround it. Hamo was a most accomplished thief: that was why Ivo had chosen him. He had been paid very well for enduring Hubert's whipping, a necessary step to allay the rebels' suspicions. Martin had denied him his chance on that first night, but on the second, supported by the men, he urged that Hereward continue the story: and this time the Lord of Ware himself fell asleep by the fire, both hands wrapped around the sword, but his grip relaxed as the wakefulness left him. Hamo had never known such fear as when he took hold of the sword: he felt that the beating of his heart must be loud enough to wake

Hereward: but, slowly, so slowly he began to fear dawn would break before he was done, he manage to slide it out of Hereward's grasp.

After that, stealing a boat and escaping the island was the easy part.

Another August night, another secret flight to the shore: Aleph's men guarded Gweek's tiny official harbour by night, but many fishermen merely pulled their boats up onto the shingle. Any enemy coming by land would have other objectives than fishing boats: and if Norse-Irish raiders came from the sea, the men of Gweek would have worse worries than losing a few smacks and coracles.

It was from this beach that Gwendolen planned to set out for Ireland. Her father would, she assured Hereward, compensate the man whose boat they stole: but neither she nor Lamorna had any experience of sailing. Hereward and Martin must not only see them safely out of Gweek, but come with them to Waterford. This was what Gwendolen had meant all along.

"It is well enough," declared Martin airily. "Lord Hannibal doesn't love us, and with the lady gone we may be suspected; and the best that can happen to us in Cornwall is to serve the Lord Aleph for the rest of our days. Prince Sitric is sure to have a place for us, if we bring him his beloved." He did not mention his own unfinished business in Waterford.

Hereward did not like rashly abandoning the place he had made for himself in Cornwall, nor yet betraying Aleph: but that he was doing anyway, by helping Gwendolen escape. And Aleph, for all his dreams, would never be a king: to be champion to a poor Cornish hundred lord was a sad end for a warrior who had fought beside the King of Scots. Martin was right: they could make a better career for themselves in Ireland. And Aleph… well, Cornwall might profit from the dashing of the unfortunate thane's hopes: perhaps a bloody war would be avoided. When all was done, too, he would have the Prince of Waterford for a son-in-law: and if he still chose to view the Lord of Marazion as a better catch, he was indeed a fool.

"Very well," he said. "And it is better that we flee as soon as possible. Are we in time to catch the tide tonight?"

"If we leave now," said Lamorna. "But some of the Lord Aleph's guests are still awake…"

"They may carouse past the tide tomorrow night, and the next, and until after your lady is wedded and bedded and carries Lord Hannibal's child."

"You're right," decided Gwendolen. "We go tonight. Hannibal and his people are still drowning their sorrows over Ironhook; they'll be too drunk to give chase if they do see us. And tomorrow we'll be in Ireland."

"So this is the famous Brainbiter," said Ivo. "It looks very ordinary, doesn't it?" The baron, his steward and his spy were seated together in his great hall, the massive sword lying across the table between them. The hall was otherwise empty: it was very early in the morning. The servants had argued for some time before rousing Ivo: on Hamo's head be it, they had insisted: but to their astonishment their lord had been glad to be woken.

All three men, whatever they might say, regarded the sword with respect.

"I know what you mean," agreed Hubert. "Somehow one expects jewels in the pommel and secret sigils on the blade, with a magic sword."

"I swear to you this is the one," said Hamo. "I took it from Hereward's own hands as he lay snoring like the Saxon swine he is."

"I've seen Hereward wield a sword that looked like this one," agreed Hubert.

"The same?" said Ivo sharply. "There's not much to distinguish it, apart from its size."

"Yes," said the steward, "it was the same. You see the

shape of the crosspiece, how both sides bend slightly towards the blade instead of forming a simple bar across? I noticed that in Hereward's sword. And I've seen that style before, too, on a mercenary captain's sword in Brittany. The mercenary was a Scot; if this is a Scottish style then the story of how Hereward came by it rings true. I only hope that will be enough to convince the people."

"They'll hear soon enough that Hereward's sword has gone missing," Hamo pointed out. "Ely must be buzzing with it already. They'll believe it."

"It would be better", Ivo mused, "if we could show we were its masters. You know the sort of stories there are about magic swords – that they turn in a usurper's hand, or cry out if wielded against their true master, all that nonsense."

"What do you suggest, my lord?" asked Hubert. "Hereward's hardly going to present himself here for you to cut him down with his own blade."

"No," said Ivo, "but there must be a way…"

"What if an English cunning man were to proclaim you master of the sword?" suggested Hamo. "Cast a few runes, put on a bit of a spectacle, make it impressive."

"Father Hugo won't approve," said Hubert.

"That dry old stick never approves of anything," said Ivo. "I'll have to see about getting a new chaplain one of these days. That scop's a cunning man, isn't he? He might have a few rituals up his sleeve for this sort of thing."

"Not Aldwine," said Hamo. "The locals know him too well. And they know he has dealings with us. No, a cunning man from out of town would be best; somebody who can bring a real air of mystery with him."

"And where are we to send for such a man?" demanded Hubert. "Where's the nearest cunning man outside Spalding? Does anybody know? Or do we just wait for a wandering one to turn up on our doorstep?"

"No," explained Hamo patiently, "we wait for a

stranger. Anyone can be a wandering cunning man if the locals don't know differently. The next Saxon stranger to come into Spalding gets brought straight here; for the right price he's sure to agree to wave his hands and mutter a few spells. And then –" He snapped his fingers. "The sword itself will declare its allegiance to Ivo Taillebois, through the stranger, in public. You will be master and Hereward will be ill-starred, rejected. We'll see how many want to follow a Jonah like that." Ivo eyed the youth marvellingly.

"You", he said, "are a quite dangerously brilliant young man."

Aleph might be convinced of Hereward's innocence, but Hannibal was not so sure. Even if Gartnait had been mistaken about the details, he still did not trust the Englishman: and he had ordered two men to keep watch on the coastal path, where Aleph had no guards – for any outsider coming that way must have come from the sea, and would have been seen by the watchers at the harbour. If Hereward or Martin attempted to leave the village that way by night, one man was to follow them, the other to report back to Hannibal.

So it was that the Lord of Marazion found one of his men, hot-faced and out of breath, shaking him out of his mead-induced torpor.

"What the hell do you want, Breok?" he growled.

"The Saxon and the Irishman, my lord – they're leaving like you said – and they have the Lady Gwendolen!"

"What!" Hannibal lurched to his feet, overturning the table.

"Glyn's following them, but there are boats down there, and –"

"Muster every man you can find that's awake," said Hannibal grimly. "I will bring them back here though Heaven and Hell stand against me: and I will leave Gweek with Gwendolen on my arm and Hereward's head tied to my saddlebow! Don't wake Aleph: this is a task for the men of Marazion."

A few minutes later, as Martin was untying the painter of the boat they had chosen to carry them to Ireland, the night peace was shattered by the sudden whoops of half a dozen Cornish warriors bounding over the dunes.

"Cast off!" hissed Gwendolen. Martin apparently did not heed her, instead dropping to one knee and gathering up a handful of stones.

The first brought down Hannibal's man Glyn, who had taken off towards the boat as soon as he had seen his comrades arrive and was therefore at the head of them, with a blow to the temple. With the second, Martin took aim at the Lord of Marazion himself: he missed, but struck another warrior in the chest; the man winced and staggered. As the Cornishmen drew nearer, Martin drew his axe from his belt and sliced through the painter, pushing the boat out into the water: but he did not board, instead standing in the surf, axe in his right hand, a third stone in his left.

"Martin!" Hereward did not hesitate, but leapt down into the surf beside his friend, drawing Brainbiter.

"Do you recognise this?" he shouted. "This is Brainbiter! This is the blade that slew Gartnait Ironhook. Gartnait died by the judgement of God, because he impeached my honour. This sword wrought justice upon him. Are you willing to face it?"

Behind him, Gwendolen had seized the tiller and turned the boat sideways to the shore. She was not going to abandon the men who had risked their lives for her.

"At them, you worms!" shouted Hannibal. Breok and another man moved forward, swords before them; Martin threw his last stone and caught the one nearer to him in the left eye, dropping him beside Glyn. As Breok neared Hereward, Brainbiter arced sideways: and the Cornishman's head fell on the wet shingle. Six were reduced to three.

The Lord of Marazion angled his sword in front of his

body, and crouched like a cat.

"I'm not afraid of you," he said.

"That's your mistake," said Hereward.

Hannibal lunged forward, but Hereward sidestepped and he staggered slightly as he missed: but he had his footing again before Hereward could riposte. Their blades rang against each other. Martin stood back, eyeing the other two Cornishmen: he would not interfere in Hereward's fight unless asked for help. He would never have turned down such assistance himself, but had learnt before that the Englishman was touchy about matters of honour.

Hannibal's missed lunge had placed Hereward between him and his men. Their lord, too, was a proud man, and might not be grateful for aid in a duel: but he would be still less so if the Lady Gwendolen escaped his grasp. They exchanged glances, then one of them charged at Martin, while the other leapt like a frog onto Hereward's back, grappling him with arms and legs. Hereward staggered backwards into the water, and crashed into the side of the boat: Martin was occupied fighting the other man, and Hannibal saw his opportunity. He licked his lips, and advanced towards his adversary.

Suddenly, Hereward felt his attacker's grip slacken. He did not stop to wonder what had happened, but wrenched his arm free just as Hannibal raised his sword, and ran the Cornishman through. Only after Hannibal had slumped lifeless into the sea did Hereward disentangle himself from the other man and see what had happened: Gwendolen had thrown a sheet from the boat around his attacker's neck, and choked him. She was still squeezing; the man was barely alive. Unable to talk, Hereward signalled her to let him go; then turned back towards Martin in time to see the Irishman bury his axe in the chest of his adversary.

He looked again to the women. Both were pale, and Lamorna was breathing very heavily: but neither was hurt. Gwendolen managed a smile.

"Well done, my lady," croaked Hereward.

"Well," she said, as calmly as she could, "let us be on our way."

"Behold Brainbiter, the blade forged by the trolls!" declaimed Hubert. "This is the source from which Hereward whom you call the Wake derived his power. And this has been taken from Hereward, captured by your gracious lord, the Baron Ivo Taillebois!" He turned, left and then right, to display the sword to the people. They watched silently, suspiciously, unsure how to react. "You all know that blades such as this choose their own masters. Brainbiter would not have left Hereward if it had not chosen to do so. But we do not know yet if the blade has chosen a new master." He paused, and let his gaze travel around the crowd. It was disappointingly small as well as unresponsive; by proclaiming this event in advance he had hoped to draw in some people from the villages. "By happy chance, the cunning man Cynric Cynewulfsson is in Spalding today, travelling towards Lincoln to offer his services to Sheriff Turaud. He has undertaken to unlock the magical voice of the sword, and to learn its choice, that all may know why it has abandoned Hereward. Master Cynric!"

The cunning man bowed low, with a flourish of the purple cloak with which Ivo had provided him for his role. The stranger had been found at an inn, and had identified himself as a pilgrim newly arrived from Gloucester; it had been established that nobody had seen him before; and his Southron speech was held to rule out his being one of Hereward's followers. That, plus the fact that Hamo had barely seen his face and was unlikely to recognise him clean-shaven, was why Methelgar had been chosen to go into Spalding in the first place. He still could not quite believe that the Normans were about to place Brainbiter in his hands of their own accord, without any stratagem on his part whatever.

Ivo was sitting by on his horse, in full armour, looking suitably heroic for the moment when Brainbiter would be presented to him. He bit his lip as he watched Hubert place the sword in the hands of the stranger. He hoped the man would play his part well; the spectators were muttering and did not seem happy, and Ivo wanted a cheer when his name was announced as the new master of the sword. He was prepared, however, for disappointment. What he was not prepared for was for Master Cynric to seize him by his cloak and haul him from the saddle, pitching him onto the dusty ground.

"Stop that man!" shouted Hubert. Guards were rushing forward, but Methelgar had already vaulted into the saddle, and, with Brainbiter tucked under his arm, was galloping through the conveniently parted crowd towards the town gates. In a few moments more he was out and away, and Ivo and Hubert were once again left impotently cursing.

The story quickly spread that it was Hereward himself who had reclaimed the sword, his appearance disguised by the magic of Brainbiter, which would not suffer its true master to come to harm. It added immeasurably to his glamour, and every new recruit to the band at Ely would ask about Brainbiter and the story of how he had acquired it.

"And did Prince Sitric marry the Lady Gwendolen?" pressed yet another eager youth.

"Yes, he did," said Hereward, smiling. "With no dowry and no inheritance, but he didn't care."

"And did her father forgive her?" At this point Hereward would generally evade the question, for the heartbroken Aleph had remained set against his daughter until the day his mead hall burned over his head and a Norman lord was installed in Gweek. And where Sitric and Gwendolen were now, Hereward could not answer, for the Gaels had retaken Waterford and installed a native King, and the Norse royal family had retreated to God knew where. Even Martin, who generally rejoiced when his mother's people defeated his father's, had shaken his head at that news.

"They want to hear happy endings," said Hereward. "But life doesn't offer many of those."

"Life offers no ends at all except death," said Martin. "Live well, die well, and earn a good epitaph, and that's as happy an ending as any of us can hope for. With the hope of salvation, of course," he added, mindful that they were on holy ground. Winter nodded affirmatively, and Hereward thoughtfully: Martin was voicing the wisdom they had all grown up with.

"I think there is one more thing at least," said Wulfric, glancing at Rowena. "Not every man who dies well dies *happy*, after all. I've known some happiness in life, and I wouldn't trade that for any epitaph."

"It's certainly rarer," remarked Martin.

"God grant", said Gwynnog, "that we may all achieve both." And Hereward answered fervently:

"Amen."

Chapter 10: *The Miller's Daughter*

Ely, September, 1068.

"A downward blow like *so* leaves the attacker's middle undefended for a moment. If you're quick you can slash him across the belly while his hauberk's still pulled up from raising his arms: but he may split your skull while you're doing it. It's much safer to block it by raising your sword sideways." Hereward demonstrated, angling his wooden weapon before his face to parry Winter's blow. The watching men and boys nodded wisely. It would take a long time to make an army out of this collection.

"Ahem." Hereward looked round, and saw that Martin was hovering at his shoulder.

"What is it?" he asked irritably.

"A courier for you. My lord," Martin added, remembering the watching recruits who had to learn to respect their leader.

"Couldn't you or the monks have entertained him until I was free?"

"I think he might have been offended by having to wait," said Martin. "It's the Lord Dolfin Gospatricsson." Hereward dropped his sword.

This Dolfin's father, Gospatric, had been one of the most powerful noblemen in the North. In the scramble for Northumbria after the death of the great Earl Siward, he had been a leading player: but a few weeks ago, caught in a plot against King William, he and his sons had vanished into the wilds of Cumberland. Norman rule did not run there, and though the King of Scots laid claim to it he could never spare the men to subdue it. The whole of the Border country was wild and fierce, more loyal to Gospatric than to either King but preferring its own chiefs first and foremost; and Cumberland was perhaps the most untamed part of the

Borders. Little news came out of its rugged mountains and dark forests; a man might hide there years and not be heard of.

Dolfin was waiting for Hereward in Abbot Thurstan's chambers, tapping his elegantly shod foot impatiently. For a man – or rather youth, for he was fresh-faced with only the beginnings of a moustache, which had his hair been lighter would have been altogether invisible – who had ridden across England, and who lived in what was commonly thought of as a wilderness, he was startlingly well clad, his hose cross-gartered, his short green supertunic stopping short of the embroidered hem of his tunic, his travel cloak secured by a golden brooch three inches across, with a large garnet at its centre.

"My lord Hereward," he said, making a bow. He spoke the Anglo-Norse of the Danelaw with a curious precision, under which lay the thick accent of the far north.

"My lord Dolfin." Hereward nodded curtly. "To what do we owe this honour?"

"You have heard that my father is in possession of Carlisle?" said Dolfin. "I see you have not. Well, he is: and from there he intends to take the North from Bastard William." He spat on the ground; the Abbot shuddered.

"To take the North from him?" said Hereward. "What do you mean?"

"Why did the sons of Harold fail?" demanded Dolfin.

"Because Godwin was a drunken fool," said Hereward. "Because the Normans took us by surprise while our commanders were squabbling among themselves. Because Ednoth took the Norman side and the common people didn't come out to join us."

"They'd have failed anyhow," insisted Dolfin. "The Normans are strong in the West, and all their support came from over the sea, from Ireland. And even if they had got a foothold, they'd have been opening up a front too long to fight on. The North is different. The Normans are already struggling to control anything north of Derby – they're on their fourth Earl of Northumbria in two years. My father's last rising would have thrown them out if we hadn't been betrayed. The front is narrower, and we'd have a friendly power at our back – Scotland."

When Dolfin had begun his lecture, Hereward had gaped, astonished at a boy presuming to tell him about matters military: but by the end of it he was looking at the son of Gospatric with a new respect. Not, however, with entire agreement.

"Friendly to Edgar Atheling, maybe," he said dubiously. "Is Scotland friendly to your father? Or to the people of the North?"

"Think of it," Dolfin urged. "The Danelaw back in English hands. Edgar as King in the North, my father as Earl. Let the Normans hang on to the South a few years longer. We'd have the perfect staging point to drive them out altogether when the time came. It's worked before, one King in the North and another in the South. You and I are Anglo-Danes, anyway, not Southron Saxons. Our people would be free."

Hereward did think of it. It had worked before, though never for very long: but then, that wasn't the intention this time. His own lands were well within the Danelaw. It would also, of course, suit Gospatric very well. The Earldom of Northumbria had grown hugely powerful under Siward, even with a King of all England set above it: if Edgar's writ were confined to the North then Gospatric would be King in all but name. Well, he might rule better than the Atheling could: but would the other earls allow it? The Normans might be on their fourth Earl of Northumbria, but the English had proved little better at keeping it since Siward's death. The old man's son, Waltheof, had been passed over because the Godwinssons, who had ruled King Edward long before Harold had usurped his throne, had wanted it for their brother Tostig; Tostig had been deposed in favour of

Hereward's own cousin Morcar Alfgarsson; and William had favoured three English claimants in a row before finally naming a Norman, Robert Comyn. The most recent Earl had been Gospatric himself: but he had plotted with Edgar Atheling and, surprisingly enough, the Alfgarssons, and King William had discovered their plans. Apparently Gospatric had not abandoned them. But Morcar and Waltheof were still alive and vigorously proclaiming their right to Northumbria. Both had petitioned William for restoration of the earldom, and been denied; and the King had been heard to wish that Siward was still alive, "for", he said, "no man else can rule these fractious, factious Northern men."

"What about King Malcolm?" Hereward asked. "He'll not want to set up any Earl in Northumbria with enough power to be a threat to Scotland – and if he did, it would likely be his kinsman Waltheof." Gospatric was also Malcolm's cousin, but dangerous for that very reason: unlike Waltheof, he had Scots royal blood in him, and might be a threat to Malcolm's very throne.

"King Malcolm will feel safer with my father on his southern border than William or one of his lackeys," said Dolfin. "He knows the Norman won't be satisfied with England if he ever finds he can hold it." He paused. "The war will begin in the spring," he said, "but it will do no harm to begin stepping up our raids on Norman manors in the north-west immediately. Your enemy Ivo Taillebois lays claim to the Manor of Kendal, does he not?"

"He does," said Hereward. Dolfin smiled.

"How would you like to be there when Ivo's barns go up in smoke?"

Hereward shook his head.

"Never burn grain," he said. "If your father plans a war we'll have an army to feed. But I'll not deny, if Ivo's getting revenues from Kendal, stopping them would give me satisfaction: and your father's plan sounds as if it might work."

"Then you'll join us?" said Dolfin eagerly.

"Not in force," said Hereward. "Ely must be defended; besides, moving troops about the country would only alert the Normans. Martin Lightfoot and I will come back with you; Winter Osredsson can take command here, and we'll send for the men when they're needed." And, of course, if this turned out to be a repeat of Bristol, he would have run only two heads into the noose and not forty.

"That will do very well," said Dolfin. "Will you be ready to leave tomorrow?"

Hereward blinked, and looked round in confusion. He had been with Dolfin and Martin at Abbot Thurstan's table in the refectory only a moment before, surely, and now he was in a wood. The air was crisp and clear and the moon was full.

"I knew you would come," said Lysir.

"This is a dream," said Hereward. "Or a vision like the ones at Frey's temple. It's not real." Lysir shrugged.

"Does it matter what you call it?" he asked. "There is something I have to show you." Hereward saw that before them, where before the trees had stretched out into the shadows beyond his sight, there was now a church – the *inside* of a stone chapel of Norman fashion, there in the woods, as if there were no walls, or at least no near wall. The far one he could see. Before the altar there lay an armoured man. His face was obscured by the thick nosepiece of his helmet and the high aventail around his chin, but the sword he clutched to his breast was familiar enough: it was Brainbiter. The man was dead, and his widow was weeping over his bier. She too was unrecognisable, hidden under a black kirtle; but Hereward could see that she was wailing aloud, though he could hear no sound.

Then, suddenly, the words came. Not from the widow: rather, they were spoken directly into his head: but he knew that the voice was hers, and that she was Torfrida.

> "I was once thought by the King's thanes
> Higher than any of the maids of Woden:
> Now am I as little as the leaf may be,
> Often storm-swept, now that he is dead.
> I miss in sitting and in sleeping
> My mind's dear one. The Gjukings made this;
> The Gjukings made this, my dole,
> And their own sister sorely weeps."

Hereward rounded on Lysir, who was still by his side.

"What does this mean?" he demanded. "'Their own sister'? Torfrida has no brothers." A smile played around the greybeard's lips. Hereward seized him angrily by the front of his tunic. "You've shown me my own death!" he shouted. "I have a right to know what it means! That was *Gudrun's Lament*. If Torfrida is Gudrun and I am Sigurd, then who are the Gjukings? Who are my murderers?"

"Your death?" said Lysir, still smiling that infuriating, mocking smile. "Do you really think it's as simple as that?" And he pushed Hereward back with a strength more than a man's. Hereward fell flat on his back, and still felt Lysir's hand on his chest: he looked at it, and saw that it had become a paw, a long, heavy paw with thick white fur and crooked claws. His eye travelled up the arm – no, foreleg – and took in the face that loomed over his own. It was still Lysir: the cloth patch still covered the right eye, though not, now, the scar that ran across it: but the face was that of a hot-breathed, yellow-toothed, snarling bear.

That was the last sight Hereward remembered before he woke up, back in his own bed.

"What's this town?" The three riders were approaching a walled settlement. It was not a major city, but considerably bigger than the likes of Spalding: large enough to be worth fortifying.

"Manchester," said Dolfin. "The Normans have

expanded the walls since they came here; I'm not sure if it's us or each other they don't trust. There are two powerful knights who vie for control of the town, Sir Henry de Manville and Sir Miles de Mountney."

"Is it a wealthy place, then?" asked Martin. Dolfin shrugged.

"A market town," he said. "The revenues are richer than their manors, but not by much. But Norman noblemen are born greedy. Besides that, there is Godred's mill."

"A large business?"

"I'll say," agreed Dolfin. "Godred provides flour to most of Manchester and half the surrounding villages – he must be responsible for feeding thousands of people. He came up from the south twenty years ago with his baby daughter on his back and not ten shillings to his name; now he's one of the richest men in the county. Stories like his are rare. Some say he's had the help of the fairies – or the Devil. Anyway, both the knights would love to get their hands on that mill, and on Godred's daughter."

"Norman knights wooing a common English girl?" wondered Martin. "What miracles money can work."

"Indeed," agreed Dolfin. "Though Emma's mother was a Norman, from one of the families who came over in King Edward's time. That's why the girl was named Emma, after Edward's mother. Perhaps they think that makes her a little more respectable."

"Anyway," said Hereward, "we're short of food. We'll need to buy some soon. I'd rather not go into a walled town; there'll be soldiers about. How far is the next village?"

"We'll not reach it today," said Dolfin. "The sun's low already. There's a bakery just inside the town gates; it should be safe enough for us to buy bread there, and we may be able to buy information, too. The baker's one of Godred's biggest customers: with the whole town going to Godred for flour, and taking all their gossip with them, he gets to know most everything that's going on in these parts, and the baker hears most of it soon enough afterwards." Martin licked his lips at the mention of a bakery. Fresh bread was a rarity: bakers operated mostly in the cities, and many villages never saw bread less than a week old. Since the rebel camp had moved to Ely, they had occasionally enjoyed the produce of the abbey ovens, but there was never enough to go far.

"Are you known there?" asked Hereward.

"Not well, but there might be some who'd recognise me."

"And there might be some who'd turn you in. I'm not letting you set foot through the gates. It'll do us no harm to sleep hungry tonight." Dolfin was about to protest when Martin held up his hand.

"There's no need for that," he said. "I'll go. Nobody's looking for me in Manchester. I'll buy us enough bread for the rest of the journey, see what I can learn about these Normans and their doings, and be back here inside an hour, two at the most."

"And if you're not?" asked Dolfin.

"No nonsense about rescuing me," said Martin firmly. "If I'm not back this evening wait for me here until an hour after dawn, then ride on."

By riding round so as to approach the town gates from the west, Martin had no difficulty in passing himself off as a pilgrim from Dublin on his way to Lindisfarne. He found the bakery easily: it was, as Dolfin had said, just inside the gate, a large wooden building with a high smoking chimney and the most delightfully homely smell to it; inside, while apprentices minded the clay ovens, the portly, easygoing baker himself was ready enough to while the time away chatting with a customer. Martin gave him a few invented tidbits of news from across the sea, and, after paying for a dozen large loaves, he began to root for news concerning the two knights. He did not have to press hard.

"Pair of Norman buzzards in peacocks' feathers," said

the baker, "and I care not who knows I said so. Hovering around poor old Godred as if they're waiting for him to die."

"Godred?" said Martin, feigning ignorance.

"Our miller here," said the baker, "and as good a man as I've met, though he may be a Southron and his bairn half Norman. He gave my sister's boy Thormod an apprenticeship when no one else would. Quiet, Thormod is, keeps himself to himself mostly, but he does have a bit of a temper and after he cracked that other lad's skull no one wanted to know, but Godred took him on. And he's been proved right, if I do say so myself. There isn't a harder worker in Manchester than Thormod."

"But Godred..." Martin steered him back towards the subject of the miller.

"Ah, yes, poor Godred. That pair of greedy Norman jays won't leave his Emma alone. Now, she's a pretty thing, I'll not deny: but it's the mill they're after, God rot the pair of 'em. To tell you the truth, I was hoping that young Thormod might marry the lass, after he's done with his apprenticeship. He's a year or two younger than she, it's true, and he doesn't talk much to girls, but I can tell he's fond on her, and Godred likes him, and he wouldn't be the first prentice to marry the master's daughter. I know Godred would sooner have him than a Norman."

"But if he married a Norman himself..."

"Ah, but that was before the war. These knights aren't just Normans, they're William's men, with English blood on their hands from Hastings – and a sight more since in that Manville's case. A nasty reputation he has, both as a landlord and with the lasses." Martin nearly retorted that he knew the kind, but remembered in time that he was supposed to be newly landed from Dublin. "Godred served King Edward when he was younger, and he's taken harder than most against William and his invasion, though he's not been hurt as bad as some – not yet, anyway. He hasn't a good word for the King, and he isn't careful who hears him. I've told him he's only giving de Manville a rope to hang him with, but he doesn't listen." The baker could have done with heeding his own advice, but Martin was not about to tell him that.

"And the Normans?" he prompted – not that it seemed necessary. The baker mopped a little sweat off his florid face, and carried on.

"De Manville has a keep down Withington way, de Mountney a lodge out towards Gorton, and they both have houses in town. They're both here now, or any road they were yesterday and I've not heard that they've left – and most folk leaving go right past my front door. They spend more and more time here these days – God knows who runs their estates." Or how any bread gets baked, thought Martin, with the baker giving every waking hour to gossip: but the work appeared to be getting done, even undirected.

"They come alone?" The baker shook his head.

"No, de Mountney has a page that goes with him everywhere, and de Manville half a dozen guards to make him look grand. And of course they've servants at their town houses. When did you ever hear of a Norman knight travelling alone?" The baker's eyes narrowed: he was, it seemed, at last beginning to get suspicious. Martin laughed it off.

"Norman ways are strange to me," he said. "When I was last in England, Earl Siward was alive." The baker nodded, accepting the explanation. He had noticed that Martin's English was strikingly good, but he knew that Dublin had swarmed with English merchants even before the Conquest, and now also played host to any number of exiles.

"Well, and speak of the – Godred!" exclaimed the baker, as a burly, grey-bearded man wearing a deep frown pushed into his shop. "What brings you here?"

"Have you seen the physician?" asked Godred urgently. "He's not at his house; I was told he came out this way."

"Bless you, he's gone out to Denton to treat a case of

maw-worm," said the baker. Martin grimaced: he was far from squeamish, and had helped dress wounds on many a campaign, but he found maw-worm more horrible than any wound he had seen. The mere mention of the parasite near turned his stomach. "He'll not be back today, nor yet tomorrow, I should say. What do you need him for?"

"Emma's fallen ill," said Godred. "One minute she was hale and well, the next she was shaking so hard she could barely stand. There's a burning fever on her." He scowled. "And it had to happen when both those bastard Normans were in the house." He spat on the ground.

"Sir," said Martin carefully, "I have a little skill in medicine, learnt in the wars. I'm no physician nor cunning man, and I make no promises, but I might be able to help your daughter."

"And who are you?" asked the miller suspiciously.

"Martin of Dublin, a pilgrim on my way to the Holy Island," replied Martin. "Is your house far?"

The miller's house, attached to his mill by the Tib, was a curious construction. Originally there had been one room in a corner of the mill for Godred to live in; as he had grown richer, he had built onto this, until his quarters were as large as the mill itself. It spoke far more eloquently of prosperity than did Godred's simple clothing: the only sign of riches on his person was a heavy gold signet ring bearing the device of an eight-pointed star. Two servants with staves guarded the door, and dipped their heads to Godred and Martin as they entered.

Emma was in her chamber – very few below the ranks of the nobility had rooms of their own, but the rich miller's child was privileged – lying fully clothed upon the bed, a sheepskin wrapped around her. Her round face was very pale, a contrast to her black hair, which hung loose and uncovered. Though it was warm, her teeth were chattering. She looked much younger than the twenty years the baker had imputed to her, little more than a child.

The room was shuttered, and lit by a single dim horn lamp. Such lamps were expensive and cast little light, but it would be foolhardy to bear a naked candle in a mill, with flammable flour everywhere: and Godred extended this rule to his house. Such light as there was fell mostly on Emma's face; it took a few moments before Martin saw the two men already in the small chamber. Sitting on a low stool by the bed, clasping the girl's hand in both his, was a tousle-haired youth in a plain grey tunic covered in flour, concern writ deep on his face, which was as white as hers. A pace away stood a tallish young man in a riding cloak: he wore a sword, and his hair was cut in the severe Norman style.

"Sir Miles," said Godred stiffly, acknowledging his unwelcome guest, then turned to the boy. "Thormod, where is Winifrid?"

"Preparing a simple in the kitchen," said the youth. Only after speaking did he look up. "You don't mind me leaving the mill, do you, sir? Only, when I heard –"

"It'll survive without you," Godred assured him. "Is there any change? Emma, how do you feel?"

"Weak," said Emma, and tried to smile. Even that one word had been an effort. "But no worse." Something about her eyes as she looked up at her father struck Martin, and he pushed quickly past the knight to lean down and peer into them. The girl drew back, startled; then began to breathe heavily from the exertion of the movement.

"This is Master Martin of Dublin," said Godred. "He knows matters of physic."

"I could mix a simple to lessen the fever and help her sleep," said Martin carefully, "but it might be no better than the one the maid is already preparing. I should like to know what is in that before I make a decision." He paused. "But first, I should like to speak with you alone." Godred's brow furrowed still deeper. He glanced at the Norman.

"Where is your friend?" he asked.

"Sir Henry", said de Mountney, in tones which suggested that the other knight was no friend of his, "remembered an urgent appointment at his keep almost as soon as you had left."

Godred tugged at his beard.

"I don't mean to be discourteous," he said, "but how long do you mean to stay?"

"Until I see the lady sleeping soundly, sir," declared the Norman. Thormod shot him an angry glance, which he ignored; Godred sighed, and steered Martin out of the chamber and into his own.

"What did you mean by asking to speak with me alone?" he demanded. "Is my daughter going to die?" Martin shook his head.

"No, master miller, I don't believe she's in mortal danger," he said. "But nor do I believe this sickness is natural."

"What do you mean?"

"I mean", said Martin, "that she has been poisoned. Not a fatal dose, or she'd be dead already: but somebody induced this fever on purpose."

Godred punched the wall. The wattle within it cracked loudly.

"That bastard de Manville!" he exclaimed. "He couldn't sweet-talk or bully her round as he can his farm hussies out at Withington, so he's tried to kill her! By Christ and the twelve apostles, do they think they can – well, I'm going to the Sheriff's sergeant -"

"Patience," said Martin. "I don't believe he ever meant to kill her – only to have her insensible for a day or two. What he's planning is abduction."

"But – but that's more monstrous even than -"

"It is the way of the great," said Martin sourly. "They take what they want. Nobility and robbery are but heads and tails on the same bad penny. But they can be resisted. Have your people be on guard. Always at least one at the door and one in her chamber. If this de Manville is coming, he will probably come tonight."

"You talk more like a captain than a pilgrim," Godred marvelled. Martin smiled.

"Pilgrims come from all professions, master miller," he said. Godred clasped his hand.

"Will you stay?" he said. "At least tonight. A man with experience of physic and war is just what we need here."

"My party has foresworn the comfort of beds," said Martin, hating to lie to the miller, though he was not straying far from the truth. "Until our holy pilgrimage is completed, we sleep under the stars."

"If you've foresworn beds then you may sleep on the floor, or stay awake all night if you prefer," said Godred impatiently. "Ride out now before it's dark, and tell your fellow pilgrims the circumstances. I'm sure they won't begrudge you bending your oath to help us. It's a Christian act, after all."

"So it is," said Martin. "So it is."

"Master! Master! It's Mistress Emma – she's gone!"

It was the maid Winifrid who roused the house. Going in to relieve Thormod of his vigil by Emma's bed in the last watch of the night, she had found the chamber empty, the bedclothes flung aside, Thormod's stool overturned, the shutters open, and on the floor a sticky patch of blood. Nobody had heard a sound. In minutes the whole household was roused, and rushing about in a panic: all save Godred, who simply stood like a statue in his nightclothes, unmoving, silent. Martin stood before him and took him by the shoulders.

"He's killed him," muttered the miller. "He's killed poor Thormod and taken my baby. He's taken her."

"Thormod may still be alive," insisted Martin. "There's no body. Why would they take it? In any case, Emma's not dead. Are you going to let de Manville have her or are you going to save her?" Godred stared at him.

"What can we do?" he demanded. "Two of us – four with these lads, but they've never had to fight real swordsmen – against the tower at Withington?"

Martin took a deep breath.

"My name is Lightfoot," he said. "I've not come from Dublin, I've come from Ely. Hereward the Wake is my captain and he's a few minutes' ride away now. I imagine even here you've heard his name. Seven months ago we not only took a prisoner out of a Norman keep, we burned the tower about its master's ears. Now, you could go to the sergeant for help, and I'll not stop you even though you know enough to hang me. But every minute lost is dangerous to Emma, and you can't trust Norman law not to side with de Manville. Or you can send one of your guards for the sergeant while you get horses and ride with me, and we see if we can free your daughter."

So it was that, as dawn broke, Godred the miller and the pilgrim who had lodged with him rode out of the southern gate of the city. The turmoil at the mill had not gone unremarked, and this fresh peculiarity excited still more comment: and some paid especial attention. There was a Norman squire lodged in the guardhouse: he watched and listened closely, eavesdropping on gossip here, quizzing a neighbour of Godred's there, until he knew enough to speed him on his way. And so he hurried through the awakening streets, towards the house of Sir Miles de Mountney.

Informed by Martin the night before of the situation at the mill, Hereward and Dolfin were not altogether startled to see Godred. That a sword, unnoticed by the town guards, poked from the miller's pack was unexpected: but he looked like a man who knew how to use it. Martin quickly explained what had happened.

"How well defended is de Manville's keep?" asked Hereward.

"When I was last there it was a single wooden tower set on a rise in the land, with stables and a hall attached," said Dolfin. "Bogs and hedges defend most of the approaches, so he hadn't bothered to build a palisade. He may have done since, what with the rebellions this year."

"He hasn't," said Godred. "He doesn't need to – there's only one approach that can be made on horseback; and he has two dozen armed men there."

"Small chance of our getting in by daylight, then, unless we catch de Manville outside it," said Hereward. "I suggest we ride as close as we can go unseen, to get a look at it and form a plan, then put it into action after dark."

"But that may be too late for my daughter!" exclaimed the miller.

"Hereward's right, Godred," said Dolfin gently. "Without a war band, there's nothing we can do before nightfall, unless we get there ahead of him."

"If we ride fast there may still be a chance of that," put in Martin. "He'll be burdened, and if he expects you to go for the sergeant he won't think to be followed so soon. It's a slim enough chance, but -" Godred had already put his spurs to his horse's side. It was some minutes before the others caught up with him.

They had been riding at speed for less than an hour when a young hart bounded across their path. As they drew their shying, whinnying horses back, a hound streaked after it, then another. Hereward turned anxiously to Godred, but the miller was still in his saddle and in complete control of his mount: he was evidently an able horseman.

"And here comes the hunter," remarked Martin. "Does anybody recognise him?" Crashing through the bushes on a huge dapple grey stallion came a tall, blond Norman with a square jaw and aquiline nose, wearing a green linen cloak edged in yellow. He swore loudly and reined in as Martin positioned his horse in his path.

"What the hell do you think you're doing?" he

demanded as soon as he'd regained his balance and dignity. He had dropped his hunting spear, but reached for the hilt of his sword as he added: "You might have killed me."

"Draw that sword and I will," Martin snapped, in French. Turning to Godred, he spoke English: "Is this Sir Henry de Manville?"

"Yes, damn you, I am de Manville," blustered the knight, "and these are my lands and that is my beast you've helped escape. What in God's name -"

"What have you done with my daughter?" thundered Godred, drawing his sword. Not only could he ride, Martin noted, he spoke French as well. Of course, that was unremarkable in a man who had had a Norman wife.

"Your daughter?" De Manville frowned uncomprehendingly. "I haven't touched the Saxon slut. I haven't even seen her since yesterday."

"Do you deny abducting her?"

"Of course I deny it!" barked the knight. "D' you think I'd risk my neck when I can take any wench from my own estate? Never mind the fact that she was afire with the Devil knows what filthy fever! I've no desire to catch my death, Englishman, nor yet to land a sickly wife. I enjoy life and don't feel like ending it just yet, and before it does end I want healthy sons that a lass prone to fevers won't give me, even if she does survive this time. And I *was* enjoying my hunting before you interrupted me. Now, I think I should warn you that there are half a dozen spearmen only a few minutes behind me: so if you fancy a long life yourself you should put that penknife away and take your friends back to Manchester before my men arrive. Who knows, if you use the ride to calm down and clear your head you might even work out where your daughter's run off to. She's either wandering the streets in delirium and infecting half the town or in bed with her sweetheart and thinking how clever she's been to get away from Daddy. Good luck finding her. Now, if you'll excuse me, I have a hart to kill. I wish you good day."

Thormod raised the taper, shielding it from the draft with his hand, and lit another candle.

"We'll be alone now, my love," he whispered. "They'll never find us here."

Emma could not hear him; she was still unconscious. He had made her a bed at the back of the cellar, three bales of straw with a sheet stretched over them and blankets on top: quite homely. Nobody else knew there was a cellar here: up above was an overgrown Roman ruin that even curious children no longer visited, not since the rumours had grown that goblins lurked there, ready to snatch the unwary. Thormod had not invented the story, but had done his bit to spread it: he did not want to share his secret place with anyone but Emma. In time, when he was sure he could trust her not to run away from him, he could even show her the way back to the town: but that would have to wait a while. He understood that she might take a few days, weeks maybe, to get used to the idea. He could wait. But he had had to get her away from the company of those Normans. It hurt like a dagger to see her laughing and joking with those evil outsiders, in a language he did not understand. He knew well enough how weak women were, and the two knights were rich and handsome and seemed dazzlingly sophisticated: it was understandable that Emma should not see their true nature. So it was his duty to save her from them.

Emma stirred, her eyelids fluttering.

"Father?" she murmured. Thormod gripped her hand.

"He can't be here," he said softly. "You're safe. You're with me."

She opened her eyes, and gave an uncertain smile.

"Thormod?" she said as he came into focus. "Where are we?"

"Safe," he said.

"Safe from what? What happened?" She looked around, her eyes becoming used to the dark. "Thormod," she said, sitting up, "what is this place?"

"That doesn't matter."

"Doesn't matter?" She wrenched her hand out of his and flung off the bedclothes, shivering involuntarily as the cold air hit her. "What are you talking about?"

"Lie down," said Thormod, placing his hands on her shoulders. "You're not well enough to get up yet."

"I'll not lie down until you tell me where we are, and where my father is," insisted Emma, pushing his hands away.

"You don't need to know!" The calmness was leaving Thormod's voice; he began to sound slightly tremulous. "You're with me; you're away from the Normans; it's dangerous in the town and safe here. It was for your own good."

"Thormod," said Emma, with all the authority and composure she could muster, "take me back to my father's house."

The apprentice shook his head.

"That's not possible."

"It is possible, Thormod," she said. "It's where I should be. You will take me back there now."

"No!"

"You will do as the lady says." Thormod spun round. Nobody could have found them, it was impossible – but Miles de Mountney was standing on the stairs, his hand on the pommel of his sword.

"You filthy Norman!" spat Thormod. "What devil showed you the way here?"

"You did," said the knight. "The blood on the floor was a nice touch, but you should have bound up your wound properly before you left – there were enough splashes in the road outside to show that you'd gone towards the river gate. I suppose you relied on it raining enough to wipe those out, but it didn't. A few coins in the right hands were enough to learn that a youth carrying a heavy burden wrapped in a blanket had gone out that way and left the road; after that any tracker could have followed your trail through the mud to the ruins. There are four soldiers outside, so don't try anything foolish."

With a wordless, strangled shriek, Thormod drew his dagger from his belt and launched himself at the knight: Emma screamed as de Mountney's sword sank into the apprentice's chest. Thormod sank to his knees with a groan, blood bubbling from his mouth, then slid off the knight's blade, collapsing dead onto the floor.

"I won't ask who your friends are, Master Miller," said de Mountney, eyeing the three "pilgrims" with a slight smile. Emma, after a tearful reunion, had been put to bed at her father's insistence, although she had in fact come through her ordeal remarkably well; there was strength there. The men were gathered in Godred's parlour for a meal of roast pork and chipped parsnips. "The answer might not be fitting for a loyal servant of King William to hear. But I know who *you* are."

Godred looked up sharply, and gripped his knife.

"Who am I, then?" he growled. De Mountney gestured at his ring.

"If you're truly concerned to keep it a secret, you probably shouldn't wear that. My family received a parcel of the old Godard estates when they were broken up, and we were sent the relevant papers. My father had his clerk deal with them – he couldn't read, and neither can I – but he showed me the seals. I remembered the signet of Sir Oliver Godard because it was so stark, so simple – an eight-pointed star. The same you wear."

"So I'm a Norman knight, then?" said the miller.

"A Norman knight banished for plotting against the Duke," said de Mountney. "And you may not have been back to Normandy, but you're certainly in the Duke's realms again now." Hereward and Martin exchanged glances. This might at any moment get bloody.

"If I were Sir Oliver Godard," said Godred, "your point is, I suppose, that I should be eager to conceal it, and that you might be in a position to help me – no doubt for a price."

"Now, Sir Oliver, if I tried to blackguard you at your own table I'd not only be no gentleman, I'd be a fool. You're four to one: I'd be dead before I could cry out. And I doubt very much if any of your friends would balk at killing one of the King's men."

"And when they're gone? Will you ask for Emma, or the mill, or both?"

"I should be very grateful for your permission to court Emma, of course," said de Mountney smoothly. "But her decision will be free and I will abide by it. You are in no danger from me, whatever happens – Sir Oliver."

"I doubt she'd be kindly disposed towards you, for all you saved her," said Godred. "She was fond of Thormod before this happened – so was I. I still can't quite believe it. And she saw you kill him. That's a hard stain to wipe away."

"As long as you don't mind my trying, that's all I ask."

"Was it necessary?" asked Godred. "Truly?"

"Truly," said the knight firmly. "He drew a knife on me. Besides, he could have been hanged for what he'd already done, if the sergeant's men had got him. Abduction is the same thing as rape in Norman law – but then, you know our laws."

There was a pregnant pause.

"I wasn't guilty, you know," said Godred suddenly. All eyes turned back to him. "It was in those bloody days after the old Duke was killed, when William was still a child and half the nobles in France wanted his wardship. I was a loyal servant of the true Regent, Alan of Brittany: after they murdered him I wouldn't accept the new regency, so I was accused of treason. I spent two years on the run; then Edward became King of England and the word went out that Norman knights would be welcome at Westminster, whatever their past. I became one of the King's bodyguards, and I served him well for seven years: but then an English thane tried to rape my wife, and I killed him. I had to flee again, but it's a harder matter with an injured wife and a baby. Rohese died on the journey north; I arrived here, where King Edward's people would never look for me, with a sword, a ring, ten shillings and Emma. And here I've been ever since. Emma knows nothing of this; I thought there was nobody left who did. I thought I'd left war and killing behind, too. But I will tell her. I can hardly let you know the truth and her not, in the circumstances."

"Then I do have your permission to woo her?" asked de Mountney. Godred sighed.

"I know nothing about you," he said. "I have no way to fathom you, no way to be sure you're any better than de Manville, or even Thormod. But I trust Emma's judgement. If you can get her goodwill I'll not stand in your way: but only if."

"If I hear of any harm to Godred or Emma," said Dolfin quietly, "not a stick of your lodge at Gorton will stand."

"That is friendship," said de Mountney, inclining his head. "And I hope that we may all part as friends – even though if we meet again, it may be as enemies."

It was nearly a week later that Dolfin, Hereward and Martin rode into Carlisle, and up to the great whitewashed stone house where Gospatric was lodging. Servants took their horses and their riding cloaks, and they were ushered into the presence of the erstwhile Earl of Northumbria. Gospatric, a tall and muscular man with a grey-flecked beard, was sitting as if in state on a dais, his purple cloak edged with a zigzag pattern in silver flung over the arms of a gilt-decorated chair, against which leant a broadsword with a massive amethyst set into the hilt. To either side of him stood fully armed spearmen, and, a little way further forward, two women. The one to the left was about Gospatric's age, straight-backed and sour-faced, wearing a long, straight, unembroidered maroon supertunic over a white kirtle, while a stark white mantle entirely hid her hair; a small wide-eyed boy clung to her skirts. To the right, there stood an extraordinarily beautiful woman in a pale green kirtle and cloth-of-silver sash, her head uncovered. She nodded to Dolfin, then looked straight into the eyes of Hereward, and smiled.

He caught his breath, and tried to think of Torfrida. But the exercise only brought to the front of his mind the ways in which their beauty differed. Torfrida was taller than the girl before him, paler, more slender than those generous curves; she was also a few years older – this one in the green must be under twenty; but the most striking difference was their hair. Torfrida's was black as midnight, the girl's yellow as the broom. Never before had Hereward seen a woman who matched the loveliness of his wife: but this girl boldly eyeing him was Torfrida's equal if any such existed. Yet he felt certain that he *had* seen her before. He knew he could not have done: he would have remembered: but she certainly appeared to recognise him.

"Lord Hereward, Martin Lightfoot, my father, the Earl Gospatric," Dolfin was saying. Hereward blinked, bowed perfunctorily to the Earl, and looked back curiously at Dolfin. "The Countess Ethelreda, my mother, and my brother Patrick," the youth continued, "and the Lady Elfthryth – my wife."

And then Hereward believed that he understood his dream.

Chapter 11: *The Atheling*

Roslyn, 1055.

Hereward was bored. After all the terror and exhilaration of his first campaign, his first pitched battle, the past few months had been singularly uneventful. They had won the Battle of Dunsinane by the stratagem of disguising their numbers under the boughs of trees, taking Macbeth by surprise: but at heavy cost. Earl Siward had lost his nephew and his eldest son, and had withdrawn to York, where word was that he was dangerously ill. Prince Malcolm, unable to press on and harry Macbeth without Siward's support, had retreated to Edinburgh and was consolidating his hold south of the Tay, leaving Scone, the traditional capital, in Macbeth's hands; Dunsinane itself had been retaken by the enemy, although with the fortress there in ruins it was of little value to them. And Malcolm's army sat and waited.

Gilbert of Ghent appeared content to wait. Malcolm had granted him the manor of Roslyn, taken from one of Macbeth's supporters, and he had settled straight in, installing servants, rebuilding barns, collecting rents, and essentially behaving as if his war and his journey were over. There had been one surprise: the former owner had left behind a log-lined pit in which there lived a bear. It was not too uncommon for the showier noblemen to keep brown bears: but Harek was something different. He had come from the land of the Frost Giants in the uttermost north; he was bigger than any land animal any man in Malcolm's army had ever seen; and his fur was pure white.

Unwilling to return to York with Siward, Hereward had entered Gilbert's service until such time as Malcolm should choose to resume the campaign: and Martin had chosen to remain with him. Martin seemed happy enough helping out in whatever tasks needed done: he did not mind being more servitor than soldier: but Hereward chafed. The one duty he did volunteer for, every day, was feeding Harek: when nobody else was by, he would speak quietly to the bear in Norse, which he felt ought to be its language. Harek had his sympathy: a caged beast was exactly what he felt like himself, and he saw himself reflected in the bear's sad eyes.

"Hereward?"

He looked down. A tiny hand was tugging at the hem of his tunic: it belonged to the little blonde girl, Elfthryth. Her father had been a landless cousin of Earl Siward's and a captain in his army: he had been killed at Dunsinane, and, the girl's mother being dead already, she had been foisted upon Gilbert. His whole household seemed to compete in spoiling her, hardened soldiers wrapped around an infant's finger: for who could refuse a child who had no one of her own to care for her? Hereward smiled, and patted her head.

"What is it?" he said.

"I want to feed Harek."

"I'm afraid you can't do that," said Hereward, crouching down to speak to her face to face, "but you can watch me feed him. Would you like that?" She looked uncertain: for a moment, Hereward was afraid that she was going to burst into tears. "I'll let you help me tip the bucket," he said hastily. "It's too big for you to tip on your own. But you'll have to be careful. We'll be right on the edge of Harek's pit."

"Oh, I've done *that* before," she said dismissively. "You can't see him properly if you don't go right up."

"As long as you take care," Hereward insisted.

The bear was restless, and shuffling about his pit, making little growls, as Hereward and Elfthryth came to the opening. He looked up, and sniffed the air suspiciously. Elfthryth gave a delighted gasp: Harek was usually asleep when she saw him.

"Now," said Hereward, "you take hold of that side of the bucket, at the bottom and the top, and I'll hold this side, and tip it slowly when I say. Now." Of course, Elfthryth's little hands had hardly the strength to hold onto the bucket of stinking scraps: but Hereward kept a firm grip on it, and slowly turned it sideways and then upside down. The remnants of meat and fish and crusts of bread tumbled down into the pit, sliding down a wall stained by hundreds of Harek's previous meals; the bear growled, and lumbered in to begin eating. Elfthryth clapped her hands.

"I did it!" she exclaimed. Harek looked up – then, suddenly, he reared onto his hind legs, pawing the air. The pit was more than seven cubits deep, but the bear's yellow teeth and long claws seemed to pass within inches; Hereward could feel its rotten breath. Elfthryth squealed, and stepped instinctively backwards: and her foot landed on a stray piece of fish that had fallen from the bucket. She slipped, and fell, and tumbled into the pit, landing with a squelch in the middle of Harek's dinner.

Hereward hesitated for less than a heartbeat. After shouting "Hey!" in the general direction of the hall, he jumped down into the pit after the child. The shock of landing jarred up through both his legs and knocked the wind out of him, but he managed to stay on his feet, which meant that Harek, now settled back onto all fours, had lost the advantage of height. That, at least, was one consolation.

"You know me, Harek," said Hereward softly in Norse. "It's Hereward. You don't want to hurt us." The bear made an uncertain noise in its throat. Hereward turned to look at Elfthryth. She was clutching her right leg in both hands and whimpering, but at least she was alive and conscious. "We'll be all right," Hereward told her. "There's nothing to worry about."

Harek had other ideas. His growl turning into a roar, he aimed a vicious swipe of his front paw at Hereward, who skipped out of reach only just in time. He looked up, but he could see nobody, hear nothing.

"Hey!" he shouted again. "Somebody bring a rope!"

Nothing.

Harek drew back his upper lip, and raised his paw again; Hereward, reluctantly, drew his dagger.

"I don't want to hurt you, boy," he said. "But I will if I have to."

Harek moved towards Elfthryth, sniffing curiously at her; she shrank back, shivering. Hereward could not wait to see if the bear meant to harm her: by the time he could be sure, she would be dead already. He did the only thing he could: he leapt onto Harek's back, out of the reach of his claws, and plunged his dagger again and again into the beast's neck. Elfthryth screamed. It took a dozen blows before the thrashing and convulsions stopped, and Harek's body lay still; the pit was carpeted in blood.

Hereward clambered awkwardly off the creature's back. Elfthryth needed comforting; but there was something else he had to do first. He leaned down over Harek, stroking the fur of the bear's face, and closed its eyes.

"I'm sorry, Harek," he whispered. "I had to do it. I had to."

Durham, January, 1069.

"Well?"

The messenger tugged at his collar. The ground was frozen and his breath condensed almost before it left his mouth, but he suddenly felt strangely hot under the gimlet eyes of Robert Comyn.

"Well?" repeated the Earl. "What says my lord Bishop?"

"Ah, my lord Bishop respectfully advises that my lord Earl should, um, should not enter the city at this time," stammered the messenger. The Earl's left eye twitched, and his hand tightened on the reins of his horse.

"He respectfully advises, does he? This simoniac

Saxon snake respectfully advises me?"

"He believes that the people's, ah, unhappiness could -"

"Unhappiness?" echoed the Earl incredulously. "This is a city in a state of rebellion! Am I supposed to consider the happiness of traitors?"

"With respect, my lord, that is the Bishop's very point," said the messenger. "He believes it is not safe for you to proceed."

"Not safe?" sneered Comyn. "The gates stand open. Half the city has already fled – it's just a gaggle of women and dotards."

"Exactly, my lord – innocents. The men who rebelled are gone, so my lord Bishop feels -"

"So we come to it," Comyn breathed. "He doesn't give a holy curse for my safety, he just wants to stop me doing my duty. Well, let him rot. Cities which foster rebellion must be punished. I have the orders of the King himself to levy this fine on Durham, and to make an example of the city in doing it. If the men are too cowardly to face me, so much the worse for their womenfolk: but if they pay promptly they will not come to harm. Well, not much harm." And he smirked.

"These are poor people for the most part, my lord."

"Then let the Bishop pay for them, if he's so concerned. His coffers are deep enough. They'll all be thankful that I have the money to spend on their defence when the Scots invade."

"You do the lord Bishop an injustice, my lord," insisted the messenger, finding a little more courage. "His first concern is for the King's peace. He believes that if you enter Durham it will be irrevocably broken."

"The people of Durham have already broken it by entertaining rebellion," snapped Comyn. "Or is this supposed to frighten me? Is that celibate English cur daring to threaten the premier nobleman of the realm? Ride back and tell the lord Bishop: I will enter Durham. I will lodge in his palace.

And I will collect the King's fine by whatever means necessary. If the people of Durham force me to resort to violence then the fault will be on their own head; if the Bishop lifts one finger to hinder me he will be imprisoned. And if you do not bear this message, I will have your head."

The stillness which greeted the Norman soldiery as they entered the city was eerie, and it was not only the cold which made many of them shiver. There was no sound of work or play: only the clack of hooves on frozen ground, and the accusing eyes of the silent women and old men who lined the streets. No lathe was being turned, no forge heated, no kiln stoked: almost every working man was gone.

At first the same oppressive silence hung over the gathering of the fine: but gradually it occurred to the soldiers that there were taverns standing empty, ale and wine unguarded: and the Earl had said they might take what refreshment they pleased, where they chose. And when the Earl complained that the money was being brought in too slowly, and ordered more thorough searches and rougher methods of dealing with those who might be holding back, it was not long before the city descended into a vision of Hell. Abandoned shops which had already been overturned and stripped of all valuables were smashed for the sheer joy of destruction; any who resisted were beaten senseless, and if they did not recover, it did not trouble the soldiery unduly; the Earl had forbidden rape, but when the first reports were brought to him he had the women thrown out into the street. Bishop Ethelwine muttered and chewed at his fingernails, but he said nothing: he was too afraid of the Earl's temper, and of the soldiers who were by now barely even in Comyn's control; so he covered his ears against the screams of his flock, and prayed harder.

The Normans had never thought to bar the gate of the city. They were here to raise a fine, not as a garrison, and what enemy could there be? It was the second watch of the night of the Commemoration of St Agnes when the men of Durham returned. Their ranks were swelled by angry folk from every village in the county; they had gathered every weapon that could be found; and they had sobriety, surprise and sheer cold fury on their side.

The first Norman soldier to see them was staggering from a house, clutching a rich garnet necklace. Its owner had long since fled the city, bestowing it on a servant as a reward for long and loyal service: and the servant had failed to hide it well enough. He raised his hand to shield his eyes and get a better look at the men approaching him, forgetting that he was holding the necklace, and dropped it. As he bent to recover it, scrabbling in the snow, his helmet fell from his head: and his skull was unprotected when the English cudgel fell.

Carlisle.

"So the news from Durham was true," said Gospatric. "The Bishop's courier has confirmed it all: Comyn is dead and his men slaughtered." Ethelwine had not yet thrown in his lot openly with the rebels – apart from anything else, they had burned a wing of his palace, and he did not take kindly to having his property damaged – but he recognised the possibility that they would win, and the need to court Gospatric's favour. He had not remained Bishop through such turbulent times without a talent for survival. "The story is the same all over the North. I received word this morning that the Sheriff of York has been killed, and Constable Malet besieged in the castle by the folk of the city. It's better than I could ever have planned it – and it's all spontaneous. The people, God bless 'em, have finally grown so weary of the Normans they aren't ready to wait for us."

He looked around the room, waiting for a response. His wife Ethelreda spoke first.

"A people tired of being ruled are a danger to any who try to rule them," she said. "We had best hope there is still a kingdom left when we move south." Gospatric waved his hand dismissively.

"What are they going to do," he said, "turn on us? They'll still need order – and protection against the Normans. They won't be lying down and letting this happen for long."

All knew that was true. The insurrection in Durham, if it had happened in isolation, would have been a small enough matter. William would simply have sent another earl with a larger retinue, and instructions to punish the city more severely. But against a general rising he would strike back, hard and fast. While Gospatric's agent had been hurrying north, William Malet's would have been galloping south: and when he came back it would be with an army, perhaps with the King himself at the head of it. A thrill ran through Hereward: he had never yet faced this usurping Duke, this Bastard William who was said to be the Devil's grandson.

"Then we must move quickly," said Hereward. "March on York. We have enough men to invest the city before the Normans get there, and more will follow. If they try to besiege us they may find themselves the ones besieged. We may even take the castle: Malet wasn't expecting a siege, and anything built that quickly is sure to have weak points." York Castle had been the Norman reaction to Gospatric's plot in the summer; it had been thrown up in a matter of weeks.

Gospatric frowned.

"Your advice is good," he said, "but I do not like to leave Carlisle without Prince Edgar."

"And why is he not here?" exclaimed Hereward in exasperation.

"Because he is a coward," said Ethelreda acidly. "Go on, my dear, tell them why your Atheling has not yet joined us."

"He fears to travel through the Border country," Gospatric sighed. "It is a lawless land, and between brigands and Norman spies he doesn't believe he can travel from Edinburgh to Carlisle in safety. William has tried to have him assassinated more than once before now. King Malcolm has refused to provide a force to escort him, and if I sent one we would have to wait for it to get back before we'd have the men to march on York."

"He could have been here now if you had sent one a month ago," said Ethelreda. This was true, but unhelpful, and Gospatric ignored it. Hereward rubbed his chin thoughtfully, and spoke:

"He could travel by sea."

Gospatric frowned.

"What do you mean?" he said. "To get here by sea would be longer *and* more dangerous than crossing the Marches."

"Not here: south of the Border," explained Hereward. "It would be the last thing the Normans would expect. If I ride with Martin to Edinburgh, with a letter or some token from you, and we accompany the Atheling onto a ship, we could land on the east coast of Yorkshire or Lincolnshire, avoid the Norman patrols and join you in York. Clinging to the coast we should avoid the worst of the weather, and while I was in those parts I could send word to Ely and summon Winter to York as well, if he doesn't have his hands full in the Fens."

"Are you sure that you could bring him safely to York?" demanded Gospatric.

"My lord Earl," said Hereward quietly, "by now I am a father. I do not yet know if my babe is a boy or a girl; I have only my heart's certainty to tell me that the child and my wife are alive. I wish to bring up that child in a free England. The Atheling offers me the chance to do that: I will not let any harm come to him."

It was decided that the simplest means of showing the truth of Hereward's message was for Dolfin to ride with him.

He had met Prince Edgar before, and his middle brother, Waldeve, was in Edinburgh with the Atheling.

This was not much to the young man's taste, as he had hoped to march triumphantly into York with his father: but Gospatric merely grunted that there would be much more to do, and God willing many more triumphs, after York, while Ethelreda – though she would have been more than happy to let the Prince grow old and die in Edinburgh – snapped that her son should do as his father told him. As they were to depart the next morning, there was little time to arrange a farewell feast: and although Gospatric gathered together his leading warriors and rustled up a couple of pigs, the night's meal was a muted affair.

In accordance with Saxon custom, Ethelreda and Elfthryth served each nobleman his first drink. Ethelreda moved stiffly, unused to bending, her expression daring any man to so much as look disrespectful, and clearly hating having to fill what she regarded as a servant's role; Elfthryth tripped merrily from man to man, laughing and batting her eyelids but never staying longer by any one than it took to fill his beaker. She bestowed a radiant smile on Hereward, who blushed: then moved on to the next place, to serve Martin. He frowned, startled. His presence near the top of the table was tolerated on Hereward's insistence, and Gospatric's people knew nothing of his unfree birth: but he remained a commoner, and it was quite extraordinary for a noble lady publicly to pour him a drink. Glancing at Gospatric, Martin saw the Earl look away, and realised that this was not a piece of politeness on his part: it must be the lady's own decision. Her mother-in-law would surely not approve.

Hereward, however, did, and now he returned Elfthryth's smile. Martin frowned, and chewed the edge of his cup. This was not the first such glance he had seen between Hereward and Dolfin's flirtatious wife: but at least it appeared to have gone unobserved by anybody else.

He saw their eyes meet again the next morning, as

Elfthryth kissed Dolfin goodbye. This time, Martin suspected that he saw a flicker of disapproval at the corner of Ethelreda's mouth: but he could not be sure that he had not imagined it.

"Saints Oswald and Edmund go with you," said Gospatric. "We will look for you in York two weeks from now."

"We will be there," Dolfin promised, "with King Edgar." Ethelreda sniffed loudly, but the soldiery nearby dutifully cheered the name of the Atheling. The Earl's son waved to them, and he and his companions rode out of the gates of Carlisle to the sound of cheering.

The two guards Gospatric had sent with them soon fell a couple of lengths behind, to the relief of Hereward, who felt he could speak more freely to Dolfin without his father's men listening.

"Your mother seems to have little time for the Atheling," he remarked. "Is he really so weak as she says?" Dolfin sighed.

"Mother's family is a branch of the House of Wessex," he said. "My grandfather had a distant claim on the throne; whenever King Edward made a decision he didn't approve of he used to grumble that if all men had their due he should have been King. Mother thinks we should be pushing my claim, not Edgar's. But we could never win support that way, and in any case, who'd want to be a king? Not I. If we succeed – when we succeed – Father will be more powerful than any English earl since Godwin, and my brothers and I will inherit that power one day: if that's enough for us it ought to be enough for Mother."

"Godwin's son did become King," Martin reminded him.

"And look how it ended," retorted Dolfin. "Nobody wants to be the new Harold."

"Some might," said Hereward. "He nearly succeeded. You are sure your brother is loyal to Edgar?"

"Absolutely," Dolfin insisted. "To the death."

They trotted on through the rocky hills of the Border country in relative tranquillity, and by the time the sun began to sink had entered the forested part of these uplands. Their Gallovidian ponies might not be the fastest of beasts at the gallop, but for long distances over tough terrain they were better mounts than any horse in Christendom. As branches closed above them, the dim February evening quickly gave place to premature darkness; the guards gripped their spears more tightly, and all five men began to glance from side to side. Here at least they were probably safe from Norman assassins, who would hardly dare to enter the forest: but there were by all accounts cutthroats behind every bush. When the light grew too dim to see the path, they lit torches and rode on, without even discussing making a camp: it was not until some hours after dark that they finally agreed to rest.

The night passed without attack; even the weather was not too harsh. It was not until they were clearing the eastern bounds of the forest the following afternoon that the outlaws finally made their sally: whether they had been following, waiting for an opportunity, or had happened upon them by accident, it was not a well chosen spot. One of Gospatric's guards, caught by the bridle, was gashed in the arm before he managed to cut his attacker down, but once clear of the trees the riders easily outdistanced their horseless foes. Binding the soldier's wound detained them only a few minutes, and they were into land that Hereward and Martin recognised from their campaigns with Siward and Malcolm by the time they made camp again.

But though the trees had not seemed friendly on the first night, when they crowded oppressively round seeming to conceal brigands and wolves in every shadow, they were sorely missed on the second. Trying to sleep on bare hillside, where a few inches of turf clung to the rock, they were exposed to the bitter winds of a Lothian winter: and Martin remarked the next morning that he had grown too old for Scotland. Hereward said nothing, but he felt the truth of it: his bones were aching like any greybeard's, and though only thirty-two he envied Dolfin's youth. That the young nobleman, used to soft beds, had in fact passed the worst night of the five was small consolation.

It was on the third day that they came to the gates of Edinburgh. This fortress of a city, clinging to its rugged hillsides, had changed hands almost as often as Carlisle between Briton, Saxon, Dane and Scot: but while Carlisle remained a bone fought over by hungry dogs, Edinburgh had in recent years settled into a kind of peace under the mostly distant and light-handed rule of Malcolm of the Big Head.

The gatekeeper of the city recognised Dolfin's name: Gospatric's family was well known across southern Scotland: and they had no trouble gaining admittance, and being guided to the gloomy-looking dun where Edgar and Waldeve enjoyed King Malcolm's hospitality. Once there, they were shown into a torch-lit feast hall, dark even in the middle of the day, and empty save at the high table. There stood a handful of young men, gnawing on fowls' legs and gulping wine while they pored over a mess of maps and papers, most of them stained by some spillage or other. They looked up when Dolfin, Hereward and Martin were shown in: and one of them, with a sudden delighted smile and a cry of "Dolfin!", bounded down the hall and swept the youth into a crushing hug.

"This is my brother, Waldeve Gospatricsson," said Dolfin, once he had regained his breath. The introduction was unnecessary: anybody could have seen that the two were brothers. The surprise was that they were not twins. "Waldeve, this is Hereward Askilsson, and Martin Lightfoot."

"I'm honoured to meet you, Lord Hereward," said Waldeve, bowing. "What brings you to Edinburgh?"

"Father sent us," said Dolfin before Hereward could

reply, "to bring the Prince to York."

"By what road?"

The speaker was a boy who looked younger even than Waldeve, fair haired and delicate of feature. Since making so poor an impression on the Conqueror at Berkhamsted, Edgar Atheling's frame had filled out a little, and he had grown the beginnings of a moustache: but his extra life experience had consisted mostly of eluding Norman traps. Looking at him, Hereward wondered if Ethelreda's harsh assessment of the rightful King of England had some truth in it: but he could not tell. He seemed to bear himself confidently enough, and that combined with his good looks would certainly help to win him loyal followers: but there is a great gap between finding men to lead, and leading them to success.

"By the sea, Highness," said Dolfin. "The Normans expect you to travel by land: this way we shall surprise them. And by the time we arrive in York, my father will already have taken control of the city, in your name."

"And then?"

"And then we face what comes," said Dolfin. His father had taught him this speech and he knew it word for word. "William the Bastard will march north against us but we do not know when. We may be able to take York Castle before he arrives, or burn it about Malet's ears. We may even be able to advance, take Derby, Nottingham, Lincoln, before the Norman army is in array. We may be able to persuade Archbishop Eldred to crown Your Highness as King in York. But even if we can do none of these things we shall have the greatest city in the North and men enough to defend it. We will beat the tanner's grandson, at York or wherever we face him. And Your Highness will be a king."

"By sea..." mused Edgar. "What do you think, Waldeve?"

"If it is what my father recommends," said Waldeve, "I am sure it is the best way."

"No way is without danger, Highness," said

Hereward. "None of us would have you take risks without need: if you fall we are all undone. But when you aim at a throne you must face danger. You face it every day whether you will or no, because your very life is a threat to the Bastard."

"I think you are right," said Edgar carefully. "But I wish there were time to consult with King Malcolm."

"There is no time," said Hereward.

"Malcolm wishes to see you restored to your right," Dolfin put in. "He has been in your position, and he endured exile until the opportunity came, then reclaimed his throne. This is your chance to do as he did. He would advise you to take it."

"When should we leave?" asked Edgar.

"As soon as we can find a trustworthy captain to bear us," said Dolfin, "and square it with the authorities here. There's no time to lose. We needn't gather men: Father has enough, and half the North will rally to him once York is taken."

"Leave the authorities to me," said Waldeve. "When they know this is what Father wants there'll be no trouble."

Their departure was quickly arranged. It was all curiously anticlimactic, and not what Hereward had expected. He had thought that there would be at least a token force of Scots sent with them: but instead they took only the personal guard which Malcolm had provided for the Atheling. He asked Waldeve if the King of Scots could be trusted.

"He can be trusted not to turn against us unless William puts a knife to his throat," he was told. "But as for supporting us in battle – he may need to be surer that we can win first. Or he may need something more basic."

"What do you mean?"

"Malcolm's wife died last year," Waldeve explained. "Then while he was still mourning, into his court came Edgar with his sister Margaret in tow. You've seen Edgar: well, next to Margaret he looks like the Loathly Worm. She's as rare a beauty as I've ever seen. Malcolm fell head over heels in lust, and with a brother who might be King of England one day she'd be a catch if she had the face of a toad and limped. But the pious princess has set her heart on becoming a bride of Christ. She's taken no vows yet, and Malcolm certainly still thinks she can be worn down: but for now, at least, she won't hear of marriage. Now Malcolm's not said as much, and nor have any of his courtiers in so many words, but I suspect he'll be readier to send troops to help Edgar once they're brothers-in-law than he is now."

"Then I hope to God the lady changes her mind soon," said Hereward fervently.

"Amen."

By lucky chance, Hereward's old acquaintance Brunman of Skirbeck was in port with his ship the *Gannet*. He had become too well known to find harbour in most ports of eastern England, but for that very reason had been welcomed in the Forth: any thorn in the side of the Normans was looked on as a friend by the Scots. Edgar took some persuading to put his trust in a pirate, but at length matters were arranged to everybody's satisfaction, and they took ship together for England.

York.

"It seems Malet's defences are better than we thought," admitted Gospatric. He had lost a dozen men in an assault on York Castle, and feared he had also been made to look foolish in the eyes of the people – and of his wife. It was to Ethelreda that he was now explaining himself. "No matter. He can't leave the castle, and nor can he withstand a long siege. If we have to detach a few men to watch him while we beat the usurper, what difference does it make?"

"The difference between victory and defeat, for all we know," said Ethelreda. "You said our army would double in size once we had taken the city. And what do we have? A rabble of peasants. And they were all here already – has one new man entered York since we did? I thought they were supposed to come from all over the North."

"They will," insisted Gospatric. "We recruited plenty on the way here, did we not?" This was true: the outlaws of the West Riding had come out of their woods to follow Gospatric's flag readily enough, but no man from the villages had joined them. "It is early yet," he went on. "Word has to get out of what is afoot. It will be different once the Atheling arrives."

"The Atheling," snorted his wife. "If he even comes! And what's become of your plan to have him crowned King by the Archbishop? The man won't even speak to us."

"The Lord Archbishop has doubts," said Gospatric patiently, "as is only natural. We could be dreamers or adventurers, the sons of Harold all over again. And do not forget that William is an anointed King. He came here with the Pope's blessing and showed God's favour by beating Harold in battle. Of course Churchmen are chary of opposing him. When we have a decisive victory behind us, Eldred will think again." But Ethelreda was in no mood to be charitable to the Archbishop of York.

"To think that such cavilling, snivelling eunuchs pass for bishops now in the Church that produced Cuthbert and Dunstan!" she exclaimed.

"I did accept office at William's hands myself," Gospatric reminded her, "and swore fealty to him, as Eldred has. I am the one in breach of my sacred oath."

"You had the interests of your sons to protect," she retorted. Gospatric was about to say that Eldred's flock could be regarded as his children, when a guard threw the door open.

"Edgar Edwardsson, Atheling of England, the lords

Dolfin and Waldeve Gospatricsson, and the lord Hereward Askilsson," he announced.

The parents' greeting for their sons and their proclaimed King was not the warmest. Ethelreda found a smile for Waldeve and Dolfin, but it grew forced when she turned to bestow it, with the merest inclination of the head, on Edgar; Gospatric bowed, and mumbled "Highness".

"We are pleased to greet our loyal servant the Earl of Northumbria," said Edgar, with a slight tremor. Gospatric bowed again. "What is the news in York?"

"As Your Highness has seen," said Gospatric, "York is liberated and has submitted itself joyfully to your rule. The invaders hold out in the castle, but nowhere else; and the castle will soon fall."

"So it should," said Edgar, seeing an opportunity to sound decisive. "So it must. An assault should be made at once."

"Highness, a frontal assault was attempted this morning. It is clear that the castle will not be taken that way. It will take a little time to discover its weak points; but you may rest assured, it will be taken."

"Would it help if I were to lead the assault myself?" asked Edgar. "To give the men heart?"

"No, Highness," said Gospatric emphatically. The Atheling, half disappointed and half relieved, let both feelings show rather obviously, and Gospatric changed the subject. "I am glad that your journey was a safe one," he said. "What news have you gleaned on the way?" Edgar turned to Waldeve, who answered for him.

"The sea was as calm as could be expected at this time of year," he said. "We landed at the mouth of the Trent, and came here with little trouble. The Sheriff of Lincoln sent men after us but we were able to outride them; they were too few and came too late. Lincolnshire is not yet in revolt the way Yorkshire is, but the Normans there are looking to the defence of their own houses and many are not answering the

Bastard's summons."

"Then he has summoned them?"

"To Nottingham," Dolfin confirmed. "He cannot be there himself yet, but that is where he plans to muster his army. Gilbert of Ghent is there already with a considerable force, and William de Warenne is said to be bringing a still larger one from the south."

"That is bold of him," mused Gospatric, "to call a muster within striking distance of York. He must be very confident."

Hereward shook his head.

"It's a front," he said. "He's sent Mathilde and their son Robert back to Normandy. He wouldn't have done that unless he were scared."

"Then we should attack," essayed Edgar. Gospatric shook his head.

"No," he said. "Nottingham is a well defended city, and we do not know when William will arrive. He might easily take us by surprise while we were still outside the walls. We are better holding our own defensive position." Ethelreda curled her lip. She suspected that her husband would have been less cautious had Edgar not been with the army. He looked to Hereward. "What of your men at Ely?" he asked.

"Martin Lightfoot has returned to Ely to find how many men can be spared," said Hereward. "With half the Normans barring their doors and the rest off to Nottingham, we should be able to raise at least fifty and still leave the island defensible."

"And when will they reach York?"

"Ten days, perhaps less. Not more than twelve."

"By which time William will probably be in Nottingham," sighed Gospatric. "Well, as long as they are here before he reaches the gates of York…"

That night, Hereward stood alone on the city rampart,

looking up towards the castle. He could see lights moving there: perhaps Constable Malet was looking down on the city, wondering when the King would come, and whether he had made a mistake in coming to York.

Martin had said once that Hereward would never be truly alone: but he could not help feeling so now. Dolfin and Waldeve might be friendly enough, but he missed Winter and Gwynnog, his childhood friends, and Martin, of course, Martin who had always been there. Above all, he missed Torfrida, and their child whom he had never seen.

"Let me live," he prayed silently. The most he had ever asked of God before past battles was that he might keep his honour: life, he had always been taught, was a matter for wyrd, and each man's wyrd was set fast. He still believed it, but he did not care about the contradiction: he clasped his hands and screwed his eyes and begged that he might live long enough to hold his child in his arms.

A soft hand fell on his arm.

"What are you praying for?"

Hereward did not need to turn round to recognise the speaker.

"Victory," he said curtly. If there was no other in York to whom he could open his heart, he was not going to open it to Elfthryth.

"We all pray for that," said Elfthryth softly. She paused. "Do you think we will win?"

"Of course," said Hereward stiffly.

"Be honest," she insisted. "Dolfin and his family can't imagine defeat, but I'm afraid. I trust you. I want to hear from you that all will be well." Hereward turned and looked her in the eyes: and he saw the same frightened child he had had to save from the white bear all those years before.

"I cannot promise that," he said. "But the city is strong, and, except for not holding the castle, we have a good position. And there will be reinforcements before King William comes. We *ought* to win. I believe we will. And inside the city you will be safe." Elfthryth threw her arms around him and hugged him.

"Thank you," she murmured. "Thank you."

Hereward stood stiffly, not returning the embrace, and after a few heartbeats Elfthryth stepped back with an awkward laugh.

"I'm sorry," she said. "I shouldn't have done that." Hereward said nothing. "Dolfin will be wondering where I am," said Elfthryth unconvincingly. "Don't stay out in the cold too long." And she pulled up the hood of her cloak and walked quickly away.

Gospatric had brought food wagons from Carlisle, and there had been some provender left in the Sheriff's stores which the local populace had not yet looted: but by the time the men of Ely arrived provisions were beginning to run low. Men were sent out to commandeer food from the villages, but with instructions to leave no community with less than it needed: they could not afford to turn the country against them. They had already had to hang a few soldiers who had taken liberties with the people of York. Methelgar shook his head.

"Is this enterprise any better organised than Godwin's?" he wondered.

"It could be better," Hereward admitted. "But it is a campaign, not a chaos. We won't be taken sleeping this time, at least: there are scouts on every road, ready to report the coming of the Normans. Gospatric knows what he is doing. Edgar knows nothing, but he does as he's told – God knows how that bodes for when he's King, but it's the best thing he can do for now. But my worry is the castle. Gospatric seems sure we can spare the men to keep Malet pinned down there, even if we have to fight William on the open field: but we don't know how many men William may bring. I'd feel much happier if we could winkle Malet out before he arrives."

"And if we don't fight in the open?" demanded

Martin. "How are we to last a siege with our food this low?"

"We can't," said Hereward. "Our best hope is to ambush the Norman army on the road, if we can. Gospatric knows that, and I'm sure William knows it too. So he'll do everything he can to make it impossible. Which means that it comes back to a pitched battle. We still ought to win: we have a strong army here."

They were standing in the barracks which the survivors of the Sheriff's garrison had abandoned when they fled the city: it was far too small for Gospatric's army, who had spilled over into civilian homes and into clusters of makeshift huts wherever there was a bare patch within the city walls. Since the King had reached Nottingham, Gospatric had forbidden his men to sleep outside the walls, and York was now a desperately crowded city. Within the barracks itself, many men had made themselves beds in the courtyard, where, wrapped tightly in as many blankets as they could lay their hands on, they braved both the elements and the frequent passage of mailed feet and horse-shoes.

A horseman clattered into the barracks now, and a few men who had been sleeping looked blearily up and swore at him before they recognised Dolfin Gospatricsson.

"Up!" he ordered urgently. "Get up, you idle bastards, before the Normans come to wake you up!"

"What's happened?" demanded Hereward.

"The enemy marched from Doncaster at dawn yesterday," said Dolfin. "They are not five miles from the city. We should have heard the day they left Nottingham, if not before – God knows what happened. Not one of our riders reported."

"So much for not being caught sleeping," muttered Martin. It was Bristol all over again. Perhaps they had an hour or two to prepare, instead of minutes – but that would hardly suffice even to round up their men, let alone get them into formation.

Ethelreda pointed this out to Gospatric at the top of

her voice. The wailing Patrick, who hated his parents' quarrels, was carried away by a maidservant, while Gospatric's page laced him into his hauberk.

"I know that," he growled. "We can get enough together to defend the main gate. We'll hold the Normans off for today and sally out tomorrow."

"Which they'll be expecting," she retorted. "You'll be cut to pieces – and you can't stay behind the walls because we haven't any food. If you hadn't been so concerned about your damned Atheling you'd have struck south before now, taken Derby or Doncaster -"

"You know that's not true," said Gospatric. "Consolidating at York was the best thing to do. We should have had word when William marched north. If we had..." But he knew there was truth in what Ethelreda had said. Continuing the march south would have been a gamble, but staying in York had been no safer, and might now prove disastrous if he could not beat the Norman army tomorrow. At least today's engagement, with the stout gates of York on his side, was one he should win without difficulty.

The second Norman assault came in the last watch of the night. Gospatric had not been to bed, but had been pacing the hall of the former Sheriff's residence, trying to form a plan. The skirmish at the gate had gone as he had foreseen, an easy victory for the defenders after no more than a token probing: and he had committed the fortifications to Hereward's command for the night and retired to try to work out the morning's strategy. He was still pondering this when Winter reported to him.

"The Normans have brought a ram," he said. Gospatric stared.

"A ram?" he echoed. "They can't have done. They haven't had time to make one here, and if they only left Doncaster two days ago they've come too fast to have brought it with them."

"I don't know how, but they have one," insisted Winter. "We were holding them off with burning arrows when I left the gate but it won't keep them away for long."

"Is this ram powerful enough to breach the gates?" demanded Gospatric.

"I don't know," confessed Winter. "But it could be. We couldn't see how big it was, but… it looked evil. And it has an iron head, with a point to it – like a giant's arrow."

"Fire arrows won't be enough," said Gospatric, "nor oil neither, if it's well roofed and they have enough men. We'll have to attack it. Has Hereward made any preparations for a sally?"

"He's ordered men to form up ready for one, but he wouldn't open the gates without orders from you."

"Good man. Good man. Get back to him as quick as you can. Tell him the ram must be destroyed."

"If Gospatric means to face William in the open anyway, then the gate won't matter in another couple of hours," said Martin. "We can't go out at the postern; we've blocked it up and anyway the Norman archers are sure to be covering it. If we can only go out in single file we'll die one by one. The only way to get to the ram is to open the gates. Why risk that now when we'll surely be marching the whole army out at dawn? They'll take nearly till then to break the gates down. In the meantime we can sit up on the walls killing them with arrows, then go out for the battle in our own good time."

"And what if we lose the battle?" said Hereward.

"Then we've lost the war."

"Well, what if we win but don't annihilate them? As long as the gate's intact we can retreat within the city, fight again another day – at least while the food lasts. No, Gospatric's right: the ram must be destroyed." The ground shuddered beneath them as the massive iron head of the ram thudded against the gate.

"Do you think he'd have been so ready to give that order if it were his own people manning this gate instead of us?" demanded Martin. "I'm sure it suits him very well that he doesn't have to sacrifice a single Northumbrian."

"That doesn't make any difference to us," insisted Hereward. "We have our orders and they're the right ones. We have to destroy that ram." He turned to the men who were waiting expectantly by the gate, their hands on the chains that held up the great bar, and nodded. "Open the gate," he said.

Just as the bar was lifted from its slots, the ram struck the gate again. Without the bar in place, it was flung open at once, knocking the closest men off their feet. Hereward's men rushed forward, but the Norman vanguard was already inside the city. What followed was fierce and bloody butchery. The Normans were driven back, but slowly and at great cost: every man wielding the ram was fully armed, and all had their swords out by the time the English reached them. They had clearly been expecting this attack. One by one they sold their lives dearly, and the area around the gate was littered with corpses by the time the English took possession of the ram.

"How are we supposed to destroy this?" wondered Methelgar.

"Get it inside and close the gate again," said Hereward. "If the Normans don't have it it's as good as destroyed. But we'll need to be quick. Get those bodies out of the way so we can move the thing."

"There's a Norman column advancing up the road," called the lookout above the gate.

"Christ," said Hereward under his breath. "Hurry up!" he barked at his men. "Or they'll be inside York before we close the gate."

They worked as if the whips of Satan were upon them, clearing the bodies aside to free the road of the ram. The corpses were clad in heavy mail and the ground was slippery with blood, but they got on with the gruesome task, then took a hold of the great wooden beast itself to haul it into the city: but it was too late. The Normans, advancing at a jog despite their heavy armour, reached the gate: and the English had no chance to close it.

Hereward managed to withdraw his men from the gate before they were massacred, and commanded the retreat through the streets of York: but the rest of Gospatric's army was fleeing headlong. Taking possession of the city was the work of hours: over sacking it, the Normans took their time. King William would record this as a glorious victory: the fact that all the principal rebels had escaped, that his army was by then in no fit state to pursue them, and that the ordinary citizens of York made up most of the victims, need not be stressed.

"So another great push ends in disaster," said Hereward bitterly. "God damn all kings."

"What became of the Atheling?" asked Abbot Thurstan.

"Edgar Edwardsson", said Hereward, "was back in Carlisle before the Normans had watered their horses. Gospatric and his family were right behind him, once we'd got them out of York. William Malet's been made Sheriff, as a reward for defending the castle, and they're building a second bailey on the other side of the city – or what's left of it. Thank God they were too busy looting and raping to stop us getting away. Oh, taking York doesn't mean they control the North: they don't, and won't, today nor tomorrow, but nor will Edgar now."

"If the Atheling's cause is lost," said the Abbot tentatively, "is it not perhaps time to think of negotiating a peace with King William? Or of leaving the country?" Hereward fixed him with a hard stare.

"Never say that to me again, Father Abbot," he said quietly. "I will never live a slave. Nor will I run, until there is no free corner of England to hold me. Ely remains. From this day I fight my own fight against William, in my own land and in my own way: but fight I still shall while there is breath left in my lungs and blood in my veins."

Outside, in what those who fled Norman rule had come to call the Camp of Refuge, the sun was sinking. Somewhere out on the marsh, a lone curlew was calling; and a small crowd of those who had taken the sanctuary Hereward offered had gathered around Wulfric the Heron, who was plucking on a rebec and chanting softly.

"We have heard of Ermanaric's
Wolfish thought," he sang.
"He ruled widespread folk
Of the Gothic realm:
That was a grim king.
There sat many a swordsman,
By sorrows bound,
Woes in their weening:
Wishing now that the kingdom
Were overthrown.
That was overcome,
So may this be."

Historical note

Hereward's family

The *Gesta Herewardi* names its hero's parents as "Leofric of Bourne" and Edith. It was later assumed that this Leofric must be the Earl of Mercia, making Hereward and Toli younger brothers of Earl Alfgar, uncles of Edwin and Morcar, and sons of not Edith but Godiva. This was the genealogy used by Kingsley and many other novelists: but it will not stand up historically. The sources agree, however, that Abbot Brand of Peterborough was Hereward's uncle: and Peter Rex has demonstrated that, of all Brand's brothers, only the eldest, Askil, is a plausible candidate for Hereward's father. The idea of a connection with the House of Mercia, however, remains attractive – and actually fits quite well with the evidence, once the idea that Hereward was Leofric's son is disposed of: so I have made him Godiva's nephew. Since Askil and his family never held Bourne, which plays a significant role in the *Gesta*, I have made them its stewards on Morcar's behalf – which is plausible enough if they were cousins.

Hereward's exile

The account of Hereward's early career is disputed. Some have hypothesised that he never in fact left England: but the Flemish part of his exile, *c.* 1064-67, as described in the *Gesta*, matches real events in Flanders in that period. Rex has suggested that he was in fact exiled *c.* 1063 and not in 1054 as the traditional account has it: and certainly the *Gesta*'s telling of his exploits in Scotland and (especially) Cornwall smacks more of romance than of history. In the interests of a good story, however, I have not excised them: after all, they *might* have happened. (I have, however, had to demote Aleph still further than did Kingsley, who made the romance's anachronistic "King of Cornwall" into a local petty king: even such could not have gone unrecorded surviving among the English thanes who ruled most of Cornwall in the immediate pre-Conquest era. If there was an Aleph he must have been a very minor landowner.)

With reference to his service in the army that installed Malcolm III as King of Scots, it is worth mentioning that I am aware of the interesting recent theory that Siward's invasion was aimed at restoring an entirely different Malcolm to the defunct throne of Strathclyde. As an historian I might reserve judgement: as a novelist, compelled to come down on one side or the other, I have chosen to stick with the traditional version.

Although it is now thought that Hereward did return to England in September 1067, rather than early in 1069 as was earlier believed, this part of his career is extremely obscure. The *Gesta* has little to say about it: as a result, this novel owes less in terms of both structure and content to that romance than its sequels will. It is not known for certain whether he took an active part in either of the major rebellions featured in this book, though in the case of at least the second one (*The Atheling*) it is probable that he did. With regard to the first, it might be thought somewhat implausible that he could have travelled safely so far from his home turf. But I could not resist the temptation to bring Wild Edric into the story, and to provide Thord Gunnlaugsson with a more dramatic exit than Kingsley gave him.

Chronology

1035: Death of Canute, last king to rule both England and Denmark.
1036: Hereward born; Ivo Taillebois born.
1037: Martin Lightfoot born at Waterford.
1039: Duke Robert of Normandy assassinated; Count Alan III of Brittany becomes regent for the young Duke William.
1040: Assassination of Count Alan; Godard flees Normandy for England.
1042: Edward the Confessor becomes King.
1044: Murder of Eithne by Thord; Torfrida born at St Omer.
1047: Martin escapes from Waterford.
1049: Godard has to leave King Edward's court.
1051: Births of Elfthryth, Edgar Atheling, and Toli Askilsson.
1053: Marriage of William and Mathilde.
1054: Hereward outlawed. He travels to York, meets Martin, and they join Earl Siward's army for the invasion of Scotland. The south is subdued but Macbeth holds out in the north.
1055: Death of Siward. Hereward saves Elfthryth from a bear at Roslyn.
1056: Arngrim of Brampton executed.
1057: Macbeth is defeated and killed. His stepson Lulach becomes the figurehead for his supporters.
1058: Lulach is killed and Malcolm III becomes King of Scots.
1059: The final crushing of Macbeth's loyalists leaves Hereward and Martin without employment in Scotland, and they travel to Cornwall.
1061: Hereward kills Gartnait Ironhook and acquires Brainbiter; Hereward and Martin flee Cornwall with Gwendolen and deliver her to Prince Sitric in Waterford, then travel on to Dublin.

1063:		Hereward and Martin arrive in Flanders.
1066:	Jan:	Death of Edward, usurpation of Harold II.
	Sep:	Norwegian and Norman invasions; Hardrada defeated and killed at Stamford Bridge, Harold likewise at Hastings.
	Dec:	Submission of England; Edric the Wild holds out alone; coronation of William.
1067:	Jan:	Hereward supplants Ascelin as Count Baldwin's champion and defeats Holbert.
	Sep:	Baldwin V dies; Hereward and Torfrida marry; Hereward and Martin return to England; Ivo's men kill Toli; Hereward meets Lysir; Hereward avenges Toli and reclaims Bourne Hall; Edith becomes a nun.
	Dec:	Hereward spends Midwinter's Eve in the Temple of Frey; the manor of Bourne is transferred to Ogier fitz Ungomar.
1068:	Feb:	Wulfric is unmasked as the Heron and joins Hereward's men. Torfrida comes to Bourne.
	Apr:	Hereward and Ivo both seek the treasure of St Edmund.
	May:	Torfrida discovers she is pregnant and returns to St Omer. Hereward and half his men travel to join the rebellion in the west, and meet Edric, but they are defeated. Death of Thord.
	Jun:	Ogier seizes Bourne; Winter relocates the rebel camp to Ely. Hereward briefly joins the Wild Hunt.
	Jul:	Hereward returns to the east. He encounters Hiccafrith and they face the Gyrvians. Death of Grendel; Starkad swears vengeance.
	Aug:	Ivo tries to steal Brainbiter.
	Sep:	Hereward agrees to join the rebellion of Gospatric. On the way he meets Godard and Emma at Manchester. Hereward meets Elfthryth again.

1069: Jan: Robert Comyn killed; rebellion begins across the north. Torfrida's child born.
Feb: York falls to the rebels.
Mar: King William sacks York. Rebels scattered. William Malet made Sheriff.

Hereward will return in THE FURY OF THE NORTHMEN.

www.ingramcontent.com/pod-product-compliance
Ingram Content Group UK Ltd.
Pitfield, Milton Keynes, MK11 3LW, UK
UKHW041257180426
11947UKWH00008B/541